Sunday Night Book Club

Clare Boylan lives in Dublin. In addition to several volumes of stories, she has written many novels including *Holy Pictures*, *Black Baby*, *Room for a Single Lady* and *Emma Brown*.

Veronica Bright is the winner of the *Woman & Home* short story competition in 2005. For many years she taught at a local primary school, which inspired her to write stories, poems and plays. She is married with three grown-up children and lives in Cornwall.

Elizabeth Buchan is the author of, among other novels, *The Good Wife*, *That Certain Age*, *Revenge of the Middle-Aged Woman* and its sequel, *The Second Wife*. She lives in London with her husband and children.

Clare Chambers was born in Croydon and read English at Oxford. Among her novels are *Uncertain Terms*, *Learning to Swim*, *A Dry Spell* and *In a Good Light*. She lives in Kent with her husband and three children.

Mavis Cheek was born in Wimbledon and has worked as a journalist and travel writer before turning to fiction. Her novels include *Mrs Fytton's Country Life*, *The Sex Life of My Aunt*, *Patrick Parker's Progress* and *Yesterday's Houses*.

Tracy Chevalier grew up in Washington, DC, then moved to England in the 1980s. Among her novels are *The Virgin Blue*, *Girl With a Pearl Earring*, *Falling Angels* and *The Lady and the Unicorn*. She lives in London with her husband and son.

Katie Fforde lives in Gloucestershire with her husband and some of her three children. Among her most recent novels are *Paradise Fields*, *Flora's Lot*, *Restoring Grace* and *Practically Perfect*.

Nicci Gerrard has worked in teaching, publishing and journalism. She is the author of *Things We Knew Were True* and *Solace* and also writes thrillers with her husband Sean French, under the name of Nicci French. They live in Suffolk.

Lesley Glaister teaches Creative Writing at Sheffield Hallam University and her novels include *Partial Eclipse*, *The Private Parts of Women*, *Now You See Me* and *As Far as You Can Go*. She divides her time between Peebles and Orkney.

Tessa Hadley teaches literature and Creative Writing at Bath Spa University and lives in Cardiff. She has written *Accidents in the Home* and, most recently, *Everything Will Be All Right*.

Maeve Haran's novels include *Baby Come Back*, *The Farmer Wants a Wife* and *Husband Material*. She lives in London with her husband and three children.

Joanne Harris lives in Huddersfield, Yorkshire, with her husband and daughter. She is the author of, among other novels, *Chocolat*, *Five Quarters of the Orange*, *Jigs and Reels* and, most recently, *Gentlemen and Players*.

Wendy Holden was a journalist before becoming a full-time writer. She is married with two children and lives in London and Derbyshire. Among her novels are *Fame Fatale*, *Azur Like It*, *The Wives of Bath*, and, most recently, *The School for Husbands*.

Cathy Kelly is the author of nine novels, including *Always and Forever*, *Best of Friends* and, most recently, *Past Secrets*. She lives in Ireland with her partner and their twin sons.

Andrea Levy was born in England to Jamaican parents. She has written a number of novels and short stories, including *Every Light in the House Burnin'*, *Never Far from Nowhere*, *Fruit of the Lemon* and *Small Island*. She lives and writes in London.

Kate Long was working as a teacher for several years before writing *The Bad Mother's Handbook*, *Swallowing Grandma* and *Queen Mum*. She lives in Shropshire with her husband and two children.

Santa Montefiore is the author of six novels, including *The Swallow and the Hummingbird*, *The Forget-Me-Not Sonata*, *Last Voyage of the Valentina* and, most recently, *The Gypsy Madonna*. She lives in London with her husband, the historian Simon Sebag Montefiore, and their two children.

Elizabeth Noble was born in Buckinghamshire and worked in book publishing before writing *The Reading Group*, *The Tenko Club*, *Alphabet Weekends* and *The Friendship Test*.

Maggie O'Farrell was born in Northern Ireland and grew up in Wales and Scotland. Her works of fiction include *After You'd Gone*, *My Lover's Lover*, *The Distance Beetween Us* and, most recently, *The Vanishing Act of Esme Lennox*. She lives in Scotland.

Patricia Scanlan was born in Dublin where she still lives. Her novels include *The City Girl* trilogy, *Two for Joy*, *Double Wedding* and, most recently, *Divided Loyalties*. She is also series editor of the Open Door literacy books.

Alexander McCall Smith was born in Zimbabwe and now lives in Scotland. His works include the *No. 1 Ladies' Detective Agency* series, of which the most recent is *Blue Shoes and Happiness*.

Adriana Trigiani grew up in Big Stone Gap, which became the setting for her trilogy *Big Stone Gap*, *Big Cherry Holler* and *Milk Glass Moon*. Adriana lives in New York City, where she has just written her seventh novel, *Return to Big Stone Gap*.

Lynne Truss is a writer and broadcaster, best known for her book on punctuation, *Eats, Shoots & Leaves*. She is the author of three novels and many radio dramas, including the twelve-monologue sequence *A Certain Age*. She lives in Brighton and London.

Penny Vincenzi is the author of twelve novels, including the *Spoils of Time* trilogy (*No Angel*, *Something Dangerous* and *Into Temptation*) and, most recently, *Sheer Abandon*. She is married with four daughters and divides her time between London and the Gower Peninsula, South Wales.

The Sunday Night Book Club

Stories by Wendy Holden, Cathy Kelly,
Penny Vincenzi, Joanne Harris, Andrea Levy,
Alexander McCall Smith and many more...

arrow books

Published in the United Kingdom by Arrow Books in 2006

3 5 7 9 10 8 6 4

All stories have been previously published in *Woman & Home* magazine.

Arrow Books
The Random House Group Limited
20 Vauxhall Bridge Road, London, SW1V 2SA

Random House Australia (Pty) Limited
20 Alfred Street, Milsons Point, Sydney
New South Wales 2061, Australia

Random House New Zealand Limited
18 Poland Road, Glenfield
Auckland 10, New Zealand

Random House (Pty) Limited
Isle of Houghton, Corner of Boundary Road & Carse O'Gowrie
Houghton 2198, South Africa

Random House Group Limited Reg. No. 954009

www.randomhouse.co.uk

A CIP catalogue record for this book is available from the British Library

Papers used by Random House
are natural, recyclable products made from wood grown in
sustainable forests. The manufacturing processes conform to
the environmental regulations of the country of origin

ISBN 9780099502241 (from Jan 2007)
ISBN 0099502240

Typeset by SX Composing DTP, Rayleigh, Essex
Printed and bound in Great Britain by
Bookmarque Ltd, Croydon, Surrey

Contents

Your Timing's All Wrong

Clare Boylan

Angela was at the bar when she felt a pair of hands moving over her haunches. They moved quite lightly and nicely, scarcely touching. She did not react, although not to stiffen or turn around was a reaction in itself. The hands had a slightly yearning feel. 'That man needs a woman,' she thought mildly.

This went through her head as she waited for her wine. When it came she drank it quickly and it had a sobering effect. The man must have made a mistake, she realised. Seen from the back, she could be any age. When the hand crept up her waist and brushed the side of her ribs towards her breast, she whispered, 'Sorry!' and turned around.

It was Pollock. Pollock, of all people! He had

scarcely spoken to her all week. When she had tried to exchange words with him, he would not meet her eyes. Now that their gaze did connect she saw that his were of the dense brown that is suited only to small children or animals. His lashes were dark except for one blond mongrel lash. His grey hair had been cut in spikes like a cartoon character.

She had seen him on deck rallying people for games. She had tried to make her escape but he'd called her back in a wheedling, nursery tone. 'Angela!' She had stood there, feeling mottled and dismayed. Around her, the fellow cruise-goers tittered in mild unified aggression.

She had come on the cruise expecting not to fit in. Her hope was to be left alone. She had elected this holiday because there might be safety in numbers. She had not anticipated that anyone would be so cruel as to make her join them. 'Pollock's the name,' he beamed. 'Everyone calls me Polly.'

'I should like to finish my book, Mr Pollock,' she said. 'I would just like to be left in peace.' Her voice shook when she spoke and she was dismayed by how angry it sounded. Polly! Ridiculous! she thought as around her grown-up people ran in a circle and fell laughing into chairs.

The cruise had cost a lot of money and Mr Pollock

was employed to make sure that people enjoyed themselves. He taught ballroom dancing to the old and salsa to the young. When the liner docked he took guests sailing or showed them how to dive. There had to be more to him than met the eye. He was good-looking, lean and tanned. Of course, he must be gay.

Now, almost a week after the embarrassing encounter, she had felt his hand on her bottom; stealthy, but not sleazy. Just for his touch, her bottom felt a better shape. She apologised, smiled her foolish smile and went to a table.

It happened on an evening when the liner was docked in a small port and they had been taken to a restaurant on stilts in the sea. First, they had waited on the beach beneath a childishly spangled sky. Out of the blackness of the sea a single point of light appeared and then gauze-skinned wings spread out on either side of it. It was a rowing boat that had come to carry them over. The wings were made by the pull of the oars. Inside the restaurant, diners sat at low tables on cushions on a deck. Planks had been removed so that their feet dangled above water illuminated by concealed light. To avoid conversation, Angela watched the feet beneath the table. It was interesting to see feet divided from their owners.

Some plump women had wonderfully slender ankles. Her toenails, inexpertly dabbed with scarlet varnish, were like half-sucked Smarties. The feet to her right were long and brown with very short white toenails that were evenly ranked in half-smiles. She looked up. Pollock! Brave of him to have sat beside her. It seemed very intimate to have their bare feet so close and she was overcome with shyness. This was relieved when one of the women went to put her handbag under the table and it was caught by another woman before it dropped into the sea and she laughed along with everyone else.

A mouth touched her ear. 'What age are you?' For once Pollock was not smiling.

'I'm fifty-four,' she told him brutally.

'I'm fifty-five.' He flung it out with the furtive deftness of someone leaving a refuse bag on another person's step. 'You don't look it,' she said. She said it because it was expected of her but, also, it was true. He smiled a smile of dazzling innocence. His undefended eyes were eager and uncertain. She noted that there was a half-bottle of whisky by his side and that most of it had been consumed.

After dinner there was dancing. Coloured lights were strung around the deck and old records were played. People looked hopefully at Pollock for he was a good dancer. He stayed where he was, humming the tunes under his breath. Angela found she knew the words. An hour ago, they would have been lost in the jumble of her brain. She sang very softly: '*I'll never let you see the way my broken heart is hurting me.*' Pollock joined in. '*I've got my pride and I know how to hide all my sorrow and pain.*' Together they belted out: '*I'll do my crying in the rain.*'

Such happiness. Such cheap happiness. Pollock took her hand and held on tightly and they sang and sang all evening.

Early in the morning she went on deck. She leaned on the rail and watched a small boy in the water working with nets, his matt-brown shoulder blades spinning like a sycamore seeds. She had the pleasant feeling of being set down upon the earth, much as Fay Wray might have felt when King Kong ceased to dangle her from his hairy fist.

She had anticipated that Pollock might be bashful about the night before and he was. His teeth flashed a tense 'Good morning' and she soberly placed herself at the table between two women. When the other women left she remained at the table to write a postcard. 'What is your name?' she asked Pollock without looking up.

'You know my name.'

'I wondered about your first name.'

'Martin.' He spoke the name uneasily as if Martin was some rival whom he had not quite seen off. 'Everyone calls me Polly.'

'Martin, why do you do this?' Her pen still pursued its end and occupied her gaze. 'It must be exhausting, keeping everyone happy all the time. Don't you sometimes long to go home?'

He said nothing. How stupid she was! She had offended him. 'Of course, you do it very well. Everyone says so.' She set down her pen and turned to him in appeal. She saw that his head was bent, his features compressed in anguish and the effort to suppress it. Tears fell down his face and jumped playfully on to his brightly coloured shirt. 'I have no home,' he said. After a time he patted the table several times, as if for reassurance. 'Playtime!' he said in a little voice and he moved jauntily away.

The ship remained in port for the day and there was an excursion to a temple. Angela decided instead to walk to the nearest town. She wanted to carry off alone what Pollock had given her. He had touched her and she, in turn, had touched him.

The little town was wreathed in innocence and reeking with filth. Tin-roofed shacks served as houses. World-weary dogs scratched fervently.

Children of breathtaking beauty played meditatively in the dirt. Behind a bank of palm trees, a golden shrine to Buddha was adorned with garlands of fresh jasmine. The shops sold opulent green fruits and holiday clothing for less than the price of a cup of coffee. Angela bought a handful of bead necklaces and then was overwhelmed by an urge to bring something back for Pollock. On the wall of the shop was a tiny shrine and it too had a fresh flower garland. 'Can I buy?' She touched the flowers with a finger.

'Oh. No!' the man said, shocked, and then: 'How much?' Immediately, he hung his head in shame. She pretended not to have heard and paid for the beads with a wad of toy notes.

Pollock was waiting for her on the boat. 'I have a surprise for you.' His radiant smile was back in place. 'I've organised a musical evening – strictly "sixties"!' He had spread out cushions for people to sit on and small glasses of wine. The light from the candles illuminated his face. With his brown skin and blameless features he had the look of a saint. The other guests arrived. Their jewels and sequins and fringes shifted in the candlelight. 'Has anyone got a request?' Pollock strummed pleasantly on his guitar.

'"Where Have all the Flowers Gone?"' someone said.

He began to play. Voices shuffled in, frail and shabby. Pollock looked anxiously at Angela. For Pollock's sake she tried to keep the concert going but her eagerness became nervousness and people begin to drift away. The music stopped. Pollock turned to her sadly. 'You're timing's all wrong,' he said.

It is an exasperating fact of female nature that once a woman has set her heart on a man almost nothing will deter her. Angela remembered it from her youth. She was surprised to discover that it was still so in middle age. She found that she was both seeking Pollock out and avoiding him. When he looked her way, she buried her face in a book.

On a particularly sultry afternoon she went to bed with a cup of tea and a cigarette and a book. She slept for an hour and then lay in the warm gloom, drowsing. In her half-wakened state a strange thing happened. A sense of self stole over her. Her panic-stricken brain was still. The middle-aged persona that sweated and fretted fell away and a different person – an Angela – slipped into place. With an overwhelming sense of sweetness she recognised that self. Here was the person who would see her though her life.

She pulled all her clothes from the cupboard and threw them on the bed to find fitting attire for this self. Several outfits were rejected before she decided she ought to shower and wash her hair. She stood beneath the shower and then threw wet towels on the bed.

A knock sounded at the door.

'Who is it?' she called out gaily.

'It's Polly!' A timorous voice, but perky.

'Oh!' She could not send him away. She pulled on a dressing gown and looked around at the chaos she had made.

'I've brought some photographs,' he beamed. He looked at her dressing gown and then past her to the shambles of the cabin. There was nowhere to sit except the bed. He lowered himself on to the vacant space and remained bashfully clamped to it. It wasn't just the mess, although she would have judged him a fastidious man. It was the disclosure. He had never meant to see that much of her.

'The photographs, Martin.'

He edged out a picture of a dog and then of a young woman who might be his wife or daughter. Still, he did not speak.

'Would you like a drink?' she asked him.

He shook his head. 'I'm not much of a drinker.' She knew it was true. She had seen him quite inebriated but understood that he did not really drink socially though now and then he got quickly and efficiently drunk. He remained slumped and silent, his photographs clasped to his chest. After a long time, he said, 'I have lost my life.'

'Dear Martin.' She put a hand lightly on his shoulder. 'I do understand. I understand better than you can imagine.'

He turned to look at her for the first time since he had entered the room. His brown eyes looked hopeful and then sad. 'You can't possibly,' he said. 'No one can.'

That night at dinner he directed his attention at a vivid young woman with a hoarse laugh and long red nails. Angela took her punishment meekly and went alone to the cocktail lounge. 'Are you married?' a woman at the bar asked her. She felt less frightened of the other passengers now. 'Yes,' Angela said, and then, 'no.'

'Oh, dear.' The woman watched her through black-rimmed eyes as she hoovered up a Daiquiri through a straw.

Angela drank rather a lot. As she picked an unsteady way to bed she found Pollock waiting for her. 'I'm going to walk you to your cabin,' he said. 'I'm going to make sure you get there safe and sound.' When they moved out of range of other people he took her hand.

'Now we can do this right,' she thought. Her cabin had been tidied again and looked decent and anonymous.

'Do what?' her fuddled brain wondered, and she realised that she meant to make love to him. She would do so with affection more than passion for her sexual hormones now ran on an economical setting. She wanted him to know that what might happen was by her invitation; that he need feel no responsibility or obligation. I'm glad we met,' she told him. 'I shall always be glad. When I go home I shall regret nothing.'

He squeezed her hand and led her up the stairs. 'Up the wooden stairs to Bedfordshire,' he said. When they reached her cabin he hugged her briefly. 'Nightie-night,' he said as he released her. 'Don't let the bedbugs bite.'

In the morning they docked at a smart little port and Angela climbed the two hundred steps to a celebrated hotel. On the terrace, with its vulgarly beautiful view of the bay, she drank coffee and thought about Pollock. It was difficult to understand men when one belonged to a generation brought up to believe that they were all after the one thing. Thirty years had intervened. Sex had become readily available and then mortally hazardous. All the rules of engagement might have changed. Pollock might really be gay. He might have braced himself to cautiously touch a female to protect himself from speculation. A plain, middle-aged woman; that is exactly what he would have chosen. On the other hand he could be heterosexual but understandably wary. He would have sought her out for some reason other than the traditional one. Comfort? Perhaps he only wanted comfort. Well, it was too late now. It was the last day of the cruise and Pollock was feverishly embroiled in preparations for the farewell party.

There was a note under her door when she got back. 'See you at the bash.' It was signed 'The Boy'. She sighed and sought him out. 'I'm not a party animal, Martin. I'll dine alone.' She had already booked a single table for dinner on the terrace of the famous hotel. He hung his head but when his face came up again it was as if a light bulb had come on. 'We might sneak out together. Of course I'll have to be back later, sort out the music and so forth, but I could play truant for an hour or two.'

She altered her booking and had her hair done. She was glad she had made an effort. Pollock wore a black T-shirt and slacks and looked very young and handsome. 'Where shall we go?' He took her hand.

'Shall we find some little bar? There might be one with old songs.'

'I've already found somewhere,' she said. 'It's a surprise.'

The walk up to the hotel made her hot and dizzy. She had to stop a moment and when she did, he swiftly kissed her. As they entered the hotel's cool, beautiful lobby, she thought that for the first time in her life she had absolutely no regrets about anything. She urged him forward to the beautiful terrace. They were brought to their table with its swooning spread of ocean, its misted champagne which she had requested, its white flowers and white linen. She turned to Pollock with shining eyes. 'This looks expensive,' he murmured. 'You should have asked me.' She realised that he was sulking. She suppressed a sigh as she poured champagne. 'It's my treat.' She pushed his glass towards him.

'I don't really like champagne,' he said.

Pollock ordered the cheapest thing on the menu. Angela said she would have the same, for the atmosphere was no longer one in which to linger. When the bill came he insisted on paying his share, working it out meticulously with a calculator. As they reached the boat again, he plunged into the party with frenzied joy.

In the morning she avoided him and he avoided
her. As the coach arrived to take them to the airport
people lined up to bid Pollock farewell. When her
turn came his tragic face pulled at her heart and she
found she could not let go of his hand. 'That's the
ticket,' he said in relief as she managed to release him.
She stepped on to the coach and heard his voice; 'Angela!' It was not the jaunty tone in which he usually
addressed her, but a little voice: full of fear. She
turned and they watched each other hopelessly. Then
he braced himself and faced the crowd. 'I've had some
wonderful times with Angela,' he announced. 'I must
just give her a hug.'

The cruise-goers cheered. His arms came around
her and he held her tight. This time, she did not think
what it might signify. In his arms the years fell away,
the childhood with a father who had frightened her,
the thirty years of marriage to a bullying man. She
had stayed with him out of fear and when, a year ago,
he had left her for another woman, she had been
terrified.

'Be good,' Pollock beamed at her. As the bus
moved away he waved to her, his hand opening and
closing like a child's. Behind his grin, the ghost of his
tragic face gradually faded from her sight. Behind her
habitual expression of dismay, a smile began to grow.

Out of the Apple Tree

Veronica Bright

I sit in the apple tree and look forlornly at the bright cover of the book. Two grinning faces. A sprinkling of freckles. Two sets of plaits. I finger a strand of my own wispy hair. Twins. About nine, my age, I suppose. That's why Mum bought the book for me. She thought I'd like to read about these two laughing, happy, lively girls. Well, I am a girl, but not those other things. And I can't read.

A noise across the lawn makes me look up. The French windows are opening and Mum is bringing Mr Lancaster out on to the terrace in his wheelchair. I almost stop breathing. Mum parks Mr Lancaster and stops to speak to him. He doesn't move. I imagine him grunting. Mum says he grunts on a good day. On a bad day he just stares straight ahead. Mum looks around the garden, probably making sure I'm well and truly hidden. Then she goes back inside Mr Lancaster's house. She's doing his washing today.

The grinning twins catch my eye again. Mum says if I read the whole book we can see any film I like at the cinema. Actually I find the cinema a loud and frightening place. Even with Mum there beside me. I stare hopelessly at the distant river, and my mind slips its moorings again. I like being up here alone. No one stares at me, or asks me how I feel about losing my hair. No one wants me to play because they get fed up when I drop things. No one calls me a rabbit because I scare easily.

Mr Lancaster's lucky. He sits beside his flowers and listens to the bees. John Jessup comes up from the village four times a week to do the garden. The terrace is a tumble of big daisies. I'd like a close look, because I like watching insects. I hope Mum brings me tomorrow, and all the tomorrows of the summer holidays. Yesterday I went to Emma's house, but it didn't work out. At lunchtime, Mum wheels Mr Lancaster away, and I climb carefully off my low branch. I walk softy to the kitchen.

'Appetite like a sparrow,' grumbles Mum. I

imagine Mr Lancaster pecking at a few crumbs. 'Did you get much reading done?' She dishes up beans on toast.

I shake my head.

'You'll never learn if you don't try.'

I feel ashamed. My mum has always tried very hard for me. Throughout my illness I remember her beside my bed, holding my hand, stroking my forehead. I want so much for my mum to be proud of me.

'This afternoon you stay in the kitchen, OK?' says Mum. 'Lie low!' she jokes. I nod. Nobody needs to tell me that. The whole village lies low when it comes to Mr Lancaster. John Jessup's son says he's got a stick he keeps handy for whacking children, and no way would he come up here and help his dad with the gardens. While I was in hospital last year, a crowd of village children crept up Mr Lancaster's drive and he caught them peering through his windows. Emma told me he threw wellington boots at them, then he screamed and bawled and waved his stick. After that he had enormous fences put all round his estate, and notices saying 'Trespassers will be prosecuted'. 'I'll push His Nibs up and down the drive for a bit, then I'll make a nice cup of tea, right?'

I nod again. I open the book. Mum kisses me and

goes out. I try the first line, slowly breaking down the words and trying to hear something sensible emerging. My shoulders sag. I try to find the word twins. It must be there somewhere. A lump heaves in my throat. Tears trickle down my cheeks. I get up and wander around Mr Lancaster's kitchen. I look in all the cupboards, and in the end set up a shop on the kitchen table, with rows of Mr Lancaster's groceries for sale. Since there's no one else around I have to play all the parts – a mother with a new baby coming to buy a tin of beans, then a girl who wants biscuits. I am the shopkeeper too of course. I have a curly perm that bobs about as I speak. Now I'm a very grumpy old man stomping into the shop.

'Eggs!' he growls.

'I have some in the fridge, sir.'

I open Mr Lancaster's fridge and take out a box of eggs.

'Jessica!' My name zooms through the shop. 'What on earth are you doing?'

I drop the eggs. All six of them crunch on the floor.

I burst into tears. Mum'll never let me come again, and I'll have to go to Emma's every day. I sob.

'Hush, hush!'

Mum clears the mess up. She takes Mr Lancaster a cup of tea. I drink my milk in near silence. All the way home I feel Mum's despair. What is to be done with me?

I am allowed back though. The next day I sit in my apple tree, with – you've guessed – the grinning twins. Mr Lancaster is in his place like a terrace statue, and John Jessup is riding up and down the orchard on the grass cutter.

John knows I'm here, but I keep quiet. Mum said Mr Lancaster likes a calm atmosphere. Funny how he likes to throw wellingtons, I think. Anyway, there are some hopes of a calm atmosphere with John Jessup about. John Jessup is one of the friendliest people on earth and he seems to make a noise wherever he goes. He does a lot of whistling. He sings in the church choir, and practises between times in a strong deep-voiced bellow. Mr Lancaster doesn't bat an eye.

John's just getting into the third verse of 'Rock of Ages' as he approaches my tree. Suddenly the engine cuts out and he stops singing. The silence is deafening. John gazes up at me.

'Lovely day!' he bellows.

'Shh. I'm a secret.'

'Sweet?' He holds up a bag of sherbet lemons.

I pause only for a moment. 'Thanks.' I whisper.

John nods in Mr Lancaster's direction. 'His Nibs is sounds asleep, never fear.'

I looked over the terrace.

'Snoring and gurgling!' he grins.

He restarts the grass cutter, and launches into 'Rock of Ages' verse four.

At lunch, John says I can help weed the terrace while His Nibs is out having a ride. Mum looks shocked. Maybe she's thinking that I'll be attacked with a stick if Mr Lancaster finds me there. Or have two large boots heaved in my direction. But she remembers the shop episode of yesterday, and agrees. John shows me which plants are evil weeds, and I start to take the sinners out. He tells me not to work so fast or Mr Lancaster will think he's been a slacker up till now. I giggle. I work slowly. There are hundreds of tiny insects to watch.

John and I weed the borders for three-quarters of an hour, then we go into the kitchen. As we drink lemonade, he spots the grinning twins.

'Good book?'

I mumble a reply. I am ashamed of not being able to read.

'I like a good story,' says John.

My face reddens. I press my lips together. And of course he knows at once.

'Aw, lass,' he says, 'I'm sorry. You've been away from school for so long.'

He pauses, thinking.

'Did your mum buy you this book?'

I nod.

'You're a fine wee girl,' is all he says.

Next time John comes to the big house it rains, so I help him water His Nibs's tomatoes in the greenhouse. John's brought something for me. He holds out a book. It's got a couple of lines of print on each page, and loads of pictures.

'Try this.'

'It's for babies.'

'I see no babies!' His eyes are twinkling, but he's not laughing at me.

I take the book, and open it. I am afraid. Afraid of not being able to read even this, this book for children half my age.

'I see a girl with courage.'

John isn't smiling now. He's willing me to have a go.

I open the book.

'Take your time, lass.'

He draws up a huge flowerpot, and turns it upside down for me to sit on. Nervously I point to the first word. John quietly turns back to the tomatoes. I begin in a whisper. Whenever I stop, John gives me the time to ponder, to sound out, to try. Sometimes he gently tells me a word. I get to the end of the book. John is busy watering. 'Well done, lass,' he says. I open the book again. I read it aloud, more confidently this time, with no help, all by myself.

John has two more books in his bag. 'For tomorrow, when I'm not here,' he says. 'Our little secret.'

Next day I sit in the apple tree and I read both John's books. It takes me a long time, and I nearly throw them out of the tree more than once. Then I finally manage to work out for myself the word 'machine', to say it properly, and to understand the sentence I'm reading. I let out an enormous 'YES!' Immediately I'm conscious of being in Mr Lancaster's tree. Is he looking at me, or is he asleep? Please let him be asleep.

I watch, horrified, as his hand picks up a small bell on his lap, and he rings it. My mum hurries out and bends towards him. She looks towards my tree, and I know I'm done for. This is far worse than the grocer's shop episode.

I watch Mum cross the terrace and head for the tree. I grip the branch.

'Jessica. Mr Lancaster would like to say hello.'

I stuff the books into my bag, and climb slowly off my perch.

'Is he going to hit me with his stick?'

'Jessica!' she says, shocked. She probably doesn't believe the stories of the flying boots.

Close to, Mr Lancaster is extremely scary. His face is wrinkly and pitted, and his mouth hangs slightly open, as if he isn't ever going to be able to shut it again.

Mum says, 'This is Jessica, Mr Lancaster. I didn't introduce you yesterday as you weren't feeling too well.'

Mr Lancaster grunts. I wonder if he's suddenly going to turn into a pig, and I giggle. Mum shoots me a look.

'Hello, Mr Lancaster,' I whisper.

'Some lemonade,' grunts Mr Lancaster.

'Jessica won't be any trouble,' says Mum, and she's off to the kitchen. If you can imagine your mother leaving you on a lonely terrace with a potentially dangerous boot thrower, you'll know exactly how I'm feeling right now.

In the silence, I blurt out a question. 'Why can't you walk, Mr Lancaster?'

The old man stares at me. He is not used to

children. Well, he wouldn't be, would he? He drives them away.

'I mean, most people walk if they can.'

Suddenly Mr Lancaster is making gravelly noises that come from a place deep inside him. I wonder if he is having a heart attack. I am rooted to the spot, when obviously I should be rushing in to fetch Mum. Then here she is, coming round the corner with a tray of lemonade and cherry biscuits.

'Nice to see you laughing, Mr Lancaster,' she says. 'Well done, Jessica. You've cheered Mr Lancaster up already.'

A wave of relief hits me as I realise Mr Lancaster isn't about to die.

'Cherry biscuits, eh?' he croaks, 'My favourites.'

'Mine too, Mr Lancaster.'

Mum smiles and I can tell I'm doing OK.

After that, summer holidays look up. I go to the big house with Mum every day except Sundays, when John's wife cooks His Nibs a nice lunch. I help John with the weeding, and he says I'm a star so often, I think I shall soon start shining in the dark. John helps me read the books he brings. I think he smuggles them out of his children's bedrooms.

I help Mum too by looking after Mr Lancaster

on the terrace. I start by telling him stories I make up specially. Sometimes he goes to sleep in the middle and then I have to tell them again the next day.

Mum usually pushes His Nibs around his grounds in the afternoons – and I like to go too. Mum says His Nibs is a recluse. I'd like to be a recluse when I grow up. John says I won't need anyone to tell me stories because I make up enough of my own. Then he says I am getting on with my books so well, I am nearly ready to give a public reading performance. I laugh, because he is teasing me. But I know I am doing well, and this makes me try even harder. One day Mr Lancaster asks me if I play draughts. I smile, because I played so many games of draughts when I was ill, I think I might be able to beat him. His Nibs tells me where to find the draughts. I set up the game on a tray, and we start. Mr Lancaster grunts. I always know he's having a good day when he grunts. I concentrate hard. Mr Lancaster looks at the board with his unblinking tortoise eyes, his neck disappearing into the shell of a scarf that is wrapped around his neck. He is very surprised when I win.

Next day he is sitting up at the table. It will help him to concentrate better, he croaks happily. I wonder if he has been practising all night, because he is much better at draughts today. We have three games and he wins the first two. When Mum brings him his lunch he grumbles that I have tired him out. But his eyes are gleaming, and I know he's had the best fun of his whole week.

At the end of the summer holidays I worry about going back to school. John cheerily tells me I'll be fine. Mr Lancaster says we must have a final Battle of the Draughts to see who is the Champion. We fix the date for two days' time, and His Nibs tells Mum to buy plenty of cherry biscuits and some lemonade. 'For this auspicious event,' he croaks.

I find John in the orchard inspecting the apples. I dance along beside him as I tell him about the Championships. Then we go to the greenhouse and I wait for him to get my next book out of his bag. My heart sinks when I look at the cover. Two grinning faces. A sprinkling of freckles. Two sets of plaits.

'Tell you what,' says John seeing the horror written all over my face, 'I'll read one page, you read the next.'

'Isn't that cheating?'

'What do you mean, cheating?'

'This is the book Mum said if I read it all, she'd take me to the cinema.'

'I thought you weren't bothered about the cinema.'

There is silence and John stops mixing tomato food.

'Jessica. You're not the same timid little thing I found in the apple tree one morning in July. Look at you. Brown as a berry. Skipping about like a young lamb. Laughing and talking to Mr Dragonface as if he's your best friend. Well,' he twinkles, 'second-best friend.' John waves his arm and bows, as if he is presenting me to the Queen. 'Jessica. Competitor in the Champion Draughts Battle. And Reader of Books.'

I laugh. I remember Mum's words. 'You'll never learn if you don't try.' So I open the book and have a go.

Five minutes later my whole world turns upside down. Mum rushes into the greenhouse shouting for John. Something dreadful has happened to Mr Lancaster. An ambulance is on its way.

Two days later I am taken to see Mr Lancaster in the hospital. Mum says he's rallied, whatever that means, and that he is asking for me. The nurses say he is insisting on it, but wonder if they ought to let me. Mum says I've lived inside a hospital myself for such a long time, I'll cope very well. We go together. I've got some cherry biscuits in my bag. His Nibs is lying very still.

'Mr Lancaster, I've brought you some cherry biscuits.'

'He's asleep right now,' says the nurse. I put the biscuits on the bedside table.

'We'll sit here a while,' says Mum. She pulls up two chairs. Mum takes out a magazine. I stare at Mr Lancaster, lying there in that hospital bed, and I remember being ill. I used to like it when Mum read to me. I open my bag and take out my book. The one with the twins on the front.

'I'm going to read to you, dear,' I say, just like Mum used to say to me when I lay in the hospital bed with my eyes closed.

I open up at page one, and begin, quite slowly at first. I sense Mum's eyes widening. I read and read. I get lost in the story. At the end of Chapter Two, Mum gently puts her hand into mine. I look up. Tears run silently down her cheeks, but her eyes are shining.

'You can read, Jessica.'

'John Jessup taught me.'

'It's a great gift, reading.'

'But the best gift of all is friendship.' The voice from the bed is like the crunch of boots on gravel. I go timidly over. Mr Lancaster grunts. And that grunt proves it beyond doubt.

Today is a good day. And I can read.

The Play is Not the Thing

Elizabeth Buchan

Nicola phoned just as Annie got home from work. 'Mum, I've got a part.'

Nicola had been auditioning for the next season's production of *As You Like It* at the Globe Theatre. It would be her first job since leaving acting school and Annie knew better than to ask, 'Rosalind?' Or even, 'Celia?' Instead she said. 'Brilliant, darling.'

'It's Phebe.'

Annie knew what was expected of her. '*Wonderful*,' she said. 'We're so proud. To do so well, so quickly . . .'

There was a small pause. 'It's only Phebe, Mum.'

This time, Nicola permitted a trace of disappointment to show. Despite having no experience, despite having just acquired the vital agent, Nicola had hoped to make the leap to a lead in one swift swoop. Her dreams ran along traditional lines and because Nicola was blood of her blood and bone of her bone Annie understood them perfectly. At this point in the conversation, Annie might also have said, *We warned you.*

A little over a year ago, Nicola had confronted her parents in the kitchen. She was blonde, lithe, perhaps not as slim as she would wish, and glowing with the fire of her decision. 'I'm going to be an actress. I've made up my mind. I can't live without it.' She banged her fist lightly against her heart. 'I've been thinking and thinking since finals, and that's it.'

Annie had been unwrapping the ready-made lasagne at the time. She reached for a cloth to wipe her hands. 'I thought you were considering being a teacher.'

'No,' Nicola replied. 'Not.'

'Good,' said her mother. 'All that paperwork.'

Nicola peered at Annie. 'I know you want me to head up Goldman Sachs or something . . . but I've been accepted for a year's postgraduate course at drama school . . . I'm sorry I didn't tell you before.'

Annie was not listening. She turned to her husband. 'Bob, who do we know who can help?'

'Mum . . . it's not about who you know. It's about my *talent*.'

'Oh Lord,' said Annie, 'I'd forgotten you're still at that stage. But, darling, it's *who* you know that makes the difference.'

Bob flashed his daughter a smile. 'Your mother is a cynic. She's too successful these days to remember being a beginner. You keep your dreams, my sweetheart.'

Annie was running various possibilities though her head. There was Peter Change, married to Amelia in the office. He occasionally pitched up in a small part in the *The Bill* or *Holby City*. There was Mary Slope who had had a brief, but fairly glorious, career in the West End. She and Annie were in touch from time to time. Their communications ran along the lines of: *You haven't changed a bit*. And: *To think it was thirty years ago*. Either one could give Nicola a pointer, or maybe introduce her to someone.

Nicola fixed a serious pair of eyes on her mother. 'Are you paying attention? I'll find my own way.'

Annie took a deep breath. 'Is this going to be expensive, Nics, do you think?'

'Yes, it will,' said Bob. 'Do you expect anything else?'

Nicola had recently emerged from Leeds University and had taken a part-time job as a yoga teacher in the local gym. It was not a job designed to bring in a healthy salary but Nicola protested that, provided she could rub along, it was fine. Anyway, opening up the chakras of people badly in need of chakra fine-tuning was reward in itself. 'The flow of energy, the spring-cleaning of the spirit are vital,' she had explained to a bewildered Bob. 'Do you see?'

Bob had not seen but, as a honed and experienced business manager, understood drama school required financing. 'So, no more chakra tuning which will be hard on the bank balance.'

Nicola flushed. 'Yes.'

'Bob . . .' said Annie. 'Wait.' She glanced around the kitchen, so warmly lit and full of nice things that Bob and she had taken a long marriage to accumulate. 'Nicola. I think your father and I have been negligent about the facts of life.'

'Mum . . .' Nicola looked distinctly alarmed. 'I have Paul, and the horse has bolted. I am twenty-two.'

'*That's* another thing,' said Annie. 'Paul.'

Here Bob intervened. 'Stick to the subject.'

'The facts of life,' maintained Annie obstinately. 'Bills, pensions, somewhere to live. *Those* facts of life.

How are you going to manage on an actor's wages? Are you strong enough to stand it? It's tough, so tough, Nics.'

'For goodness' sake, Mum. There's no need to make a drama of it.'

'The danger is that you will spend your time being envious, or making comparisons with Hollywood stars. How are you going to prevent yourself becoming neurotic and self-obsessed and miserable? That's the important question.'

Nicola looked bewildered. 'Like everyone else does,' she replied. 'Only I won't be sitting in an office, but doing something I'm passionate about. *Loving it.*' She took her mother's hand. 'Are you passionate about what you do, Mum, and, if you aren't, wouldn't you like to be?'

Good question. Even so, Annie had known from that moment on that it would be necessary to guard tight her terror for her daughter's future disappointments.

Now, Nicola was going to be Phebe.

Thirty years earlier, Annie stepped out of her clothes in the dressing room of the university theatre and sat down in front of the mirror. A gentle breathing sound emanated from the intercom and, occasionally, a curse uttered by the stage manager escaped from it. *Damn, damn.*

She hunched forward and put cream over her face, before applying Leichners Number 5 and 9. The greasepaint spread obediently across her features, a helpful mask. *Bring me the head of Jokanaan.* Salome's vengeful thought flowed through Annie's fingers which trembled with fury as she applied eyeliner and fixed her false eyelashes. That she should have been so rejected – by a prophet and a man so puny that he scarce could be called a man. 'I am writing a play,' declared the playwright Oscar Wilde, 'about a woman dancing in her bare feet in the blood of a man she has craved for and slain.'

Someone stuck their head around the dressing-room door. 'Thirty minutes, Annie, OK?'

She barely heard, for she was concentrating on the wounds inflicted by the puny man. She was slender, ripe and powerful. He was dried up by the desert and religious fanaticism, an outcast, crying in the wilderness, and she had offered him the riches of her body and, who knew what else for Herod's court was lavish, but he had said no. He had pushed aside her ripeness and beauty . . . and she could not let that pass.

The false eyelashes stung, and she blinked hard.

Then she rose, and stepped into a black shift, over which she pulled a black chiffon tunic and fastened it with a jewelled belt and placed the gold circlet on her head. She was Herod's stepdaughter, and dance she would in Jokanaan's blood.

In the wings, Continuity pushed past Annie carrying a bowl of fake fruit for Herod's banquet. 'Sorry, darling, don't mind me,' he said.

What was the smell? Probably Annie's own fear, the greasepaint on her face, the mix of heat, scent and sweat from the cast.

There was a touch on her elbow. It was Neil . . . but it was Jokanaan. Scrawny, battered Jokanaan who, in real life, said things such as: *Annie, duck, could you feed me that line again?* And: *Now's the time for a pint, troupers.* But on the stage, he declared in hatred. 'Back! Daughter of Sodom. By woman came evil into the world.'

The noise slid snakily past Annie's defences. The triple beat and thud of her heart, pulse and groin. The mutter of the stage manager into the intercom. The low pitch of exchanges between the audience. Phlegm in throats. Seats snapping up and down.

Phlegm in her own throat. Her stomach constricting.

In a matter of minutes, Annie would walk on to the stage with the words of Oscar Wilde's curious, over-wrought text hovering on her lips. She would offer herself to this man, endure his rejection and demand his head. In order to become Salome, Annie must strip the vestiges of who she was to the bone. In turn, Salome would dance the dance to rouse a powerful king's lust, and let fall the seven veils to expose the flesh that would inflame Herod. This acting process – the striven-for metamorphosis, ran the entry in the acting diary that Annie faithfully kept – demanded that she denude herself of reason, of rationality, of logical pursuit of thought, of all things that she had been taught to revere. Becoming Salome demanded that Annie renounce her privacy and step forth bare, unadorned, vulnerable.

The lights dimmed, the audience hushed. The opening lines between the Nubian, the Cappadocian, the young Syrian, the soldiers and the page went back and forth between them.

Eventually, the stage manager said. 'Break a leg,' and a finger was jabbed into Annie's buttock. 'On yer go.'

Annie stepped forward into the lights.

For a second, she hovered between one world and the other, and an exultation bore her upwards. It was a moment of exquisite sensation, of balancing on a wave rolling towards a horizon where everything, anything, was possible.

A woman in the audience coughed, a nasty, chesty sound. The chiffon tunic billowed out, and settled around Annie's legs. She glided towards the hot, white light, so bright that it succeeded in blotting out the other world in which the audience sat, and opened her mouth. 'I will not stay, I cannot stay . . .' she addressed the dazzled Syrian.

At the finale, having danced in front of the lustful Herod and demanded her prize, Salome held up the head of the butchered Jokanaan, and the pieces of papier mâché soaked in stage blood fell at her feet, leaving a stain on the stage. She stepped over it to take her bow, bent her head and listened intently to clapping. With each smack of one palm on the other, she was lifted ever upward. *The words had made it happen. The play had made it happen. I made it happen.*

The sweetness and seduction of the conclusion caught the breath in her throat. She lifted her head and made out the shapes of the bodies in the seats. I have never been so happy, she thought. I have never been so right. I possess the power to do this.

Annie and Bob shuffled into their seats at the Globe

Theatre. Bob settled himself and then got up again, smartish. 'The seat is like rock. I'll go and hire those cushions.'

It was a warm evening, so the extra jacket Annie had brought would be redundant. She checked over the emails on her Blackberry. During the week the market had risen significantly, and she had been busy profit-taking for her clients.

Annie did well for her clients and for her small stockbroking firm. She believed in dealing in the spades: the unglamorous, practical, realistic commodities on which the world was built and on which it relied – concrete for building, glass, iron. She had great faith in those, and enjoyed beating the markets with them. They made her money, and with that money she and Bob had established their life together.

The sky was summer blue, and birds dived over the theatre's open roof. Shakespeare must have looked up at a similar skyscape as he waited, as she did, for the play to begin. From the stage area, a hidden musician struck a note on a stringed instrument. For a moment, it reverberated, sweet and husky-toned. Bob reappeared with the cushions and Annie accepted hers gratefully.

Bob shifted close to his wife, and their thighs

touched, familiar and comforting. 'It's worse than being . . .' He stopped. 'What if . . . ?'

'What if . . . ?'

'She forgets her lines. Trips over the stage. Can't move for terror.'

'She might, but a lot of things pass unnoticed on the stage, Bob.'

He looked at Annie. 'Do you regret it?'

She did not have to ask as to what she might regret. She laid a hand on his knee. 'No.' Bob looked a little sceptical. 'Well, perhaps the odd moment. It catches me. The old longing, but nothing serious.'

In the wings the music from pipes and tabors swelled into harmony, and several figures dressed in motley strolled on to the stage singing, '*There was a lover and his lass . . .*'

'Oh God,' said Bob, 'it's going to be one of those productions. *Very* Shakespearean.'

'Shush,' said Annie.

She barely noticed anything until Phebe/Nicola appeared. Beside her, Bob stiffened. 'Is that *her?*'

For a second or two, Annie did not recognise her daughter. The fair hair was hidden under a long black wig, and the clumsy shepherdess's kirtle hid the figure she thought she knew so well. 'You see, Mum,' Nicola had explained earlier, 'you must think about Phebe as

Shakespeare thought of her. Phebe would have been played by a boy actor, and he/she must fall in love with Rosalind, another boy actor playing a girl who is disguised as a boy. It's complicated.'

And so were Annie's feelings. Her disguised daughter wooed both Rosalind and the audience, with surprised petulance, and with the vigour of her suddenly acquired passion, and ignored Silvius, the shepherd who truly loved her. Phebe/Nicola spoke and Annie strained every sinew to listen. She remembered so well the requirement to catch the breath just so and, thus, get through the sentence. She remembered the exhaustion of wearing unfamiliar clothes as if they were a second skin. She knew how half of the mind has to concentrate on the moves – step too far in one direction and the lighting goes wrong; forget to move, and the spotlight misses you. Yes, the part of Phebe was small, but important. It was there, she was sure Shakespeare intended, to remind the audience that it is luck as much as anything else that divided the happy couple from the unhappy one.

Almost breathless and unmoving, Annie sat and willed her daughter through the play – willed her to be so good that she, Annie, forgot Nicola was her daughter. Phebe shrugged and let slip the remark that

Jaques was 'an old gentlemen' and Annie thought: No, I would have not said the line in quite that way. Phebe smiled at Rosalind and Annie: Yes, that was absolutely right.

Phebe tossed back her long, black hair and opened her eyes wide. And, Annie, drawn deep into the performance, shuddered at the inevitable pain that Phebe was going to have to endure at the hand of Rosalind. And, at the end of the play, after all the words had been spoken and the situations resolved, the lovers had drifted into a dance in the enchanted Forest of Arden, Annie found she could not speak.

'Brilliant,' said Bob, eyes glued to the stage.

'Poor Phebe,' said Annie at last.

'Nicola did brilliantly.'

'Yes, of course,' said Annie.

Her eyes were fixed on the cast who, linking hands to take their bow, moved to the front of the stage. More than a few wore the glazed look of woken sleepwalkers. Still in character, Nicola moved forward and clasped her hands and raised her eyes. The applause sounded, not too bad, not over-whelming. Yet, Annie could tell, it was enough. She knew the sound of palm smacking on palm lifted her daughter on to the crest of the wave, and carried her towards the horizon where anything, everything, was possible.

It had been the photographer who begged admittance into the dressing room after the final performance of *Salome*. He was thin, red-haired and hungry. He was a stringer, he explained, for the big newspapers and he had been very, very interested by her dance of the seven veils. If *he* had been lucky enough to have been Herod, he would have granted her anything. Would Annie care to let him photograph her performing the dance again because he had an idea that the *Sun* would be interested, particularly if she was planning to be a professional actress? The publicity would be useful, he pointed out, with a flickering smile.

Annie remembered staring at him, the creep of nausea at the back of her throat taking her by surprise. Yet it was not the photographer and his invitation – he had made what he wanted perfectly clear in a perfectly open manner. If she took off her clothes, he would give her publicity. What could be plainer, or fairer? No, it had been Annie who had changed in that instant. A spotlight had been trained on the future: a harsh, white light which spared Annie nothing. In that small exchange, she knew that she would have to live with precariousness and a hunger such as his as daily companions. Each time she stepped on to the stage, she would have to obey the demands of the acting process which she had written about so carefully, and expose both her body and her soul to others.

And she did not wish to do it.

That was it.

Simple.

Annie watched as the actress playing Rosalind bowed and smiled, and waved to the audience. She observed Nicola, still holding hands with Silvius, watching Rosalind. Nicola's evident ambition for the big role had, once, been Annie's own, but she was perfectly content that it was that way round. She thought briefly of her spade commodities which, no doubt, would bring in increased yields overnight.

Again, the cast moved forward to take the final, final bow. Nicola/Phebe tossed her theatrical black locks, and tippled into a curtsy which showed a pair of ripe, provocative breasts to naughty advantage and the audience laughed. For a moment, Nicola claimed its full attention, and Annie thought, yes, my daughter, that was clever, that was good.

Hands on his knees, Bob bent forward. 'Maybe . . .' he uttered. 'Maybe, she will do it.'

'Maybe,' echoed Annie.

Smiling, she gathered up her jacket as she and Bob prepared to go backstage.

Summer at the White House

Clare Chambers

I never read obituaries. In fact, I never buy newspapers at all, but someone had left one beside me on the train, so naturally I glanced at it, and was shocked to see a name I recognised among the departed. The photograph, which was captioned *France mourns its adopted son*, showed the great man reclining in a planter's chair, and I was instantly transported back to that summer years ago, when I met the famous poet, and fell in love for the first time.

When I was sixteen, my parents persuaded me to go on an exchange visit to France during the summer, with the aim of 'bringing me out of my shell'. In fact, they were in the process of divorcing and wanted me out of the way while they carved up the house.

The arrangements were made through school, and
I was duly matched with a girl called Laure Bougerol,
from a small village near Lisieux in Normandy. We
exchanged letters – a brief, stilted note in each other's
language, followed by more heartfelt ramblings in our
native tongue. It seemed so promising.

On the appointed day a whole group of exchangees
travelled down to Portsmouth together, and we were
met off the ferry at Caen by the French rep, whose job
it was to see us on to our trains for the next leg of the
journey. We had been assured that our host family
would be there to pick us up at the other end, but
when I alighted at Lisieux in the early-evening
sunshine no one came forward to greet me. I watched
as one by one the waiting cars swung out of the
station and the last few passengers melted away,
leaving me alone. Half an hour passed, then an hour.
With a sense of rising panic I extricated Laure's
address from the sheaf of documents in my rucksack:
La Maison Blanche, Merivel, St Pierre, followed by a
phone number. I steeled myself to make a call in
French. The phone box was as hot as a greenhouse
and stank of urine, and the door, which had an
awkward un-English way of folding, slammed shut,
sealing me in with the heat and stench. I had trouble
deciphering the instructions, and each time I started

a low washing line slung between two trees held various balled-up items of clothing, which must have been thrown at it from a distance. I approached the front door, which was ajar to reveal a heap of empty bottles.

'*Bonjour?*' I quavered. There was no reply, so I wandered round the back. At the end of the garden, beyond a scatter of apple trees, was a caravan and in front of it stood a man tossing bundles of paper on to a bonfire. I approached cautiously – he looked slightly unhinged.

'*Excusez-moi. Je cherche La Maison Blanche.*'

He looked up and smiled. 'Would it be impertinent of me to answer in English?' he said, and I was so surprised and relieved that I could only laugh. He had a warm, educated voice, and was perhaps fortyish. 'I shall escort you to La Maison Blanche if you tell me your name,' he went on, as another ream landed on the pyre.

'Amanda Wetherall,' I said. 'I'm staying with the Bougerols. They were supposed to meet me at Lisieux station, but no one turned up.'

The man stirred the fire with a thin branch. 'What could be grander, than to philander, upon the veranda, with charming Amanda?' he mused. 'It's nice to be speaking English. You must come and visit me while you're here and tell me how England is managing without me.' I laughed, again, out of embarrassment; he was so strange.

'What are you burning?' I asked, looking at the typewritten pages, crinkling in the flames.

'Oh, my latest masterpiece. Nothing important.'

'Are you a writer?' I was still at an age when it seemed an impressive thing to be.

'Apparently not.' He pulled a letter from his pocket and passed it across. It was from a London publisher. *Dear Mr Rafferty*, it read, *Thank you for your recent submission, which is not suitable for our list. Since you asked for an honest appraisal I must tell you that our reader found it 'ponderous, implausible and overwritten . . .'*

'Oh,' I said. 'Do they all say things like that?'

He twitched it out of my hand and on to the fire. 'Mostly. Come on.'

We had got no further than the road when a shabby Citroën pulled up beside us. A woman with cropped black hair leapt out of the passenger seat and rushed over, blethering apologies. She kissed me on both cheeks, and then carried on jabbering at my companion.

'Madame Bougerol is desolate to have missed you, but her mother had a fall and had to be taken to hospital for an X-ray,' he translated. 'She hopes you didn't have a difficult journey.'

Reassurances and apologies having been exchanged, I allowed myself to be driven the last hundred yards to La Maison Blanche. The driver, whom I assumed to be Monsieur Bougerol since Madame had squeezed his knee as they set off, remained silent on the journey and vanished into the house unintroduced, which struck me as rather ill-mannered. I discovered at dinner that he was in fact a Belgian house guest whose car Madame had commandeered.

La Maison Blanche was a large, three-storey house crowded with vast, ugly furniture – the kitchen table alone would have filled our whole through-lounge back in Chertsey. I was shown to my bedroom by Laure, who was as paralysed by shyness as I was and could do little more than smile and blush. This, as it turned out, was the high point in our relationship.

There were six of us at dinner: myself, Monsieur, Madame, Laure, the injured granny with her arm in plaster, and the taciturn house guest, Monsieur Salin, who smoked throughout the meal. He had the air of someone who had dropped into the scene from another era, in his high-waisted tapered trousers and stiff-fronted shirt.

As soon as the meal was over, Monsieur Bougerol

went off to a political meeting, Monsieur Salin
clumped upstairs to his room and shut the door, and
Madame Bougerol waved aside my offer to do the
washing up, so that Laure and I could chat and plan
the days ahead.

Laure explained that we would be spending
tomorrow in Deauville, about forty minutes away.
Madame would take us early in the morning, and
bring us home after work. We could look around the
shops, sunbathe, swim, etc. Laure seemed extremely
eager to promote this scheme, though I would have
been happy to spend a day getting my bearings and
exploring the tiny hamlet of Merivel. . .

The reason for Laure's insistence soon became
clear: she had a boyfriend, Serge, who worked in
Deauville, in one of the overpriced car parks on the
promenade, designed to keep riff-raff off the beach.

Laure introduced us, and then they spent the next
twenty minutes snogging while I stood around
feeling spare. She finally dragged herself away when a
queue of cars began hooting indignantly, and we went
on to the beach to sunbathe. I had just stripped down
to my bikini and oiled myself, when Laure announced
that she was too hot and was going back to the car
park. I told her to please herself and that I would
meet her there at the end of the day and she seemed

delighted with this arrangement, and loped off up the sand, her dark hair swinging. Not having anticipated long periods alone, I hadn't even brought a book, so I lay back on my towel beneath a film of sweat and oil, cooking on the outside and seething on the inside.

While we waited for our lift back home Laure asked me not to mention Serge to her mother. Oho, I thought, but I said OK. With the vocabulary at my disposal, not mentioning things was a pleasure.

The next day followed the same pattern but on the third day I rebelled. 'I don't want to go to Deauville today,' I said at breakfast.

'Why not?' Laure asked, ever so casually, but shooting me imploring glances. Her mother was within earshot.

'I want to stay in Merivel.'

'But there is nothing at Merivel.' This was true – it was a hamlet of five houses and an ossuary reputed to contain a toe of St Peter.

'What about the menhir?' Madame suggested. 'You should take Amanda to see the menhir.' Laure rolled her eyes.

'I have a headache,' I said. 'I'd prefer to rest.' As I climbed the stairs I could hear angry whispers being exchanged, and no sooner had I flopped down on the bed than Madame tapped on my door and asked if I needed anything. I said no, and that I was quite happy on my own and she went away, satisfied.

Eventually I heard the car starting in the driveway, and I ventured out on to the landing, setting the floorboards creaking. From Monsieur Salin's room, opposite, I heard him whisper 'Justine?' but as that was Madame's name, not mine, I didn't reply. Then the door opened and he stood there bare-chested, his funny tapered trousers half unbuttoned. He recoiled when he saw me, muttered *'Pardon'* and slammed the door again.

I crept out of the house and made straight for Les Bouleaux. It didn't occur to me that its eccentric occupant might have company, but when I rang the doorbell it was answered by a blonde woman in a towel. She was holding a home-made cigarette, which smelled of herbs.

She peered at me blearily.

'Is Mr . . . er . . . at home?' I faltered.

'Mr Rafferty? He lives in the caravan,' the woman said, in a foreign accent.

I thanked her and wandered round the back, past the patch of scorched grass, and stood listening at the caravan door. I could imagine my mother's voice. *Are you quite mad?* From inside came the clatter of an ancient typewriter. The sound faltered as I knocked, then resumed. I knocked again, more loudly.

The tapping stopped and a voice said, 'Please go away. I'm working.'

I flinched as if I'd been slapped, and then scurried back up the garden, mortified. How could I have been naive enough to take his invitation seriously when clearly it was just a frivolous comment, uttered then instantly forgotten? As I slipped through the gate I heard the caravan door clang but I kept running, past La Maison Blanche, out of Merivel and along the lanes, for about a mile, following signs to the menhir, which turned out to be a fallen slab of rock, like an altar, at the edge of a field of stubble. It was there, looking at the glare of sunlight on stone, that I realised I had dropped my sunglasses – probably at Les Bouleaux.

When I arrived back at La Maison Blanche I found the glasses perched on the crumbling wall beside a wilting posy of wild flowers. I took the flowers to my room and pressed them between the pages of my diary, where over time they turned brown and tissue-thin, like dead moths.

I didn't dare go near Les Bouleaux again, but the strange thing was, every few days there would be a fresh offering of flowers on the wall. I began to wonder if it was in fact me they were intended for, so

I left these where they were, and they stayed on the wall unclaimed until they were crisp and dead.

Two days before my departure I bumped into him on my way out of the post office in St Pierre. I had popped in there to send off one last postcard, while Madame Bougerol waited in the car.

'Amanda!' he said, as if anxious to detain me.

'Oh. Hello.' I said, primly.

'You spurned my offerings of flowers. And I don't blame you, after my appalling rudeness the other day.'

I couldn't help smiling at his melodramatic way of talking. 'Um . . .' Across the square I could see Madame Bougerol staring at us through the car window.

'I asked you to come and see me which you kindly did, and I was rude for reasons which are no fault of yours and I apologise.'

'That's perfectly –'

'Please come tomorrow instead.'

'Well, it's my last day. They might have plans for me.'

'I'm prepared to grovel.'

I laughed, embarrassed. 'I can't stop – Madame's waiting,' and I scuttled down the steps to the safety of the car.

I knew I would go, of course, whatever their plans.

It was as if I had been waiting all my sixteen years for this summons.

The following morning there were fresh flowers on the wall and a note, which read simply: *Menhir, 1 p.m.* It was easy to give Laure the slip. We had been swimming at St Pierre, and were back by noon, when I said I was going to pack. Only Monsieur Salin saw me leave. I noticed his pale face at the window as I crept down the drive, and he gave me a conspiratorial smile, almost as if he knew.

The sun was high overhead as I jogged along the lanes between fields of maize and dry paddocks. Inquisitive cows, cropping the brown turf, followed my progress with blank stares.

At the menhir, Mr Rafferty was sitting on the altar stone, which was laid with a picnic of wine, bread, cheese and apricots.

'I'm so glad you've come,' he said, as I approached. 'Eating this much cheese on my own would have given me nightmares for weeks.' He poured me a glass of strong, black wine.

'You're not trying to get me drunk, are you?' I laughed. It was something women said in films.

'God, no,' he said. 'You'll be no use to me at all drunk.' And from the floor beside him he picked up a Scrabble set and began to lay it out on the flattest part of the stone. 'It's impossible to get a decent game around here. It's the only thing about England I actually miss.'

As we played he explained the reason for his grumpiness on the occasion of my visit. He had been working on a story when one of his tenants had disturbed him by bringing the post, which contained another crushing rejection letter. He had done his best to summon inspiration again, but my interruption had been the last straw. 'Still, it's no excuse and I'm justly punished.'

'Punished how?'

'I thought when I first saw you how nice it would be to get to know you and now I can see I was right, but it's your last day so I never shall.'

'I might be back for another visit one day.'

'To the Bougerols? Is that likely?'

I had to admit it wasn't. 'I could phone my parents and tell them I'm not coming back tomorrow,' I suggested. 'I could stay with you for a few days. If you like.'

He seemed mildly amused by this idea. 'It's tempting. But only a very bad man would say yes to that, and I'm not a *very* bad man,' he said, selecting an apricot. 'A very bad writer, yes,' he added.

When he had beaten me at Scrabble, he packed the

remains of the picnic in a canvas bag, then he took my hand and we made our way back to Merivel. Where the path joined the road he stopped and kissed me, and we didn't say goodbye, but fell out of step, so that we wouldn't reach La Maison Blanche together.

I never saw him again. The next day I returned home and my mother said how much more confident I seemed, and how I'd changed, and wasn't it all down to the experience of finding my feet in a foreign country. And I just smiled my newly confident smile and said nothing.

I tore out that obituary and took it into work with me. Nearly everyone had heard of him; he had apparently won quite a prestigious poetry prize the year before.

'Did you meet him?' people kept asking. 'What was he like?'

And I had to admit that we'd hardly exchanged a word, though we were living under the same roof. But I stuck the clipping on the wall above my desk – *Henri Salin 1927–2005* – and often look at it and think of those two writers: one very good, and one very bad.

A Touch of Scarlet

Mavis Cheek

Betty Barker put her key in the door, took a deep, *deep* breath – the kind you take when you need all your courage – and entered her home. She closed the door behind her, put her keys into the empty blue-and-white dish on the hall table and felt the familiar pain. It was right there, just beneath her heart, an ache that she had never known before, physical and real, so that she gave a little gasp. The blue-and-white dish was once home to two sets of keys, hers and Ronnie's. Minnie must have discreetly put the others out of sight. Hard to know what was best; to have the tangible constant reminders of him, or to have every trace removed. Neither consoled. Minnie was a good daughter-in-law but perhaps she had too much of the practical about her, and Alexander was too bound up with his own sadness and loss to help much with hers.

What Betty really wanted was a good laugh and a good cry and sometimes both. Bereavement, so the doctor said, caused as many reactions as there were motes in the universe, so it was not a good idea to compare and contrast. Nevertheless, the path towards ease did not look very encouraging. Lydia George went religious when her husband died, Mandy Plowright was still drugged like a zombie since her son's suicide – and from what Betty remembered, her own mother had never quite shed the bitterness of early loss. The one person who might have understood was Ronnie, and Ronnie was dead. There was that little flash of anger again. Ronnie always *was* good at wriggling out of things and you could say this was the Big Wriggle. She was left to mop up as usual. As she looked at the blue-and-white dish and the single set of keys she knew that she had to have a plan, a long-term strategy, if she were to avoid going completely off her trolley. Already she had started to have a few stern words with that missing husband of hers along the lines of *How could you do this to me?* Next she'd be attending séances. Something positive must take shape in her new and solo life. Something.

She hung her coat over the newel post. It slowly

slid to the floor. A pastiche of how her own body felt. Slack and useless and ready to lie down and die. In the kitchen she put on the kettle. Very determinedly she put on the kettle. A cup of tea. A nice cup of tea. Not a stiff drink. No more stiff drinks. The funeral was more than two months ago. The time for justifying stiff drinks was well past. Séances or alcohol. Neither presented a pretty picture. The trouble with recent widowhood was that you didn't know what you wanted but you wanted something. Usually what you thought you wanted, you didn't when you got it, like meeting up with her old friend Simon for lunch – a tentative step which she thought would make life normal again – and seeing red mullet on the menu and dissolving. Ronnie loved red mullet. Simon stared at her and then at the menu as if it would unlock its secrets – and quickly offered his handkerchief. 'Sorry,' she said, as she fled from the restaurant. 'Not ready yet.' Now she must try harder.

A week later, as she stood fiddling with her card at the cash machine, a bright female voice, a far too bright female voice, said 'Well, hello there. And how are you?'

It was Nancy Barlow, she of the many dogs and the striking physical similarity to her corgi. Ronnie always said that he could not imagine how she moved so fast with such short legs. She was always breathless. Now she was bright and breathless. 'How are you?' was not an enquiry so much as a statement of association. Betty was surprised to hear her usually sharp self, the one that could not suffer fools, say, most amenably, 'Not bad at all, Nancy. And yourself?'

'Fair to middling,' she said, and gave a tug on the lead of her accompanying dog – not a corgi and therefore not a breed Betty had a hope of recognising. She did not like dogs very much. Oddly, though, she found herself stroking its head as it slavered over her skirt. It seemed the right thing to do. Nancy, at first surprised, now looked upon the head lovingly as Betty stroked it.

'Nice doggy,' said Betty.

Hard to tell who was the more surprised. Betty, Nancy or the Dog. Whatever breed it was. On enquiry she was told that it was a borzoi. 'Really?' she said, apparently with the same deep interest she once reserved for matters more substantial.

'From Russia,' added Nancy.

They both stood considering on the pavement, presumably dwelling on the engaging idea that a dog could travel all the way from the Urals, before saying their farewells and parting.

The result was an invitation to dinner at the Barlows'. The first dinner party she had been asked to since Ronnie's death. She was aware that it was a brave act on Nancy's part – widows were notoriously difficult things until they either remarried or got too old to count. Whatever the test for such a bestowal, she had obviously passed stage one. Now she must get stage two right. No second chances in her little community. Betty had seen enough of the way single women were treated, and indeed – to be fair – how single women sometimes warranted being treated if they laughed too coquettishly at another's husband's jokes. Banishment. Similarly, if the woman held forth on any subject at all at which she excelled, she was – generally speaking – for the chop. In the old days, with Ronnie by her side, Betty was inclined to be sharply witty, with a low boredom threshold, and perhaps overly intolerant of the banal. You could do that when you had a husband. Especially an amusing, tolerant husband like Ronnie. She must be careful now.

'I will buy a suitable garment,' she told herself. 'In London.' Her appointment with the dentist was for early afternoon (using Ronnie's unrequired appointment, the existence of which temporarily brought back that unwelcome pain again), so there would be time afterwards to go to a suitable garment shop. Something like Jaeger, she thought. You couldn't go wrong with Jaeger. Well cut, good quality, nothing outrageous. She drew the line at beige and taupe but apart from that it would be restrained. Nothing in scarlet. She smiled as she swung through the doors of shop. It was all play-acting, of course, but it was also about solo survival in the jungle of middle-class lives. In her position the best thing was to be calm and quiet and light on the social shoulder. Maybe it would be different if she moved in more artistic circles (or would it?), but she was an ordinary woman who worked part-time in an ordinary bank and her world was graced with few wild cards.

It was the strangest experience. Like being inside another's skin. There she sat, in a satin Jaeger shirt (brown was very tasteful the sales assistant said), sandwiched between a woman who made jewellery and a man who sold what he called *special* cars. This sounded so like a sex shop offering under-the-counter pictures, that she almost laughed and said so. Then she remembered. Instead she blinked, looked serious and asked him, eyeball to eyeball, what *special* meant. And he, most definitely, told her.

Out of the corner of her eye Betty saw that the

special-car man's wife was observing them. The one thing you must not do, Betty reminded herself, apart from wearing low-cut tops in bright colours and pouting at passing husbands, was to antagonise wives into thinking you're after their (usually) very unattractive mates. So Betty turned to her and said, 'Do you drive one of these remarkable cars?' To which the wife relaxed and said that she preferred her little Peugeot. 'Me too,' said Betty. 'As long as it goes that's all I care about.' And the two women were off on the very fascinating subject of what they drove and why.

Nancy's husband Oliver joined in and eventually turned the subject towards the far more knotty problem – he assured them – of greenhouse gases and emissions and the awful arrogance of the USA. In the old days Betty might have reminded him tartly that responsibility had to start somewhere and why not at home and that he had scarcely got a leg – or wheel – to stand on with his big fat BMW. Instead she nodded. America was shocking in its irresponsibility, shocking. Big fat BMWs were not mentioned. Betty even managed a simper. Things were going well.

The jewellery woman, who was married to a vicar further down the table, sitting a few chairs away, did not address her conversationally though she did once ask for the butter. Betty passed it to her with a winning smile, so she thought, but it was apparently not winning enough. In the old days Betty might have taken her on – asked about the jewellery-making process and the materials, for example – but now she accepted that she was not striking in any way, that she wore small gold studs in her ears and not dangling garnets, and instead, giving the vicar a fleeting and humble smile, and accepting his little embarrassed eye-screw of sympathy (so he had clearly been told of her loss), she returned to Oliver Barlow and began a neutral conversation about golf.

She did not get what Ronnie used to call *all het up* about the masculine mystique surrounding the local golf club, preferring the safe ground of asking Oliver to explain the terminology. Birdies, handicaps, shouting Fore! *Very* safe ground.

'How I should like to have a go,' she said to him, quite untruthfully. And he said, very seriously, that she might find it helpful and beneficial in her present predicament. It was the only reference all evening to her widowhood – not that she expected – or wanted – more – but it was a disturbing one. One to which she would have responded quite crisply in the old days by at the very least saying that the balls were, in her opinion, far too small to help with her *predicament*

– and let them think what they would. But now she merely nodded and agreed that he could, indeed, fill her glass again.

She left suitably early and was offered, and accepted, a lift from the Redmonds. Nancy gave her a little hug at the door and patted her on the back as if she were another of the dogs, and Oliver took both her hands in his and held them and gave her a big, patronising smile as he suggested that she should think over, very carefully, the benefits of golf. She smiled her humble agreement. On the way home the Redmonds both agreed that it was very brave of her to come and that golf would be a very good way of Sorting Herself Out – which went rather well with Having a Predicament she thought. When she got home she did not know whether to shoot herself, have a stiff drink or go straight to bed. She did both the latter, missing out the adjective *straight*.

There followed several more similar occasions at which she behaved with perfect decorum. She even found herself in conversation with the jewellery woman after about the third attempt. 'I've got a wonderful piece of raw amber that Ronnie found on the beach in Suffolk,' she told her. The woman's eyes finally engaged. She could turn it into something lovely for Betty to wear, she said, a nice pair of teardrop earrings or a pendant. But Ronnie found it uncut, untouched, and that was the way she wanted it. It caught the sunlight on the bedroom window sill and made her happy. So Betty smiled and nodded at the jewellery woman. Although she had no intention of doing anything with it she was not rude enough – or assertive enough nowadays – to say so. Instead, at the Redmonds' barbecue when she saw the jewellery woman coming towards her, she dived for the first person she could find, which was Oliver, and immediately – and desperately – renewed the subject of playing golf and her Predicament. If Ronnie could see her now, she thought, but then she reminded herself that he neither could nor ever would, and she must get on with it. She had worked hard to prove to her new world that she was harmless and agreeable and they had let her in. It was a relief not to see people crossing the road when they saw her coming, or stamping that bright look of patient understanding on their faces.

Then the unthinkable happened. Oliver Barlow invited her to his golf club and Nancy encouraged her to go, waving a dismissive hand and saying 'Never go near the place myself. Full of bores going on about balls. You might like it.'

Betty was startled to find herself saying, 'Why yes,

Oliver, thank you. But I have no gear.'

'We can sort that out,' he said, almost tenderly. 'And we don't call it *gear*, we call it *kit*.'

'Sorry,' she said.

The following weekend, at ten o'clock on a bright August morning, off they went. With Betty saying all the way there how much she was looking forward to it and how kind he was and thinking *Pinch me, pinch me, pinch me – this cannot be happening*. She wore dark green slacks (the kind of trousers she remembered on those unyielding women of yore – Nancy Spain, Katharine Hepburn and the like), not in the least designed to entice but only to be chic and comfortable. Quite proper, she felt, for a golf club.

Nancy was right. The place was full of bores going on about balls. But she passed no comment. Instead she swung her swing, missed the balls (too small as she had guessed), drank her G&T at the bar and accepted, with downcast eyes, Oliver's rallying compliments regarding her action. 'Not bad for starters,' he said. 'We'll get you there. Same time next weekend? Good.'

Then came Ladies' Night, dinner dancing, and Nancy had a sore throat, she asked Betty if she would accompany Oliver instead. A dinner dance was the kind of activity she used to deplore and she very nearly said so – then didn't. Instead she said how sorry she was that Nancy would miss it, and agreed. She wore a pale dress with a little sparkle and no cleavage and ate the leathery steak en croûte and the curious chocolate mush without a murmur. It was lifestyle balancing, she told herself. Throw the disgusting mush in the catering manager's face and she would never be asked anywhere again. Smile sweetly and accept all, and she would.

Oliver approached her inability to dance in the same way he dealt with her golf. 'Practise, practise, practise,' he said cheerfully as he whisked her around. 'We'll have to do this more often.' Doing complicated footsteps to Abba struck her as taking the amenability a little too far. 'Enough is enough, Oliver,' she said, with irritated amusement but he saw only amusement and whirled her out of doors. Ah well – anything was better than 'Fernando' and the cha-cha-cha. Anything. She agreed that it would be very nice to take a turn around the golf course, the night being balmy and the moon so bright.

Betty laughed at Oliver's jokes, admired the sweep of perfectly cut green shimmering in the silver light, jumped at the hoot of an owl – and let him kiss her. Indeed, she kissed him back. So this, she thought, is how you get another husband – even if it *is* somebody else's. If she married him she wondered quite how long she would be able to sustain her new amenability. But then the blue-and-white dish would contain two sets of keys again which, she thought firmly, was a very fair bargain.

In her bedroom that night – alone – she hung up her discreet dress and smiled at the way it nestled against her old red satin. That red satin had seen a thing or two in its time. She could still see Ronnie's face when she first wore it – and hear his *Wow!* And see Alexander's shocked teenaged expression. She fell asleep smiling at the memory.

The next morning Betty met a croaking Nancy accompanied by a bright-eyed Oliver in the high street. Oliver smiled at her in a come hither way. Nancy sneezed. 'Thanks for standing in for me,' she said. 'Did you enjoy it?'

Betty, carrying several carrier bags of assorted clothing, was entering the Oxfam shop. She looked Oliver straight in the eye and said, 'No. It was absolutely bloody awful. Horrible food, silly music and boring puffed-up people. And the balls really are too small.'

Oliver's opened his mouth, closed it and went rigid. Nancy croaked a laugh. 'Quite right,' she said. 'Same every year.'

This time Oliver moved his rigid face to stare at his wife. She smiled at him. 'Should have told you years ago. What a relief to miss it.' She sneezed again.

Later in the day the Oxfam shop displayed in its window a series of garments worn by amenable, sensible, quietly disposed women, among which was a brown satin shirt and a pale, slightly sparkly, not too low-cut frock. As well as a very pretty blue-and-white china dish.

The Gift of Giving

Tracy Chevalier

Everyone has her own favourite Christmas moment, that point during the holidays when all the fuss suddenly seems worthwhile. For those who have thought ahead, it can be that day in late November when the kitchen fills with the aroma of the currants and nutmeg and rum in the Christmas puddings they're making. Others love the moment the tree goes up, with a special thrill when the fairy lights are plugged in for the first time. Others like Midnight Mass, when they can feel both virtuous and naughty for staying up late. Children love waking up early on Christmas morning and creeping downstairs to inspect the wrapped presents under the tree or poke at the distended worms their stockings have become.

Cooks may like that moment when the dinner is ready at last, the table overloaded with food, and no one has yet tasted how dry the turkey is. Others are happy when the formal festivities are over and they can sit in front of the telly with a big tin of Quality Street to watch *Casablanca* for the twentieth time, chanting along with the well-worn lines.

Eileen's favourite Christmas moment occurred every year at her dining table on the afternoon of 23 December. Her husband Peter would be at his last day of work before the holiday break, and any guests had either not yet arrived or were out last-minute shopping. She had not yet become a slave to the kitchen; nor was she running about ironing extra pillowslips, or loading the dishwasher once again, or having her annual arguments with her daughters Rose and Daisy, or sending Peter out for more nuts after her son Jack ate them all during a late-night snack. She would have been to her favourite paper shop, and made her yearly pilgrimage to a special ribbon shop to buy her supplies. She was ready. Eileen's favourite moment of the season was wrapping presents.

Eileen always prided herself on giving good presents. For her, Christmas shopping was not seasonal, but a year-round activity. She was constantly vigilant for possible Christmas presents, whether it was November or April; a charity shop (good vintage buttons and costume jewellery) or a National Trust property (lovely aprons, coasters, trivets), or even a petrol station (AA membership). Indeed, she disliked the idea of going out specifically to buy a present for someone. The best gifts, she felt, were those she stumbled across while looking for something else. 'That colour matches Rose's eyes perfectly,' she would think of a jumper as she was meant to be buying knickers for herself; or, 'Those are just the sort of cushions that would refresh Daisy's old sofa,' when she was getting new curtains. She would then buy the perfect present and save it for when it was needed.

She had a gift drawer as well – items she'd come across and knew would make a good gift for someone some day. Eileen hated to be caught out without a proper present. To go to a birthday party with merely a box of chocolates or a bunch of flowers picked up on the way was vulgar; to visit someone in hospital with simply a novelty balloon or a card was unthinkable.

After years of experience, Eileen had established a few rules that governed her gift-giving. Practical rather than frivolous is best – frivolous may make a bigger initial splash but practical will be more appreciated in the long run. Link the gift to something you are sure the person likes or needs – extending their hobbies, for instance, or supporting a project they're doing around the house. Pay attention to what they like and file that information away for future use. Never personalise gifts with names – it's tacky and smacks of trying too hard to make a gift special. Eileen shuddered at coffee mugs with people's names on them or T-shirts imprinted with a personal photograph.

Finally, never, ever give a scarf to a woman. Scarves admit to desperation and a lack of creativity on the part of the giver. If you really can't think of anything, give her a book token or a gift certificate for a beauty treatment.

By following these rules, Eileen had sailed through many a Christmas under a shower of compliments. 'Oh, Eileen,' her friends would crow as they opened their presents, 'it's perfect! You clever thing! Just what I needed! How thoughtful of you!'

Of course she never expected others to be so skilful at choosing gifts. Her family in particular had never managed to learn any lessons from her. Rose often gave her clothes that were too tight and colours that were too bright; and since having her own children, her presents were even more poorly chosen and hastily wrapped. Eileen's son Jack was known to do all of his shopping at the local chemist on Christmas Eve, with the uninspiring results you might expect – soap, talcum powder, moisturiser. Daisy gave Eileen yoga lessons she wasn't flexible enough to do, books on feng shui-ing her house, and, last Christmas, a goat – which she was relieved to discover was going to an African family on her behalf rather than being tethered in the back garden. It wouldn't have surprised Eileen if Daisy had tethered a goat back there – she was the sort of daughter who constantly challenged her mother. 'I'm just trying to broaden your horizons, Mum,' she would say. Daisy was broadening her own horizons by switching jobs often; she was between them at present.

Eileen expected little of her husband on the gift front. Peter had no imagination; indeed, he knew it, and had the sense to ask her what she wanted each year. It was a practical solution – of that Eileen approved – but it did sometimes make her sad. It would be nice to be surprised just once. Still, he was a lovely man in many other ways, and you couldn't expect everything from a husband.

Now, as she sat at her dining table surrounded by carefully chosen items for her family and a pile of silver and gold gift wrap (Eileen used only these colours for Christmas presents) with accompanying satin ribbons as trim, she felt a satisfaction akin to having the main course placed before her at a really fine restaurant. Humming along to 'Oh Come, All Ye Faithful' on the radio, she reached for the scissors.

An hour later the gifts were arranged around the tree, edges of the gift-wrap tidily folded, Sellotape concealed, ribbons glistening, and the boxy shapes promising the perfect present experience. As much as she liked choosing them, Eileen sometimes wished that gifts never had to be unwrapped, but could remain more powerful for being mysterious.

After the joy of gift-wrapping, for Eileen the holiday itself never lived up to the promise the presents held out. This year, for instance, the problems began on Christmas Eve, when Daisy waited until the shops were all closed to announce that she was now vegan rather than simply vegetarian and wouldn't be able to eat the cheese and onion tart Eileen had prepared for her as an alternative to the traditional turkey. (Eileen got out a package of nut burgers from the freezer.) Then Jack went out to the pub with friends and didn't come back till hours after closing time. (Eileen lay awake in bed till he stumbled in at 3 a.m., but she would've been awake anyway, going over what needed doing in the kitchen the next morning.) Rose forgot to tell Eileen until she arrived with the children Christmas morning that her husband had decided to stay with his ailing mother that day, adding that one-year-old Michael was teething and three-year-old Tessa had a tummy ache. (Eileen removed her son-in-law's place setting from the table when no one was looking.)

Each time an obstacle presented itself, Eileen would picture the pile of gleaming gifts and feel better. She'd done a good job with her presents, and had held up her side, even if the rest of her family didn't.

The family always gathered Christmas morning in the sitting room by the tree for coffee, Buck's Fizz and panettone. This tradition at least had everyone's approval now – even Daisy tucked into the sweet bread, and Eileen refrained from reminding her that there were eggs in it.

Despite her tummy ache, Tessa wolfed down her slice, then began dismantling the artfully displayed pile of packages under the tree. 'Where are my presents?' she cried, and grabbed the largest box. 'I want to open this one!'

'That's not yours!' Eileen snatched the box – her present to Peter – back before Tessa could tear the gift wrap. Tessa began to wail. Rose was changing

Michael's nappy, and since it seemed she was not going to say anything to comfort or to discipline her daughter, Eileen added through gritted teeth, 'Tessa, dear, wait till we're ready and Grandpa will play Father Christmas for us.'

Tessa slumped down on the sofa next to Daisy, her tear-stained face made even uglier by the scowl she directed at Eileen.

Peter handed out a round of presents. Eileen never paid much attention to the presents she unwrapped; she was focused instead on the unveiling of her gifts to others. Now, for instance, Jack was unwrapping a gold box from his mother. He held up a popular consumer magazine, a puzzled look on his face. 'Mum?' he asked, which translated as 'Explain?'

'It's a subscription for a year, to help you with setting up your flat,' Eileen answered. 'Think of all those appliances you'll be buying – washing machines and food processors and microwaves. You'll need to know which is the best to buy, won't you? Didn't you tell me last month that your toaster caught fire? That wouldn't have happened if you'd done a little research and bought the best model.'

Jack opened his mouth to speak, then stopped. Daisy snorted. 'Right. Cheers, Mum,' he said at last. Eileen bit her lip, wondering if he was reverting to the sarcasm he had so often aimed at her during his teenage years. Perhaps the subscription was a bit serious for a boy who had just finished university. Still, he would doubtless find it useful.

Rose tossed a package to Jack. 'Never mind – here's another magazine that will cheer you up,' she said, rocking Michael on her hip as he grizzled.

'Oh, don't open it until the others have presents too!' Eileen cried. She preferred rounds of present opening so that she could keep an eye on what was being given; she hated the anarchic tearing open of gifts, with piles of gift wrap strewn about and presents jumbled together. Jack seemed not to hear his mother, however, but tore open the poorly wrapped cylinder Rose had thrown him. Grinning, he held up one of those men's magazines that isn't quite porn but features women with improbably large, barely covered breasts on the cover. 'Cool,' he said. 'Thanks!'

'Don't know what you see in it, it's such trash, but you've always got your head buried in it at the newsagent's,' Rose said as Jack began leafing through the magazine, the consumer magazine abandoned at his feet.

In the next round Daisy got a smart tweed jacket that would be useful for interviews – 'Cheers, Mum,' she intoned in the same way that Jack had, then rolled her eyes at Tessa, making her giggle – and Peter got a new tackle box for his fishing gear, which he normally kept in a tangled mess in the garage. 'Thanks, love,' he said to Eileen, and kissed her.

Jack handed Eileen a plain white envelope. 'This is for you, Mum. Well, it's sort of for everyone.'

At least it's not bath salts, Eileen thought as she opened it. She couldn't help thinking that he might at least have used a coloured envelope. Inside was a voucher for Boxing Day lunch for the whole family at the local pub. 'You complain every year about having to cook on Boxing Day, so I thought I'd save you the trouble this year,' Jack said. Eileen opened her mouth, then shut it – just as Jack had done when he got the magazine subscription from her. She'd been about to say that she'd planned to try a new recipe she'd seen in a magazine for leftover turkey using apricots and pilaf rice. But her son looked so pleased with himself that she said instead, 'Thank you, Jack. That's very thoughtful of you.'

'Thanks, Jack,' Rose said. 'Good one,' Daisy added, and Peter clapped him on the shoulder. To Eileen's surprise he said, 'Why don't I pick up the wine on the bill? We know it's hard for you now, what with just starting out on your own.'

'Thanks, Dad.' Jack looked relieved. Eileen

frowned at Peter, though she wasn't sure why she was irritated.

In the next round Rose opened her present from Eileen one-handed while the other held Michael back from pulling the lights off the tree. She managed to get the box open only after Daisy lured Michael away with a balled-up piece of gift wrap. Rose reached inside the box and pulled out a lacy white bra. 'Mum?' She sounded as baffled as Jack had with his magazine.

'I think you'll find it fits you better than your old ones, dear,' Eileen said. When Rose continued to stare at the bra she added, 'Now that you're – you know – smaller there.' Post-breastfeeding, Rose's bust had indeed shrunk so that she was smaller than before she'd had children, though she hadn't seemed to notice, and was still wearing her old bras.

Rose burst into tears.

'Mum, for God's sake!' Daisy cried. 'How can you be so tactless?'

'Mummy, what's wrong?' Tessa trundled over from her growing pile of toys and patted her mother's head, while glaring over her shoulder at Eileen. 'Who's hurt you?' Michael, never one for restraint when there was crying to be done, joined his mother's wails with his own.

'But I only meant –' Eileen began.

'Well, now,' Peter interrupted. 'Anyone for more Buck's Fizz?'

It took some time to restore equanimity. Rose had just begun to calm down when she caught sight of the busty girl in a Santa bikini on the cover of Jack's magazine, and renewed her sobs, crying, 'I'm just so tired! I'm just so tired!' Daisy passed Michael to Eileen to quiet him down (Eileen unwrapped the teething ring she'd bought for him and stuffed it in his mouth) and handed an envelope to her sister. 'Here, this may help,' she said. Rose read aloud from the scrap of paper inside: it was an offer to look after Tessa and Michael for a weekend so that Rose and her husband could go away alone. Rose burst into tears again – this time from joy.

'Look, I've found one for me!' Tessa cried, waving a silver box. 'T is for Tessa, isn't it?'

'It is,' Eileen said, 'and it's from me. I know you're going to like it.'

Tessa tore off the silver paper and held up the box with its transparent window. 'Ew, a doll!' she shouted, throwing it down. 'I hate dolls!' There was a moment's silence, and then Rose, Daisy and Jack began to laugh. Even Peter smiled. Eileen felt obliged to chuckle along with everyone else, showing what a good sport she was. She stopped laughing as soon as she could, though. She had spent a long time choosing that doll.

Eileen rubbed her eyes. She had the beginnings of a headache and there was still all the cooking to do. She poked under the tree. Satisfied that all of the presents had been opened, she got a rubbish bag from the kitchen and began collecting torn gift wrap and ribbon, setting aside the bits that could be recycled. She would add them to her present drawer, along with Tessa's doll, when no one was looking. There was no point in wasting it. She found Daisy's jacket and Rose's bra, folded them, put them back in their boxes and placed them under the tree, where Peter's tackle box already sat. She couldn't find Jack's consumer magazine (months later she discovered it shoved under the sofa).

Eileen hardly noticed that Peter was beside her, holding out a box professionally wrapped in green-and-red holly print. 'You've forgotten one, love,' he said. 'Happy Christmas.'

'Oh, darling, I'm sorry. Thank you.' Eileen set down the rubbish bag and examined the long flat box. She'd asked Peter for ceramic hair-straightening tongs, and couldn't see how they would fit in a box this shape.

'I was going to get you what you asked for,' he said, 'and I still will if you want me to. But I saw this and thought you might like it instead.'

Eileen ran her finger along the edge of the gift wrap, lifting the Sellotape without tearing the paper. It was beautifully wrapped; for a moment she wanted to ask her husband to let her keep the present as it was, but she knew he wouldn't understand. She tried to look enthusiastic rather than apprehensive. It had been so long since Peter had chosen a present for her himself.

Eileen opened the box and pulled out a long, crushed velvet scarf in burnt orange. It was the ugliest scarf she had ever seen.

Jack looked up from his magazine, Rose from the large glass of champagne Daisy had poured her, Daisy from a book she was reading to Tessa. 'Wow!' they said in unison.

Peter beamed. 'It made me think of you when I saw it.'

'Try it on, Mum,' Daisy said. 'It goes perfectly with your hair.'

'Good taste, Dad!' Rose said.

Eileen looked around at her family. She took a deep breath. 'Oh, darling, it's perfect,' she said, and meant it.

Fear of Forty-Five

Katie Fforde

'Remind me, why have you got this state about being forty-five, Rosie?' said Marcia, sipping her cocktail. 'Seems barking to me.'

'It's her old granny,' said Helen. 'Weren't you paying attention?'

'I was in the loo.'

'Well, her granny said that women stopped being attractive to men when they were forty-five.'

'Have an affair, then. Prove her wrong.'

Marcia seemed to think this was a simple solution. Rosie, the unlucky owner of the hang-up, felt this was like being told to run a marathon when you've just announced you've broken your ankle.

'I couldn't,' she said. 'Apart from the fact that now

I'm forty-five and so no one will fancy me, I'm happily married, have been for years.'

'To a man who forgot your birthday,' Helen reminded her. 'Which is part of the reason we're here.'

'Here' was a restaurant several brackets up from their usual lunch venues.

'He just doesn't do birthdays,' said Rosie, trying not to sound apologetic and resentful at the same time. 'He likes to give me presents at other times.'

'Like when?' asked Marcia.

'And what was the last thing he bought you?' said Helen.

Rosie thought about this. 'It was a thermometer.'

'Very romantic. What kind?'

'Oh, you know, a medical kind.'

'Why did he buy you that? You're not trying to get pregnant, or anything, are you?' Marcia sounded revolted.

'No,' said Rosie, 'it was because it was only a fiver if you bought over ten litres of fuel.'

'For goodness' sake! Another round of cocktails!' Marcia waved her elegant, over forty-five-year-old hand and summoned the waiter. 'An affair would not only be good for your ego, it would be good for that damned husband of yours.'

Margaritas were wonderfully empowering, thought Rosie, as she fell into a cab, only just managing to give the address to the office without slurring. She'd have to leave her car at the office when she went home, too. There was no way she'd be fit to drive until tomorrow.

She spent the afternoon doing mundane tasks that didn't require her brain to be fully functioning. When it was teatime, she produced the cake she had baked at home to bring in for her work colleagues. She could have bought one, of course, but she was old-fashioned, and unless it was some fabulous French patisserie, to her, cake wasn't cake unless it was home-made.

While she was clearing up the crumbs in the bottom of the tin, after the others had gone back to their desks, the telephone rang. She answered it, still slightly high on margaritas and chocolate icing. 'Hello!'

'Is that Rosie Morgan?'

The voice was deep, attractive, and faintly familiar. 'Yes,' she said cautiously, hoping that tea and cake had muted any alcoholic overtones.

'Giles Lennox,' said the voice. 'I heard you give a paper at the Guildford seminar last week. We met briefly in the bar, afterwards.'

'Oh yes.' Rosie blushed. Now she knew why she recognised the voice – it belonged to a very attractive man, and she was talking to him while not in command of all her senses.

'I was impressed.'

'Were you?' Frantically, Rosie tried to remember what she'd said. She sat down and tried to bring the piece up on her computer screen.

'I'd like to discuss it. I think some of your ideas should be taken further.'

'Oh.' She thought this too, but until now, no one had seemed to agree with her.

'What about lunch?' Giles Lennox had the confident tones of a man who often suggested lunch to discuss recently given papers. 'I could bring my ideas along, and see how they fit in with yours?'

Giles Lennox worked for one of the sister companies to her own. He was senior to her, by quite a bit. A productive lunch with him could mean promotion. Or could it?

'You wouldn't prefer us to fix up a meeting at another time?' The thought of lunch had made her all nervous. It must have been Marcia's suggestion that she should have an affair. It had made her silly – that and the margaritas.

'Love to, but I'm so pushed this week. Lunch I can manage. I hope you can too.'

'I probably can,' if I can think what to wear, she added to herself.

'What about Enrico's?'

Enrico's was where she'd had lunch that very day. 'Fine,' she said, thinking it would be all right as long as she didn't have cocktails.

'Tomorrow?'

Far too short notice if it was a date. Just as well it was business. 'Tomorrow looks free. What time would suit you?'

'One o'clock?'

'Fine.'

Rosie did dress extra carefully, and she did put on special cream that claimed to make you look younger, as well as form a base for your make-up, but that was only good sense, wasn't it? Even though it was her ideas he was interested in, he would be more interested if she was well presented. She wouldn't put out a report that had spelling mistakes, on crumpled paper. A smooth, professional finish was definitely required.

He was waiting for her when she arrived. She walked carefully to the table where he stood, smiling. Something suspiciously like wind bubbled up from her stomach, causing her to swallow. He was even more attractive than she had remembered. He looked into her eyes and took her hand. He didn't hold either her gaze or her hand for a second too long, but it was enough to make her feel like she'd felt when she was fifteen. I'm forty-five, she reminded herself, firmly, reminding herself of her granny's words of wisdom, 'After forty-five you're just invisible to men' – she'd said, often enough to engrave the words into her brain – 'they just don't see you.'

'What would you like to drink?'

Rosie settled herself into her seat and was horrified to see the waiter was the same one who'd served them the previous day. 'Tomato juice,' she said firmly. 'And some water. Still. Please.'

'But you'll have some wine with the meal? They have quite a good cellar here.'

She nodded agreement, irritated to note that Giles Lennox must have been at least ten years older than she was, and yet his grey hair, and the reading glasses he was now using to study the wine list, only added to his attraction. As did the crow's feet at the corners of his eyes. She sipped her water, and then her tomato juice. If she had wine as well, there'd be no room on the table for the plates.

'So, Rosie, I may call you Rosie?'

'No one ever calls me anything else.'

'I'm not surprised. It's a lovely, sexy name.'

This brought her up short. It turned politeness into flirting, instantly. And yet he couldn't be flirting with her. She was past her flirt-by date.

'I didn't think that when I was at school.'

'Which was when – about ten years ago?'

Now she knew for sure he was flirting, it was easier to flirt back, in a restrained, stay-in-your-basket, sort of way. 'No, ten years ago was when I went back to work. Now about my paper.' She produced a copy of it and put it in the table, struggling to find space for it.

'I did find it fascinating,' he said, 'although I confess to finding its author fascinating first.'

This was a bit full on. 'Sorry?'

'Terribly unprofessional of me, I know. But I do remember being delighted that such an attractive woman could write such a good paper.'

Rosie felt herself blush and hoped the lighting of Enrico's would hide the fact. She also felt herself succumbing to his charm. It was not only that he was obviously interested in her as a woman, but as a fellow professional.

'Shall we order?' she said, picking up her menu. 'Or we'll be here all day.'

By the time they left, she wished they could have been there all day. She had rarely, if ever, enjoyed herself so much. Flirting with an expert awoke dormant skills she didn't know she had. She felt girlish, attractive and nothing like forty-five.

She didn't say anything to Helen, who she worked with, because she would tell Marcia and she really didn't want her to find out. Usually she was a confiding person but Marcia would insist she have an affair with Giles Lennox and that was an area Rosie wasn't even ready to think about.

There was no doubt that the offer of one was there, and there was no doubt that she fancied Giles Lennox rotten. But being unfaithful to her husband was not something to be done lightly. On the other hand, if anyone had told her that the sensible thing was never to see or speak to Giles Lennox again, she would have shot them.

They spoke on the telephone often, although Rosie never phoned him. She started taking more care of her appearance, varnishing her nails, watching her weight, thinking carefully about what to wear each morning in case he should call in. She held herself better, she smiled more, and she thought about Giles, all the time.

There was no way her friends wouldn't notice the

difference and they did, but Rosie didn't tell them anything. She just said that she felt silly for worrying so much about being forty-five, and was just determined to make the best of herself, of life, of everything.

Rosie and Giles met for lunch again. This time Rosie insisted on paying. She wanted the relationship to be absolutely equal. This time, as she knew it would, the subject of the Conference came up.

Had Giles not been in the picture, Rosie would have signed up without a second's thought. She needed to go, she always went and, in fact, she'd have to come up with a very good excuse not to go. But Giles *was* in the picture, and Rosie felt that she would have to make the decision, before she went, whether she wanted an affair or not.

There was no question that she wanted to sleep with him. She thought about him while she made love to her husband – one man in her head and another in her arms – and that had felt quite unfaithful enough.

But could she just jump into bed with Giles? She was an old-fashioned girl, infidelity was not something she would usually consider, even for a moment. Was this feeling for Giles more than just passing lust? It was hard for her to tell – Rosie didn't fancy many people, and she fancied him so much!

'Of course I'm not going to sleep with him,' she told herself as she packed her case with new, pretty underwear, a nightdress and dressing gown set that wasn't quite a negligee, but wasn't her usual mundane nightwear, either.

In the car, on the way to the hotel, sharing a lift with two other colleagues, she realised it was the not knowing that was so exciting. She didn't know what she was going to do, and she loved the feeling, the uncertainty, the fear.

The day went to plan, to the programme. There were papers delivered, brainstorming sessions held, coffee was drunk, and, come lunchtime, alcohol. Rosie deliberately didn't speak to Giles, but they acknowledged each other in the quick, furtive way that secret lovers do. Rosie spent all day mentally tossing coins, pulling the petals of daisies, reading tarot cards and examining entrails. If any of these omen-giving activities had actually been available to her, she wouldn't have done anything else. But even coin-tossing would look strange, so she just kept changing her mind, this way and that, yes, I will, no, I won't, until dinner, and she still hadn't made up her mind firmly, one way or another.

It was the dinner jacket that decided her. Giles looked so utterly heavenly, so entirely sexy, so unbelievably gorgeous in his that Rosie no longer vacillated. She made up her mind. She'd have one, glorious night of fabulous, passionate sex and then go home to her husband, a thoroughly fulfilled woman.

They had texted each other their room numbers but hadn't made any arrangements. She went up to her room to redo her make-up before she was due to meet Giles and others in the bar. They hadn't spent long enough alone together to make a plan, but love – or should that be lust? – would find a way.

While removing mascara from under her eyes she made herself consider what it would be like to have sex with someone else after so many years of fidelity. She was not naive enough to think it would be perfect – how could it be? But somehow she knew it would work. She wanted him so much. He wouldn't have to do a lot to make it work for her.

Then her grandmother's voice came into her head. 'What about your cellulite? Stretch marks? You won't even show your bare arms to people except in high summer when they're tanned. How are you going to take your clothes off in front of a strange man?'

'For goodness' sake, Grandma!' Rosie said to the mirror. 'You didn't talk to me about things like that when you were alive, so don't start now. And taking my clothes off will be fine. I'll arrange for very dim lighting, and let him do it.'

She added a layer of lipgloss, something she'd only recently started adding to her layer of lipstick, smiled at herself, pulled back her shoulders and left her room.

Giles smiled at her as she joined the group, and while he did, she felt she was the only woman in the room. She knew she'd made the right decision. Sex with him was going to be fantastic.

She was on her second brandy, wondering how long they'd have to sit down there and drink with men who, now they were quite drunk, had become extremely boring, when Giles clapped his hand to his pocket and took out his mobile phone. He answered it.

Rosie tuned out the old jokes that were being retold around her and struggled to overhear and understand what Giles was saying into his phone. She couldn't make out any detail but she knew it was bad news.

He put his phone back in his pocket. 'I'll have to go. It's my aunt. She's fallen and the home think she might not make it.' He made a rueful face. 'I'll take a taxi.'

Rosie went to him. 'I'm so sorry. How awful for you.'

'I'm very fond of the old dear, but she's well over ninety, but I'm all she's got in the way of relations, so I must be there if I can.'

After he'd gone, Rosie made her excuses. The party was breaking up anyway, sobered by Giles's news. Rosie made her way up to her room, disappointed, yet almost relieved.

Her phone rang just as she was about to turn her light off. It was Giles. 'I'm so sorry, darling. I so wanted us to get together tonight. But it will happen. This is just a rain check.'

Rosie didn't hear from Giles for a few days and she realised how much she missed his sexy voice. When he did call it was at a bad time and she had to break her rule and ring him back.

'Darling,' he said. 'I've booked us a weekend in Paris. Meet me at the check-in at Waterloo. I've got first-class tickets and a wonderful hotel. Can you manage that?'

The date was for two weekends hence. She could easily manage it, she had plenty of time to make up a reason for her to be away.

'Of course. It'll be wonderful.'

It felt wonderful until she saw his back, waiting for

her at the coffee shop at Waterloo. She needed to go to the loo and it made her think of her husband, David. He could always find a loo if she needed one, even in a strange place. He mixed perfect gin and tonics. He brought her tea in bed and cooked her breakfast on Saturday mornings. She loved him and he loved her, even if he did wilfully forget her birthday. She had her little case on wheels. She'd packed her pretty nightie and dressing gown. She'd had her hair done, painted her toenails, waxed her legs, and yet when it came to it, she couldn't risk her marriage for a weekend in Paris, however wonderful.

She didn't say anything. She just went home.

David was pleased to see her. 'What happened? Everything all right?'

'I just decided not to go. Work can manage without me for once. I might change my job, anyway.' She'd probably have to, now.

He kissed her. 'I'm very glad. I've just been into town to pick up your birthday present. Sorry it's so late. It took them ages to make it.'

He handed her a paper bag. In the bag was a ring box. She took it out and opened it. It was an eternity ring set with alternate diamonds, sapphires and pearls.

'I didn't like any of the ones they had, so I told

them what I wanted and they made it up for me. Took them for ever, of course.'

She swallowed hard and put the ring on. It looked wonderful.

'You never had a proper engagement ring and I'm so dreadful about presents. I wanted this birthday to be special, because I knew you were so worried about being forty-five. You don't need to worry, you know. You're a very attractive, sexy woman. And I love you very much.'

It was a long sentence for David. She realised she didn't mind being forty-five any more. She didn't need to have an affair any more. She knew she was an attractive woman, now, and she needed to be with the husband who loved her.

'I love you too,' she whispered. 'Let's go to bed.'

After a Long Time

Nicci Gerrard

It took me a long time to decide what to wear. I lay awake the night before, going through items in my wardrobe in my mind, discarding them. Not the black trousers and nearly matching jacket (too staid and respectable), not the new lacy top (too partyish), not the silk maroon skirt and wrapover top (a bit too formal, perhaps, as if I'd made an extra effort, just for him) nor the three-quarter-length beige skirt that fell in layers and made me feel a bit like a Christmas tree, though in the shop's soft mirror a few months ago I'd loved it. Perhaps the spotty shirt I bought in the January sales for its cheerfulness in the grey winter light; or the red shirt. Perhaps my green coat or my lovely jacket that I only wore occasionally, always saving it for the special occasion that never quite arrived. I knew how I wanted to look, I knew what person I wanted him to see walking towards him across the Heath: attractive of course, but also happy, successful, poised, self-possessed. Someone who hadn't lain awake at night worrying about what she would look like for the meeting. Someone who no longer cared about what had happened all those years ago or even thought about it, whose life had moved on and whose heart was mended. Of course, I wanted him to fall half in love with me all over again, and realise what he'd missed.

In the end, I put on jeans, scuffed ankle boots that I may even have owned when I knew him, a three-quarter-length, strawberry-pink shirt under my jacket. Casual. Small earrings, a bangle. Hardly any make-up. Hardly any perfume. At work, just before leaving the office, I stood in front of the mirror and stared at myself, trying to see my face through his eyes. It had been thirteen years. My hair had been longer then, perhaps lighter. My face had been smoother, with the lustre of youth. I leaned into the mirror: grey eyes, chestnut hair, freckles that would become more prominent now that summer was nearly here. I was a wife and mother, a house owner and a professional, no longer a lovesick young woman, hardly more than a girl just out of university, soft-boned with precarious, blossoming happiness because he loved me too and that made the whole world seem new and charged with wonder. I dabbed lipgloss on to my mouth and tried to smile. My mouth was dry with nerves.

Will had rung me three days before, on a trans-atlantic line that gave his voice a slight echo. 'Is that Eleanor?' he'd asked, and I knew who it was at once. The way he drew out the last syllable of my name, making it sound faintly exotic. I heard myself reply: friendly, a bit distant, as if he was just an old acquaintance who'd made contact. It was hard to get the tone quite right. I was appalled at the way my heart was thundering.

He was coming over on business, he'd said, and he'd hoped we could meet up, just for an hour or so. He was here for a ridiculously short time before flying on to Paris. But maybe we could have a light lunch together.

'Why now?' I asked before I could stop myself.

'I've got a baby, a son,' he answered, as if it was an entirely logical connection.

So we agreed to meet on the Heath, where we used to walk arm in arm together, and then go to a café for a snack. And I put the phone back in its holster with hands that trembled. And I didn't tell my husband about it at first, but then the following day I did – very casually, in the middle of cooking supper, as if I'd only just remembered it.

'By the way, I'm having lunch tomorrow with Will. You know, Will Pascali. Strange, after all these years.'

'That'll be interesting,' he'd replied cheerily, stealing a slice of red pepper and popping it into his mouth. I wondered if he was pretending too. Even when you live with someone, love them, lie next to them night after night and wake to them each morning, know all their most intimate habits, you have a whole world inside of you that's full of secrets and shadows.

I had met Will when I was twenty-one and in my final year at university. He was American – a few years older than me and over in London on a scholarship. He was gangly, disorganised and clumsy in a dreamy and endearing way. People liked him, men and women, perhaps because he always seemed to see the best in others, recognise something in them that they hadn't seen in themselves, or perhaps because they wanted to protect him – I know I always wanted to protect him, from the moment I set eyes on him. He was idealistic, hopeful, full of passion for ideas, books, art. Sometimes he seemed set alight by them, or intoxicated. I had never met anyone with such an appetite for life. Such an appetite for me. He told me he loved me on the night we met. He trembled when we made love in front of the bar fire in my cold and poky student room. He recited poems to me in his lovely American drawl. He made me feel beautiful. Life spread out in a bubbling wake behind me; it unfurled in front of me. I was scared by my own happiness.

At the time, I was going out with Lawrence, whom I'd known since I was sixteen and whom my mother thought the world of – but he didn't stand a chance; he seemed to melt away like a dream fades when you wake. Will was the first man I was wholeheartedly in love with. Nobody else mattered. Nothing. Now, years later, I looked back on that period with a kind of tenderness for the woman I was then: so full of hope, so blithe. So ludicrous and foolish.

Will went back to America and he promised he would write and phone every day and that very soon he would return to fetch me. There was a kind of pleasure in anticipating the agony of missing him and the bliss of our reunion. So I said goodbye and I let him go and I never saw him again. There were no letters and there were no phone calls. I was living with my mother when he left, in that strange limbo time between university and job. While all my friends went away, on their last fling of freedom, and while my mother steadily drank herself to death, I just waited. I waited for the post, the fat envelope with his hasty scrawl across it; I waited for the phone to ring. I waited for the doorbell to ring and to find him standing there with his crooked smile and his messy hair. It took a long time to stop believing he would come. I'm not sure when I actually did; I would wake each morning and misery would come flooding back. I kept looking back over the past and trying to decipher in those weeks of giddy happiness the signs that it wouldn't last. Maybe Will could only love what was in front of him. Perhaps that was the secret of his impetuosity and appetite: that he was like a child who needed instant gratification. Perhaps my face had faded from his mind as soon as he'd turned away from me at the airport. Perhaps he'd met someone else and lavished on them all the romantic fervour I'd thought was for me alone.

Now, after all these years, I would see him again. I smiled at myself in the mirror in encouragement and left the office. I took the Underground to Tufnell Park, and then walked to the Heath in the soft May light. It had rained in the night, and everything was clean and new. The leaves were bright green, the sky was a pale turquoise, the sun lemon yellow. The air felt like silk on my skin. I'd first met Will in the wintertime. We'd walked through the Heath together when it was snowing; everything was still and silent then. Now it was quick with life. Couples sat on the grass, entwined; dogs chased sticks and balls and low-flying pigeons. Runners loped past in vests.

We'd arranged to meet beside the enclosure, and as I approached I slowed down, tried to collect myself. What if he had grown fat and old and I didn't recognise him? What if he didn't recognise me? I tried to think of what my first words should be, but my mind was blank.

'Eleanor?' He'd come from behind and I swung round, aiming for the right smile, the smile that said I didn't care.

'Hello, Will.'

'Eleanor! I would have recognised you from miles away. Wow, I can't believe this. I can't believe it's been so long.'

'Time flies,' I said inanely. I gave a small laugh. I would have recognised him too – not fat and old at all, though not as tall as I had remembered. His face both the one I had stored in my memory and yet altered and creased, his hair was already peppered with grey. Same smile, though. I wanted to punch him just to see it fade.

We looked at each other, unsure of whether we should kiss each other on the cheek, hug, shake hands. In the end, we did nothing, just grinned foolishly and then Will said 'Wow!' again, and to my surprise and relief I felt a stab of irritation at his perpetual boyishness, as if he was stuck in a time warp. He pulled off his tie and stuffed it into his jacket. 'That's better.'

'Shall we walk for a bit,' I said. That would be easier than looking at each other across a table.

'Sure,' he said. 'We came here before, didn't we?'

Memories were easier for him, I thought: he had been the victor, after all, and I the vanquished.

'So you're well, Eleanor?'

'Yes,' I said. 'Um, fine.' I winced at the threadbare words. 'You?'

'It's hard to know what to say, isn't it? I was as jumpy as a coot before coming here.'

'As a coot?'

'Don't you say that?'

'Are coots jumpy?'

'Jumpy as a Mexican bean then.'

'Were you?'

'Yes. Were you?'

'I was a bit . . .' I petered out. 'How long are you over for?'

'I arrived this morning, and fly to Paris for a conference tomorrow.'

'Conference on what?' I continued politely.

'Oh – human rights stuff. I teach international law, you know.'

'I didn't know.'

'No, well, of course you didn't. What about you? What do you do?'

'I publish music books.'

'Great,' he said. 'Great.'

'And you said on the phone that you have a son?'

'Ralph.'

'Like Ralph in *Portrait of a Lady*?' That had been his favourite book.

'You remember.'

'I remember.'

Oh, I remember everything, I thought crossly, and walked a bit faster, towards the kite-flyers on the hill. In an hour or so, this meeting would be over and Will would have gone again and I could return to my life.

'How old is Ralph?'

'Nine months. Do you have kids?'

'Two girls, aged two and four. Lottie and Rebecca.'

'Cute,' he said. 'It changes your life, doesn't it?'

'Yes,' I said.

'Right.'

We walked in silence. I glanced at him and found that he was glancing at me, and I looked away. We were never going to talk about why he had left and probably that was good. It was just a scar now, not a wound. No point in scratching away at it.

'So you're fine?' I asked at last.

'Fine,' he said. 'Sure. Great. I just wanted to – you know. I suddenly thought that it was insane not to see you again. I thought it would be difficult but I just looked you up in the phone book, it was as easy as that. I thought I'd be searching for months, but there you were, saying hello. I almost put the phone down, I wasn't ready.'

'I'm glad you didn't.' Was I?

'And you?'

'Me what?'

'Your life's good too?'

'Yes. It is good.'

And it wasn't a lie. My life was good. I loved my husband, my children, my job, my friends. What more can anyone ask for? I knew how lucky I was.

'I never understood –' he began, then stopped.

'What?'

'Nothing.'

'Tell me what you never understood. Will?'

'Let's go and grab some coffee or a snack from the café. I need to leave just after two for this meeting.'

'OK.'

We made our way down the hill and into the café. I sat at a table outside, and Will queued up for coffee and cheese sandwiches. I watched him and thought about legging it.

'Here.'

He put the tray down between us, and I picked up the coffee and took a sip, burning my lips, letting the steam dampen my cheeks.

'You hair looks nice shorter,' he said.

'So does yours.'

'Hmmm. Here. Have a sandwich. So how's Lawrence?'

'Lawrence?'

'Yeah.'

'Lawrence – you mean Lawrence Weaver?'

'You never took his name, anyway.'

'I don't understand. What are you talking about?'

'I thought you married Lawrence.'

'No. I mean, of course not.'

'It didn't work out, then.'

'Why would you think that I married Lawrence?'

'Your mother told me.'

'My mother? My mother died, not long after you went back to America.'

'I'm sorry. Though she always hated me.'

'When did you speak to her?'

'When I phoned.'

'What do you mean, when you phoned?'

'When I phoned from America, she said you'd decided to make a go of it with Lawrence after all.'

'Hang on.' I gripped the edge of the table and stared at Will. 'When did you phone me?'

'When I got home.'

He was staring at me too.

'She never said,' I said faintly. 'She never said you phoned.'

'My letters,' he said. 'What about all the letters I wrote?'

'I never got any letters. I thought, I thought you didn't write.'

'I wrote to you and you never replied. Then I called and your mother said –'

'My mother lied. She lied.' My mother's gaunt face swam into my mind. In her last few months she'd become like a caricature of herself, burning up with rage and drunken disappointment.

'You didn't go back to Lawrence? After me?'

'No.'

'This is – I can't take this in.'

'But I wrote to you too. Only once, after I never heard. I wrote and asked you to explain at least. Didn't you get –?' I stopped and put my head in my hands. 'My mother said she'd post it for me.'

And then I was too proud to write again. You can't beg someone to love you. Love's a gift, not a duty.

'So you –?' He stopped and rubbed his cheek in a way I recognised from all those years ago.

'How odd,' I said, brightly. 'After all this time to discover.' I could feel sweat gathering on my brow and there was a faint ringing in my ears. I aimed an embarrassed smile in Will's direction.

'Yes,' he said slowly. 'Odd. That's a good word for it. It's certainly odd.'

'Oh well,' I said. I sipped some of my cooling coffee. 'It's all water under the bridge, or whatever they say.' I hesitated. 'Did you mind very much?'

'Why would she do that?'

'She was mad, those last months – drunk and bitter and mad. And she was scared I'd move to America and leave her alone. And she didn't trust you. I don't know what to say, Will; it was unforgivable of her.'

'You thought I'd just left you and forgotten about you?'

'Yes. And you –'

'Yes. Me too. This is – well, I don't know what to do with this.'

'There's nothing to do with it.'

'No. I guess not. But did you –?' He stopped.

'I missed you,' I said in a low voice. 'Is that what you wanted to know. Yes then, for a very long time I missed you.'

He almost put his hand over mine, then didn't.

'Life, eh?' he said.

'The strangest thing.'

Everything had changed; every meaning had shifted and the shape of the past dissolved. He had loved me after all. My mother – my poor, deranged, spiteful mother – had betrayed me. I felt queasy with a kind of euphoria, a kind of horror.

'I love my husband,' I said at last. 'And my children. I'm happy now. Very happy.'

'I know. I know.' He rubbed his cheek again. 'Me too.'

'It makes everything so precarious,' I said. 'This life I've got now, it could have never happened. There was another life I didn't have.'

'Would you have come to America?"

I looked down at my hands. The finger with the gold band. 'I guess so. I thought I would have, but who can tell? It's one of the thousand "what ifs". I don't know whether I'm glad to know or not. I'd got used to what I knew before; my life's been kind of built on it. And now it's all changed.'

'Yes.'

'Our coffee's going cold.'

'Eleanor . . .'

'I'm not saying I wish my life had been different. I can't say that. I mean, there's Lewis and the girls. How can I regret anything when I've got them?'

'I know.'

'But it just feels so strange. If I'd got the letters or the phone call – just one of them. Or if I'd written to you one more time and posted the letter myself –'

'Or if I'd done what I thought of doing, and just got on a plane and come to find you.'

'You were going to do that?'

'A hundred times. I thought about it every day.'

'There, then.'

'We might have fallen out, of course.'

I giggled. 'Probably. You were always a bit too sunny for me.'

'On the other hand –'

'Yes, well. We'll never know now, will we?'

'I guess not.'

'I'm glad you didn't just forget me, though.'

'Jesus, Eleanor, you've no idea.'

'All those years,' I said. I didn't really know what I meant by that.

We sat for a moment in silence, leaning towards each other across the small table, gazing into each other's eyes. If anyone had been watching us, they would have said we were lovers.

'I hate to say this . . .'

'You've got to go.'

'Will you walk me to where I can get a cab?'

'Sure.'

We left the café and walked through back to the road. I felt the sun warm on the nape of my neck. Soon it would be full summer. I should buy a paddling pool for the girls, plan our holiday. Cherries, I thought, and asparagus, and cold white wine sitting outside in the small garden at the back of our house. When I thought of Lewis, my heart felt as tender as a bruise.

'Here,' I said. 'Shall I wait until one arrives? It shouldn't be long.'

'No. You go ahead.'

'So this is goodbye.'

'I don't know.' He looked at me, frowning. 'Do you mean we won't see each other again?'

'What do you think?'

'Maybe next time I'm over . . .'

'But really, we're ghosts, aren't we?' I said. 'Each other's ghosts.'

'Don't haunt me,' he said, and for the first time he touched me, putting a hand against my cheek just for a moment, and just for a moment, just one blind moment, I closed my eyes and let myself drop back into my past.

'Take care,' I said. 'Will.'

'You too, Eleanor.'

'Goodbye then.'

'Bye.'

I turned, so that he wouldn't see my face any more.

'I did love you,' he said to my departing back, and I lifted a hand in the air and waved and walked away. As I approached the Underground station, I saw a taxi go past, and there was a man sitting in the back who I recognised from a long time ago. But he was a stranger again and he didn't see me. I watched him go and then I continued on my way.

'Good day?' asked Lewis later as we lay in bed together, under the thin sheet in the balmy warmth of the May night. I could see the new moon through the gap in the curtains.

'Fine,' I said. I held his hand in the half-darkness. I put it to my lips and kissed the knuckles. Memory could drown me, but love would steer me through.

The Clutter Rut

Lesley Glaister

Are you stuck in a rut? Are you discontented? Did you know that clutter in your home and in your life can prevent you from reaching your full potential? For one-to-one advice on freeing yourself from the clutter-trap phone Trudi Wise on . . .

Toto whined, tugged at his lead and pulled Marilyn away from the ad in the post-office window. She looked back over her shoulder at the pale blue card with its simple, uncluttered lettering. It felt personal, somehow, as if meant for her. Her house was cluttered; there were no two ways about that. And she had been feeling discontented lately, just a little disgruntled with no particular cause. She'd tried talking to Ian about it but he'd put it down to her age.

'But I'm only forty-five!' she'd said. The tone of his voice had made her feel middle-aged. Middle age seemed to suit him. At fifty, he was comfortable in slippers and cardigans, happy it seemed to spend the evenings in front of the television, or playing war games in the cellar.

It was an early evening in spring. Cherry blossom was silhouetted against a lemony sky. She felt a twist inside her ribs, a wrench of longing. For what she didn't know. She turned the corner into her road and Toto lifted his leg against his usual lamp-post. Maybe it was a rut. Same job for ten years, part-time school secretary. She liked the job, the children – in the absence of any of her own – and the staff. There was nothing wrong with it except that it was the same thing, week after week, year after year.

She'd been married to Ian for twenty years. Happily, she supposed, though she couldn't remember the last time she'd felt actual joy. Perhaps it was the clutter that they had gathered about them over the years. Stuff accumulates and neither of them was any good at throwing things away.

'Hang on, Toto,' Marilyn said, suddenly certain that the advertisement was a sign. She must waste no more time. She dragged the dog back to the post office and, with the stub of a pencil, on the margin of an old shopping list, she jotted Trudi's number. Even the act of copying it down made her feel better, lighter, fully resolved.

She went through the front door into the hall, unclipped Toto from his lead and forced her coat on to a hook over bulging layers of coats and jackets and trailing scarves. Underneath the hooks was the shoe rack: a jumble of sandals, gardening shoes, boots and one stiletto heel jutting rudely out.

She picked up that shoe and tried to find its twin in the jumble. Patent leather with a little bow; foxy and dusty. She'd worn them last to a Christmas party, she remembered staggering in that night, kicking them off and swearing never to inflict such torture on her toes again. And now it was spring and there they still were – at least one of them was. Ian's muddy walking boots had left squiggles of dried mud all over everything. She rubbed the shoe on her sleeve so that she could see the reflection of her face, distorted in the patent leather, and then she dropped it and surveyed the whole lot in disgust. No wonder she was in a rut. Who would not be in such a mess?

In the kitchen she narrowed her eyes, trying to see it from Trudi's perspective. The fridge door was covered in magnets, notes, tickets, pizza and curry-house flyers. The top of the fridge overflowed with envelopes, torn-out recipes, half-burnt candles, loose change. Tea towels and oven gloves were draped over the radiator, which sheltered three chewed slippers and a bone. Even Toto was guilty of cluttering.

Marilyn took a deep breath and, before she could change her mind, dialled Trudi's number. An answerphone clicked on and she almost lost her nerve, was about to put the receiver down, when Trudi's voice broke through, soft and silky: 'I'm sorry; I've just got in. How may I help you?'

'I saw your ad . . . in the post office,' Marilyn said. 'It caught my eye, where it says "Are you stuck in a rut", that caught my eye and I thought yes that's me . . .' She heard herself babbling and winced. It was the verbal equivalent of clutter, the way she chattered. It irritated Ian and now it was probably irritating Trudi too.

'Wonderful,' Trudi said. 'Perfect timing. As it happens, I have a window tomorrow. Would that suit you?'

When she put down the phone, Marilyn felt quite faint. What had she done? Tomorrow a stranger would be in here peering at all the cosy layers of her life. Poking in all the private corners. She stared at her startled face through the smears on the hall mirror. Not frightening, *exhilarating*, she told herself. Now she just had to tell to Ian.

She baked potatoes and grilled lamb chops. 'Why not open a bottle of wine?' she said as she set the food on the table.

Ian put his paper down and blinked at her. She saw a flicker of panic in his eyes. 'Have I forgotten something?'

'No, but we can have a glass of wine, can't we? We don't have to keep it to Saturdays do we?'

Ian shrugged and gave her his baffled look – but he fetched a bottle and opened it.

'Here's to the future,' she said, raising her glass and holding it up for him to clink.

'The future,' Ian said. He sat down and took a mouthful of his food. 'Very nice chops. Capital. Now if you don't mind . . .' and he went back to his newspaper.

Marilyn trimmed a frill of fat from her chop. 'I want to talk to you,' she said. 'I think we need a shake-up, don't you? Don't you think we're in a bit of a rut?'

Ian raised his eyes from the paper. 'In which department?' he asked, looking nervous. 'Not the er . . .'

'In all departments,' Marilyn said.

He frowned at her and she noticed how deep the lines on his forehead had become. How his hairline was creeping back. 'I feel comfortable,' he said. 'If that's a rut I like it. It's a good rut.'

'There's no such thing!' Marilyn laughed, the midweek wine arriving suddenly in her brain. 'A good rut!'

'I do hope you're not heading into another fad,' Ian said.

Marilyn frowned, feeling her forehead pucker, hoping her lines were not as deep and serious as his.

'The vegan spell?' he reminded her. 'The meditations? The detoxification?'

'I only want to fulfil my full potential,' Marilyn said, thinking that that did not sound quite right. She fed Toto the scrap of fat and watched him lick the stained white fur round his mouth. 'We must move forward.'

'But we are moving forward. We move forward every day.'

'No we don't.'

'Because you remember what happened on those occasions . . .' Ian warned.

Marilyn nodded. On those occasions, he had gone to stay at his mother's while she got the 'fad' out of her system.

'It's not a fad,' Marilyn said, and it's not just for me it's for both of us. It's an ad I saw in the post office, a woman called Trudi who'll help declutter the house, declutter our lives. All quite simple. There's nothing spiritual about it or anything. She's coming tomorrow.'

Ian blinked, humphed, took a pen from his pocket and began the crossword. Marilyn clashed the plates together a little louder than was necessary as she cleared the table.

'As long as she doesn't touch my cellar,' he called as she left the room. 'I'm in the middle of Culloden.'

Marilyn looked at the window sill as she washed the dishes: three dead cuttings, a cork, an earplug, some tweezers and a jam jar full of dead Biros. But soon it would all be clear. She smiled at her reflection in the kitchen window.

Trudi rang the doorbell at exactly 10 a.m., swept past Marilyn into the hall and before she'd even said hello, began to shake her head.

'Do you need me?!' she said. 'Oh boy, do I enjoy a challenge?!'

Do you? Marilyn thought. 'Would you like a cup of tea?' she asked.

'Hot water will do for me,' Trudi said. She was a tall woman with a sleek, uncluttered silhouette. She put her head into the sitting room. 'What on earth are these?' she asked, grabbing an armful of cushions. Cushions were Marilyn's weakness: fluffy ones, glittery ones, witty ones. Wherever she went, she bought a cushion as a souvenir. The sofa was piled high. 'Oh dear,' Trudi said, 'oh dearie me.'

Marilyn led her through into the kitchen and, looking round, Trudi made a small excited groan. Toto wagged his tail and came to meet her. Trudi brushed the hairs off her trouser legs and, sweeping the seat of a chair with her hand, sat down. She took a clipboard and pen from her bag.

'Right,' she said.

Marilyn poured herself some tea and Trudi a mug of boiling water.

'Biscuit?' she offered, holding out the tin, but Trudi just waved her hand.

'Clutter is stuck energy,' she said. 'Do you understand?'

Marilyn nodded.

'Clutter can only accumulate when energy stagnates. I sense a great stagnancy, I can smell it, a pervasive odour.'

Marilyn found that she was blushing. 'Really?' she said.

'Do you feel constantly tired?' Trudi asked.

'Well, sometimes,' Marilyn said.

Trudi pushed Toto, who was trying to lie on her feet, away with her toe. 'Why am I not surprised?' she said. 'All this stuff is holding you back. The question is: are you brave enough to strip it away?'

'Brave?' Marilyn said.

'On some level you must have needed to be held back,' Trudi said. 'I have rarely seen a clearer case of clutter rut.'

'Clutter rut,' repeated Marilyn. 'Is that what I'm in? What . . .' she ventured, 'would you define as clutter?'

'Excellent question. Clutter is anything that has no purpose in your life. Anything you don't use or wear, anything that you keep for "just in case".'

Marilyn's mind sped to the wardrobe in the spare room bursting with 'just in case I'm ever size 10 again' clothes.

'Cushions, for instance,' Trudi said and gazed at Marilyn for a moment as if she was a particularly interesting specimen.

'If you want my help, then I'll have to ask you to trust me. I'll be asking you to do some painful things, things that might feel painful. But it will be worthwhile, I can guarantee you that.'

Marilyn shivered. She looked down at her shabby

fake-fur slippers, one of many pairs. She suspected that they would have to go.

Trudi continued: 'And I'll have to ask you to pay in advance for . . . at least five sessions.'

'Five?'

'At least.'

'Can't I pay as I go along?'

Trudi took a sip of her hot water, smiled and put her hand on Marilyn's. 'I ask you to pay in advance for your own sake,' she said. 'You see, you might find the process such a challenge that you'll want to give up. If you've paid in advance you are less likely to do so. It's for your own benefit. Do you want to be a new woman, Marilyn? Do you want to be liberated from stagnation?'

'I . . . I think so.'

'Sign here.' Trudi pushed the clipboard with an agreement form towards her. 'Write me a cheque, and then we can begin! Am I going to enjoy this?'

They began in the attic, stacked with boxes that had been undisturbed for fifteen years – things that had seemed essential when they left their last house though not essential enough to unpack; a higgledy-piggle of tennis rackets (from a Wimbledon fad years ago); a wedding present picnic hamper – never used; a mouldy sleeping bag; a pile of mothy blankets.

Trudi, who had put a white coat over her clothes, went up and down the stairs carrying things towards the door. Sometimes Marilyn offered a timid objection: 'My granny gave me that . . .', 'That's my favourite . . .' but Trudi was firm.

Two hours later she drove away with a van stuffed with Marilyn and Ian's belongings.

Marilyn stood in the attic and waited for her spirits to lift. The light that filtered through the dusty skylight showed nothing now but a water tank and boards.

Because Ian never went into the attic, he noticed nothing. Marilyn was very nice to him all week, with beef and pies and a supreme attempt not to chatter over meals. It was only after Session 2 that he began to grumble.

He had gone upstairs to change his cardigan and Marilyn had followed him. He'd stood in the doorway for a moment and blinked. Trudi had taken the rugs from the floor; the dressmaker's dummy; the big sick yucca plant, and she'd swept the tops of the chest of drawers and the wardrobe clean. She'd removed the heaps of cushions from the bed, the pile of paperbacks and jokey ornaments from the bedside table.

'Doesn't it look nice?' Marilyn said.

'It looks cold,' Ian said. 'I liked it as it was.'

'You'll be more energised,' she said. 'You wait.'

Ian humphed and, as soon as he'd eaten his pie, went down into the cellar to finish off Culloden.

When the sitting room, dining room and hallway had been cleared, despite loin of pork and apple snow, Ian ran out of patience. He finished his meal, put down his knife and fork.

'I'm going to pack,' he said.

He looked at her for a moment, giving her a chance to beg but Marilyn was beginning to feel empowered. When her feet clacked on the bare floorboards in the hall, and her eyes skimmed the four pairs of cleaned shoes on the rack, the empty window sills, the clean sweep of the bare kitchen floor, her spirits began to truly rise.

'All you need is two minutes a day with a damp mop,' Trudi said, 'instead all of that skirting round things. And the less things, the less dust.'

'Yes?' Marilyn had said, eager to agree though doubtful of the logic.

Ian had taken his toothbrush, dressing gown and shaving things. Consequently the bathroom was less cluttered. 'Fewer people, less clutter,' Trudi had said. Listening to Ian's car driving away, Marilyn wondered if Trudi lived alone. She went and sat

down on the sofa. Trudi had suggested removing the
lace curtains and the windows were bare and clean.
Not an ornament on the mantelpiece; not a picture on
the walls; not a witty cushion in sight.

Now it was time for Session 5. Marilyn had woken
with a peculiar sensation under ribs, almost a pain.
When she had gone downstairs that morning it had
been absolutely quiet. Toto was outside in his new
kennel. A dog causes mess and clutter: footprints, dog
hairs, chewed-up sticks. Trudi would never have an
animal in her house. But the house did feel quiet
without him in it. And without Ian. As she washed
up her bowl, cup and spoon, she gazed out of the
window at Toto. He was lying on the grass in a pool
of sunshine looking quite happy, but he had whined
all night. She had hardly been able to sleep for the
whining.

At bedtime, as he'd done every night since he'd left,
Ian had rung to say goodnight.

'Is it over yet?' he'd said.

'What?'

'The fad?'

'It's not a fad,' she'd said. Although there was
nothing to talk about she'd tried to keep him on the
phone. It had been nice to hear his voice.

This week Trudi was determined that they should

do the cellar. 'You're a success story,' she'd said to Marilyn. 'Don't you feel the energy surging around you? Except for the stagnation in the cellar. Deal with that and then my job will be complete.'

Marilyn had nodded, but she knew that if she let Trudi into the cellar she'd dispose of Ian's soldiers: no way she'd tolerate a war down there. Imagine the negative energy of that. But if Marilyn let Ian's soldiers go then . . . She'd been cold last night, listening to Toto whining and without Ian's body to snuggle round.

Marilyn stood in the hall, admiring the way the sun shone in a honeyed rectangle through the glass panels of the door on to the clean bare floor. She heard the postman's footsteps on the path; saw his outline; saw the post spill through the slot.

'Junk straight in bin,' she thought, as Trudi had taught her to think. As she carried it away, a catalogue caught her eye. It was a glossy catalogue, the cover of which showed a tumble of cream and apricot scatter cushions. Soft and squashy. She sat down at the kitchen table. It wouldn't hurt to look. She flicked through the pages at chenille throws and bright rugs, porcelain dolls and stuffed toys and cushions, cushions, cushions. She turned to the order form in the back of the catalogue. Choose any six items and get a squeaky cushion free! A squeaky cushion, she thought; that would make Ian smile.

The doorbell rang, loud in the empty hall. It rang three times and then she heard the letter flap open and Trudi's voice: 'Marilyn? Are you there?'

Toto whined and scratched at the back door and Marilyn let him in. He licked her face as she bent down to stroke him. She crouched with her arms around his neck – hidden behind the table, in case Trudi looked through the window. And once she was sure that Trudi had gone, Marilyn rang Ian at work and left a message: 'OK. It's over. Beef Wellington and treacle pud. See you later.' Then she sat down at the table with a cup of tea and began to pick her cushions.

Sweet Vanilla

Tessa Hadley

On my way to a meeting, I realise I'm early, I've got time to kill. I think how nice it would be to stop for a cappuccino and read the paper, and then I cross the road and peer into a place that looks possible. More than possible; promising, atmospheric, with a gleaming espresso machine, high mirror-glass shelves of cups and glasses, enticing pâtisserie, a proprietor standing contemplatively in a clean white apron. The lighting is either original sixties-style or tasteful retro, with long creamy cylinder lampshades suspended over the tables. The few customers are sitting alone; the shadowy depths of the place seem a womb of calm in contrast to the blare of traffic and polluted air outside.

I don't live in London, although I come up here often for work (I'm a freelance graphic designer) and I simply presume that in London I will never accidentally meet anyone I know. But now, of all people, sitting halfway back in that café, there's Barbara – doing exactly what I had thought of doing, paused with her coffee cup lifted halfway to her mouth, absorbed in something she's reading.

It's extraordinary that I don't for one moment doubt that it's Barbara, even though I haven't seen her for twenty years, even though the last thing I heard of her they were moving away – not to London, but up north. I know without hesitation that it's her; it's as if the sight of her claims me, all my memory of her seizes hold, as vividly as a hand on my shoulder. She must be in her late forties like me, but in those first moments, before she looks up and recognises me, I can't see that she's changed at all. That subtle lighting of course does women our age a favour. She's wearing her hair differently – it's rather wonderful red hair, not carroty red but a deep browny auburn like the colour of conkers (although I can't see its colour exactly through the café window, I'm remembering that). She used to wear it loose and long. It was silky and had a slight natural curl and went, in those days, with the gypsy dresses, the kohl eyeliner and baking our own bread; hanging on to hippiedom when everyone else had moved on to power dressing. Now she has her hair cut shorter, layered, shoulder-length. It's a good cut. She's taken her arms out of the sleeves of her coat and wears it slipped across her shoulders. It's a good coat, too – beige, heavy, understated, flattering. I stand peering in; the glass in the café windows is slightly smoked, so I have to press close to see her. And then, just as I'm about to pull back in shock from the glass and hurry away from her down the street, pretending to myself that it couldn't have been Barbara, pretending that I must have been imagining things, that some trick of resemblance in a stranger's appearance must have triggered a memory of her, Barbara looks up from her newspaper and sees me.

I can't believe that, outside in the bleak light, I don't look more changed to her than she does to me (it's March, a gritty wind in the street scours stone and skin indiscriminately). She surely doesn't know at once who it is she's recognising, or what makes her put her coffee cup down untouched on its saucer and half rise from her chair. There's a question in her face that might mean she knows me but can't place me; or might mean she thinks she knows who I am but isn't sure, because of how I've altered. And then we've exchanged smiles, waves, extravagant surprise; I've no choice but to push open the door and go inside. The change of air is absolute as if I had dropped suddenly under water – instead of the nagging wind, coffee steam and sweet vanilla warmth.

'Barbara? It is Barbara, isn't it?'

'Cath? I can't believe it's you.'

'Oh my God! Isn't this amazing?'

'Don't tell me you live nearby?'

We create a flurry, a hiatus, in the absorbed quiet of the café. Customers lift their heads from their papers, from studying the circling foam in their coffee cups. I feel a pang of regret that the spell of peace is broken, although I get the impression the proprietor doesn't mind. Perhaps he had been thinking that the place was a bit dead this morning and he's reassured by the excited chatter of two wealthy enough women in good coats, their appearances glossy with all the careful tending of middle age. It's not like the days when we used to pile into cafés with our noisy crowd of kids, in our clothes that we deliberately made to look as if they'd come from some extravagant scrap-bag, breastfeeding at the table, smoking little liquorice-paper rollies. But then, in those days, we would never have chosen to come into a place like this.

The last time I saw Barbara was at a party at our house, twenty years ago. Or perhaps not quite that long, perhaps more like sixteen or seventeen.

My three boys were little then, Ruby, who's fourteen now, wasn't born or even thought of. Ours were the best parties. I can't remember what the excuse was for that one – Pete's thirtieth birthday? We had a live band, some Irish musicians Pete knew; we'd cleared all the furniture out of our big middle room for dancing. Barbara and Ben were there of course; our families did everything together for a while. Always at those parties the children – fifteen or twenty of them sometimes, if enough families came – provided a sort of undertow to the crazy adult goings-on. They would develop some fantastic game of mayhem up and down the stairs of the tall old house; or suddenly they would all be underfoot, on the hunt for food, shoals of quick bright fish moving through an adult sea. We young mothers, I remember, loved to dance with our children, holding them up on a hip or jiving with them if they were older; we found a place where the two tides of our lives crossed, the maternal with the sexual. Also we were showing off – we thought we looked wonderful, our hot young flesh juxtaposed with their uncalculated angel beauty.

I only remember a few things in particular from

that night. I remember that Jodie, Ben and Barbara's middle child, had made a maraca out of an ice-cream tub filled with lentils and she was dancing and shaking it to the music, when the lid flew off and the lentils went everywhere. I was vacuuming lentils out of the carpet months later. Jodie was a handful; she must have been about three or four years old then. She'd loved being the centre of attention with her maraca. When the lentils flew out, she ran at Barbara and hid her face against her in a rage of self-consciousness, pounding at her with her fists and kicking her. Barbara held off the frenzy at arm's length until it was spent, with an expression that looked like mild curiosity.

I envied her detached, ironic approach to mother-hood. When I first met her at the play park, it was the way she sat reading a book while her children ran perilously in and out among the swings that made me want to talk to her, and then ask for her telephone number. I hadn't managed to read a book since Hal was born. Barbara wasn't nearly as organised and domesticated as me; her house was untidy to a depth of three or four feet. She seemed easygoing (she didn't quarrel with Ben the way Pete and I quarrelled) but I thought she was tougher than I was, clearer about what she wanted, less easily distracted. She had at some point rigged up electricity in a shed in their garden, put a camp bed and a desk in there, hung the walls round with shawls and Indian prints and declared her den off-limits to husband and family. The shed got damp in the winter and the shawls went mouldy, but the idea of it entranced me – the absorbing privacy, boiling a kettle for tea for one, sleeping alone, almost under the stars.

Ben, who was a social worker, had applied for a job, a promotion, in the north. Shortly after that party, he was interviewed and appointed and they moved away. The party can't have been the last time I saw Barbara. There must have been farewells; we'd been close friends.

I must have looked after the children while she packed up that chaotic house, she must have given me her new address. I seem to have wiped all that from my memory. I don't know how I managed to wriggle out of the promises, postponing visits, making excuses, until one day it was too late and our friend-ship was something we'd left behind us.

Now those wild tribes of our children – barefoot, long-haired, face-painted – are grown up into civil servants, an IT consultant, a BBC research assistant. We compare notes. Barbara's younger son, who was such a sweet-tempered roly-poly baby, is in the army, on standby to go out to Iraq. 'Isn't it funny?' Barbara says. 'How things turn out.'

I search her face for signs of the desperation I'd feel if it was one of my sons; but I'm not convinced, just because I don't find anything, she doesn't feel it. I don't know how to read her, that's all. Now I'm sitting across the table from her, free to study her close up, she looks so changed I wonder if I really knew her at all.

In the first minutes, while I was settling my portfolio beside the chair, fetching myself coffee, taking off my coat, my vision of the young Barbara was shuffled away behind this new appearance of hers – elegant, nuanced, with decisive puckers drawn in her fine skin when she smiles or frowns. Her face used to be quite plump, I think; her round cheeks used to have a peachy bloom. Her hair still has red glints in it, although maybe she has it coloured. She's interested that I work in graphic design; she's had a job for years, she says, putting together one of those magazines that sells books in schools. We try for a minute or two to establish an overlap, someone or some company we've used in common, but we can't find anything. She lives in London, just round the corner. She often comes into this café for a break if she's working at home. 'And how is Ben?' I ask her.

Her eyes are amused at the idea. She's dabbing the icing sugar from her lips with a paper napkin – I've persuaded her to have a pastry with me. 'Oh, we haven't been together for years,' she says.

Carefully, I put my pastry down on the plate. 'I'm surprised,' I say.

I have imagined them together, often. Whatever happened in my life, I have counted on Ben and Barbara existing somewhere together, their minds on higher things, their house in chaos, their relationship mostly unspoken, steady, somewhat enigmatic.

'He was so boring,' Barbara says. 'In the end, he just bored me. I thought it would be more interesting to be by myself. I waited to leave until the children were old enough to be out of the baby stage at least, although needless to say they all hold it indignantly against me whenever anything goes wrong for them.'

'Oh, really?' I say. 'Was he boring? Quiet, I suppose; but I always thought he had an intensity. Whenever he walked into a room, he was one of those.'

'No, he just had beautiful eyes. It was the eyes that did it, for women. But honestly, those eyes were just a trick. Biology. They looked as though he was listening with intent involvement to whatever you said. But behind them he was the kind of man who lies awake at night worrying about where to get his car insurance. Believe me. Boring.'

I pick up my pastry and I have to laugh, sending up a white puff of sugar. Is this true? I ask myself. Is it possible?

'And are you by yourself then?' I ask. 'Is it more interesting?'

She makes a rueful face. 'What d'you think? Aren't women weak? No, I succumbed of course. I'm living with someone else. Actually he's the headmaster of a school where I used to try out my book days. Doesn't that sound dodgy, getting off with the headmaster? "Come here, I understand you've been a naughty little girl." All that sort of thing.'

She's made this joke before, I can tell. She's introduced it now to bring the idea of this man into the conversation, simply because she loves to talk about him.

'Whatever he is, anyway, he isn't boring. And are you still with Pete?'

I am, I tell her.

'Now that surprises me,' she says. 'As it happens. Isn't life full of surprises? Good for you, for staying the old course.'

My affair with Ben wasn't much of a thing. We collided in the dark on the upstairs landing at that party (Pete was supposed to put in a new light bulb). We had both drunk quite a bit. Ben pulled me into the bathroom, locked the door behind us, kissed me, caressed me, worked me up into a state of incandescent desire that I had forgotten was possible. You have to remember that I was spending all my days changing nappies, washing them, cooking fish fingers, cleaning floors and toilets. Someone desperate to pee hammered at the door; I didn't care who saw us come out from the bathroom together.

A couple of days later Ben telephoned from his office at a time when he knew Pete would be out at work. He said that a friend of his who had a flat in town had given him the keys while he was away. I said I went to an art class on Wednesday evenings. We managed to meet three times.

The lovemaking was never as good as it had promised to be when we were pressing up against the toilet-roll holder in my bathroom, stumbling into the kids' bath toys, knocking over the Badedas bottle. All the time we were meeting, we knew that if Ben got that job in the north we would be separated. Or perhaps I also allowed myself to think that if we found we couldn't bear to live apart, Ben would leave Barbara and I would leave Pete. I can't remember now how seriously I considered that possibility.

Later at that same party, I remember I was dancing alone to Bob Marley's 'Lively Up Yourself' in one of the band intervals (the more the band drank, the less Irish their music became – they got on to Cream and the Doors by three in the morning). Ben had said he liked the way I was so spontaneous and as I danced I was hugging this idea proudly to myself. I was thinking, yes, I could see, from one point of view, that Barbara might seem too careful, not spontaneous at all.

I have a meeting to get to, I mustn't be late, I'm hoping they'll give me some work on a new contract for a company that organises video conferencing. It's only when Barbara and I have said our goodbyes and exchanged email addresses and I'm back out on the street with my shoulders hunched against the wind that I allow myself to wonder about Ben.

It shocks me to realise how much I've thought about him. I've probably done it every day since that party – at first in an agony of hope, doubt, anticipation.

We did speak a few times on the phone after they moved north; once, we even tried to arrange a meeting, but then one of the boys got quite poorly with chickenpox and I had to cancel. In the years since, Ben has been my treasured secret, my reassurance that I've had my share of adventure. I think in turmoil now – was he boring? It comes back to me that he was annoyed, once, when I tried to play the stereo in his friend's flat. He told me not to touch anything in case I messed it up.

Also, he talked earnestly and at length about some of his clients, teenagers with drug problems, while I lay there, longing for him to get back on to the bottomlessly interesting subject of 'us'.

I don't know whether Barbara knows about me and Ben. She might have intuited our treachery from the very first moment. Ben might have told her later, at some crisis of closeness, or when they were separating.

Did she say the thing about him being boring because she knew; to punish me? I'll never be able to ask her. I won't keep in touch; I'll probably never see her again.

As soon as I'm in my meeting with the conferencing people, none of this stuff from the past will matter. My real and sturdy self will resume control; I'll be fine.

Until I can reach the safety of real life, however, I have this sensation of collapse inside. I can't breathe the filthy air, I'm searching for that familiar place where I keep my memory of Ben: it's almost a shrine, with its own rituals for daydreaming and conjuring up his spirit.

For the first time, I can't recover the reality of his physical presence, or the sound of his voice. I have relied on these things for years, to melt me, undo me; but I've worn the idea of him out with too much handling, until he's transparent and paper-thin, a limp doll.

What I'm afraid of is that when I look into that innermost place I'll see Barbara instead, the old Barbara, absorbed and smiling, dancing by herself at my party.

No Baggage

Maeve Haran

'*Buon giorno, signora*. Welcome to Amalfi!'

Julia opened her eyes to find an impossibly good-humoured waiter smiling at her. 'Where shall I put the tray? On the balcony?'

Without waiting for her to agree he swept open the curtains to reveal a rattan table and chairs set against a backdrop of such luminescent beauty that it took Julia's breath away. The hotel, and her room with it, seemed to perch like an eagle's nest in the brightest of blue skies. Hundreds of feet below the sea, still veiled in a slight mist, shimmered like turquoise taffeta.

Julia sat on the balcony feeling that any minute the scene would dissolve and she'd be back home in drizzly England. The holiday had been her daughter

Sadie's idea. At first she'd insisted that she couldn't afford it. Life was a struggle when you were unexpectedly single, but Sadie had been insistent. 'Right, Mum, no moping at home this summer. Dad isn't moping. He and Adrienne are going to Biarritz.'

Julia had tried not to feel bitter or envious, but it was tough. France had been *their* place. For eighteen years they'd spent almost every family holiday there, camping when they were broke, and staying in comfortable hotels when their finances improved. She'd always thought Bill would be more tactful than to go to France. Maybe it had been Adrienne's idea.

'An activity holiday, that's what you need,' Sadie had insisted. 'They don't have to be all windsurfing and sailing,' she'd added catching sight of her mother's appalled expression. 'This firm called Solo Adventure does painting and cooking and tours of classical Greece and Rome. They even do Pompeii – you've always wanted to go to Pompeii. And since all their clients are single they can negotiate better rooms.'

Julia had been sceptical. It was a fact of life that single people always got the worst rooms, but here she was with this fabulous view.

Julia tucked in to the delicious croissant and tiny sweet rolls and sipped her caffè latte. In half an hour she would meet the other guests downstairs in the lounge.

Julia looked round the group of twelve. They seemed a nice enough bunch. A mother and daughter, the mother probably in her eighties, rather stern, the daughter perhaps sixty. A librarian type carrying an enormous tome entitled *Classical Rome: a Reader*. A distinguished-looking man who could be anything from a judge to a senior businessman. Another man, neat and quietly dressed, who might be an accountant or lawyer. Two more, flamboyantly dressed, who rather than actually being single, seemed as if they were gay. There were also several women around her own age, smartly dressed, probably in a similar position to herself, Julia guessed, from the way they were glancing interestedly at the men in the party.

But there was one guest who stood out like a blini topped with caviar among a plate of Ritz crackers. He was probably Julia's own age, lithe and tanned, wearing immaculate chinos, a crisp cotton shirt, with a pastel cashmere jumper slung over his shoulders. He had well-cut dark hair, swept back from his face, and extremely dark eyes. Julia wondered why he wasn't sunning himself in the Costa Smeralda or some other jet-set haunt.

'Hello, everyone, I'm Hilary,' a hearty Home Counties girl announced. 'Your rep from Solo Adventures and I'm here to make sure you have a really good time.'

They all introduced themselves. The women Julia's age were Suzanne and Erica. Maud was the eighty-year-old with her daughter, the unfortunately named Desiree, the distinguished man was Oliver and the handsome man's name was Marcus.

'Forty-five, barrister, happily divorced,' whispered Erica, one of the two single women, who had obviously been doing her research. She winked at Julia. 'And best of all, No Baggage. He and his wife decided against children, apparently, because of her career. He feels very sad about it, but says maybe since they split up it's for the best.'

'You're a fast worker,' Julia commented, both impressed and slightly embarrassed.

'At our age you have to be,' Erica grinned. 'You know the statistic, when you're over forty more women get killed by a terrorist than find a new relationship.'

'That sounds a bit harsh.'

'You obviously haven't been on the market long.'

Julia repressed a shudder. She hated the idea of being 'on the market'. In fact, if it weren't so damned lonely, she'd prefer to be on the shelf.

'Hello there.' The object of their discussion had joined them. 'You're Julia, aren't you. You're in the right place, then.' He smiled warmly at her. 'Your name's Roman. Julias were very important in Rome. They gave birth to a lot of emperors.'

'Lucky Julias,' Erica responded drily. 'Were there any Roman Ericas?'

Marcus shook his head. 'More Viking. Ericas are Scandinavian as a whole.'

'Just my luck. I'd probably have ended up as the booty. How about you, Marcus? You sound a bit on the Roman side yourself.'

Marcus laughed self-deprecatingly. 'There was an aristocratic Marcus or two.'

'And my name's Antoninus,' interrupted a new arrival whom none of them had noticed. 'But Tony will do.' The owner of the voice provided a stark counterpoint to Marcus's sleek sophistication. He was slight, with a humorous voice and big black-framed glasses, just visible under a floppy hat. His combat trousers had more pockets than a squaddie's. 'No Roman connections for me, I'm afraid. Though there was an Antoninus in *Spartacus*. Played by Tony Curtis with a Bronx accent. *Gee, Emperor, we who are about to die salute you.*'

Julia giggled. His Tony Curtis accent was perfect.

'Here's your itinerary, everyone.' Hilary handed them a sheaf of notes. 'Today we're doing the duomo in Amalfi and a drive along the coast road to Positano. Pack your credit cards, girls, for some serious shopping. Gucci. Fiorucci. You name it.'

Julia's heart sank at the thought of expensive boutiques for thin rich people.

'Don't worry,' Tony confided, 'I last went shopping in 1975.'

'And it looks it,' Marcus murmured.

The following day would be a boat trip round the coastline, after that a day in Capri and then, the trip Julia was really looking forward to, the ruins of Pompeii.

'It'd be just my luck if it erupted again,' Erica quipped, taking Julia's arm. She seemed to have taken a shine to Julia. 'Isn't Marcus gorgeous? And how often do you find a man like that who's had an amicable divorce and isn't even going to make you a stepmother to his horrible brats?'

They all went in to lunch together.

As she sat on the sun-drenched terrace looking down at Amalfi, Julia felt as if she'd landed on another, altogether better planet. For almost three years she'd struggled with the loneliness, money worries and sense of failure that came hand in hand with divorce.

Even the food was fabulous. Featherlight tartlets made with the tiny local tomatoes called *pomodorini*, laced with the heady tang of basil and accompanied by a wonderful red wine.

'Lacryma Christi.' Marcus leaned over with a smile that seemed to be just for Julia, and filled up her glass. 'Christ's tears. They say its taste comes from the volcanic ash of Vesuvius.'

'He was probably crying because Judas was such a bloody know-all,' Tony murmured.

The trip turned out to be glorious. Positano was a tiny gem of a town spilling down the hill towards the glittering sea, and Julia even managed to find the perfect present for her daughter in one of the smart boutiques.

At dinner she discovered that Marcus had saved a place for her next to him.

'You're in there, if you play your cards right,' commented Erica enviously. 'You're the classy type. Latin and all that. I'm common as muck, me.'

Erica didn't look too downcast in her plain black dress with an incredible diamond necklace. Clearly her ex had been generous. Unlike Julia's. The shock still hit her that Bill, so open-handed in marriage, had become so penny-pinching in divorce. Maybe it had been Adrienne.

She wasn't going to think about it. Tomorrow was Pompeii, the highlight of the whole trip.

They were all about to get on the coach next morning when Julia heard a hubbub in the lobby. Two children, a boy of about fifteen and a twelve-year-old girl, stood there looking as if they'd rather be anywhere else on earth. Hilary and Tony were standing next to them, arguing.

'I'm sorry, Tony,' Hilary was saying, 'and I sympathise, believe me, but it's company policy. This is a singles holiday and positively no children are allowed.'

'What's up?' Julia asked.

Tony shrugged, looking distraught. 'My wife, or rather ex-wife Marina, has changed her holiday plans and disappeared to some Greek island without leaving a forwarding address. She's sent the children on to me.'

Julia bit her lip. She could see the problem.

'Caspar would love to go to Pompeii more than anything on earth. He knows all the legends and history. And Claudia's missing her mum.'

'Sorry,' Hilary began, 'it really isn't possible.'

Julia took in the anxious expression in the young

girl's eyes, and the exhaustion in Tony's. Clearly this sort of thing had happened before.

'I can see that,' Julia chipped in, 'but what if the guests all agree to have them along and promise not to complain afterwards.'

'Thanks,' Tony said gratefully. 'But it'll never work.' He gestured towards the octogenarian Maud. 'Judging by her expression, the only way she likes kids is fried.'

'That's because I haven't persuaded her yet.'

Julia was as good as her word. Marcus looked mutinous but Julia smiled seductively and said she'd take him out to dinner.

By the time they got on the coach for Pompeii, it was with two extra passengers. Caspar and Claudia. 'Thank you for persuading people.' Tony's eyes held hers for a moment. His smile held warmth and real gratitude. 'Thank God you've got one of your own.'

The journey on the A3 Salerno–Naples highway was nerve-tingling and Julia felt distinct relief when they turned off.

Pompeii was magnificent, its sense of a town stopped in time both eerie and moving. There was street after street of temples, baths, markets, Roman shops, mosaics, brothels and even a Roman version of a fast-food outlet.

'The Romans loved their nosh,' Hilary explained. 'And boy could they eat. You've heard of the vomitorium where they made themselves sick when they'd eaten too much, so they could start again?'

'They drank sea water laced with mustard,' Caspar pointed out enthusiastically.

'Or else they tickled the back of their throat with a feather,' Claudia added.

'Charming,' commented Erica. 'I could have done with that when I was a teenager. Cheaper than Weight Watchers.'

As they moved back out into the sunshine, Marcus imperceptibly took the lead. He seemed to know everything there was to know about the eruption of Vesuvius and the tragic loss of its inhabitants. 'Of course, the terrible irony was they'd only just had an earthquake and rebuilt the whole place fifteen years earlier.'

'Seventeen,' interrupted a voice. To Julia's amusement it was Caspar. Marcus ignored him.

'So when the big earthquake came in AD . . . er . . .' He glanced at his guidebook.

'Seventy-nine,' supplied Caspar. Marcus looked distinctly irritated now. 'The locals all said it couldn't happen again and refused to leave.'

'How does Caspar know all this?' Julia asked Tony

as they walked towards the next site.

'*Revolting Romans* or some such book. Ever since Marina and I split he's devoured history. Especially the gory bits. You were lucky he didn't tell you how, outside the laundries, the Romans left pots for passers-by to pee in. Human pee is excellent for washing clothes, apparently. And he read me out another choice bit this morning. What do you think was a favourite item for Roman dessert?'

'I dread to think.'

'Mice dipped in honey and poppy seeds.' They both laughed. 'Do you have any children? Or were you lucky enough to miss out on that pleasure?'

'Just one. Sadie. She's twenty-one. It was her idea I come on this holiday.'

'I hope Claudia's that thoughtful one day. Poor kid. All she wants is boring security, and she gets Marina and me for parents. And, believe me, with Marina life's one long firework display.'

When they got back to the coach, Julia found herself sitting next to Marcus. 'Of course, one day isn't nearly enough for Pompeii,' he began. 'Free day tomorrow so I thought I might come back again. Do you fancy coming as well?'

Julia knew he was right, Pompeii deserved much

more of their attention, but the thought of the hotel pool, tiny though it was, was just too tempting. She wanted to go home with at least a faint tan or Sadie would accuse her of spending a week in the shade with her book like an ancient spinster. 'Actually, I think I'll pass. I'd like to catch up on my reading.'

'Have dinner with me tonight then.' Marcus flashed her a smile which had the rest of the ladies on the bus swooning. 'The Palazzo Palumbo. Three stars in the guidebook. Panoramic views over the bay. Their octopus in its own ink is famous as far as Naples itself.'

Julia smiled. He sounded faintly like a timeshare salesman, but, she had to admit, he was very attractive.

'Lucky you,' Erica whispered as they queued up for their keys. 'He earns a hundred grand apparently.'

'Erica,' Julia teased, 'you're beginning to sound like Mrs Bennet in *Pride and Prejudice*.'

'Well,' Erica shrugged, 'maybe Mrs Bennet was the only sensible one in the book. It's no fun being broke. And single.'

The thought of an empty home and a pile of bills flashed into Julia's mind and she knew exactly what Erica meant. Maybe those diamonds of Erica's were fake.

Some instinct told her that Marcus would dress for the occasion so Julia put on a simple blue sheath with a pretty sparkly necklace. Her faithful pashmina with the beads on the end would add extra glamour if called for.

In the lobby she bumped into Tony with Caspar and Claudia. Tony had taken off the nerdy hat and was wearing sunglasses and a crisp white linen shirt. He looked almost attractive, 'Off for a pizza in the square,' he smiled. 'Don't suppose you'd like to join us?'

'Actually,' for no reason Julia found herself blushing, 'I'm planning to eat in the hotel.'

He glanced at her dress and the beaded pashmina, and, in a mock serious voice, said: *'Whenas in silk my Julia goes,/Then, then (methinks) how sweetly flows/ That liquefaction of her clothes.'*

Julia laughed. 'Herrick. What a cultured family you are!'

'Makes a change from gory facts gleaned from *Revolting Romans*. What have they got in store for us tomorrow?'

Julia consulted her itinerary. 'Tomorrow I'm spending by the pool. Then it's Capri . . .'

'Gracie Fields and the Emperor Tiberius,' Tony laughed. 'What a combination.'

'Thursday, shopping in Amalfi town. And Friday home.' Julia realised with a shock that her holiday would soon be over.

'Have a good time,' Tony shouted as he linked arms with Claudia and Caspar. 'And let Marcus pay. He's rich enough.'

The restaurant was everything Marcus had promised. He had even managed to book the best table, placed in a tiny tower jutting out over the sea below.

'It makes me feel like the Lady of Shalott,' Julia laughed.

Marcus looked blank.

'I've already ordered, if you don't mind. The *fritto misto del golfo*, followed by their special thyme-roasted lamb. They both get three stars in my restaurant guide.'

Actually Julia did mind but before she could say so a glass of champagne and peach juice appeared at her elbow.

'I hope you like Bellinis. The best are in Venice, of course.' He smiled again. 'You and I are different from the others, Julia. We've got taste. And culture. I would love to take you to some of my favourite places.'

Julia sipped her Bellini as a vista opened up before

her of well-heeled security. No more worrying if she could afford a week's break *and* pay the gas bill. No doubt Marcus did everything in style. It would certainly make Bill and Adrienne sit up. They were always patronising her but with Marcus in her life she could say things like; '*Have you ever been to Venice, Adrienne? You really ought to go in February for Carnival.*' Even the thought brought a wicked grin to Julia's lips

Marcus, noticing, took her hand and looked as if he might be about to say something.

The nearest table to theirs was a twelve-seater. Now it began to fill up with a vast Italian family, with noisy representatives from every generation from aged parents to the smallest grandchild.

The moment Marcus reached for her hand, one of the toddlers, probably hungry and bored, let out an echoing wail.

'Wretched children,' murmured Marcus. 'You can't get away from them anywhere.'

Marcus stood up and smiled. Julia was conscious that women all over the restaurant were casting admiring glances in his direction. To his credit Marcus didn't seem to notice. He leaned towards her.

'I won't be a moment. Just going to see if we can move to a quieter table.'

Julia looked out over the bay as the last sliver of setting sun slipped down towards the horizon, suffusing the entire scene with a shimmering pinkish glow. She glanced across at the Italian family. It was noisy and complicated. Like family life. For a moment Julia looked back on her own marriage. There had been fabulous moments and terrible disasters. Bill and Adrienne probably wouldn't have children. Adrienne was certainly young enough but Julia couldn't imagine sticky fingers and pongy nappies in Adrienne's fragrant world view. Adrienne was probably grateful that Bill came with only one problem-free, grown-up daughter. Not much baggage, as Erica would put it. But wasn't baggage another word for having lived and loved? For life? She thought about Tony and his attention-seeking ex, the ghoulish but engaging Caspar, the troubled but likeable Claudia. Anyone who hitched their star to that family would get everything they deserved.

Across the balcony she could see Marcus beckoning her to a discreet table. Julia put down her napkin and got to her feet.

If she ran down to the square she might just catch Tony and his children at the pizzeria.

Al and Christine's World of Leather

Joanne Harris

Christine reached for her cup of tea, stretched her cramped spine and sat back to examine her handi-work. Quite a good job, though she said it herself: nice straight seams, no puckering in spite of the difficult fabric, a good, strong line. That was going to make someone a very nice, durable pair of work trousers – unusual, perhaps, but hardwearing. Vaguely she wondered what the flap was for.

Not that it mattered. Nowadays she just did what she was told and let Candy deal with the artistic side of things. Doing what she was told, after all, was what Christine Jones was best at. Imagination was Candy's department.

They had met at a Weight Watchers' meeting.

Candy was ten stone three and wanted to get down to nine and a half; Christine was thirteen ten and, as her husband Jack put it, letting herself go. She was planning to let go of at least three stone, anyway, but somehow had never quite made it. Instead, she'd gained six pounds and a social life of sorts, consisting of Candy, her friend Babs and the Weight Watchers' mascot, Big Al Maguire.

Big Al had been going to the club for over three years. A huge man who never seemed to lose any weight, he was tolerated because he made even the fattest women feel better about themselves. Christine wondered what he got out of it and decided he just liked the company. Babs worked in a shoe factory and was desperate for a man; Candy was a divorcee, now a mature student at the local poly, studying textiles and design.

She had taken to Christine at once.

'What a lovely sweater,' she had said, as Christine stepped down from the weighing machine. 'Missoni, is it?'

Christine flushed and admitted that she'd made it herself.

Candy was impressed. She couldn't sew or knit herself, she said, but she had lots of ideas. Perhaps they could get together sometime and talk. And so the 'knitting coven', as Jack called it, was created. Every Sunday after church, Candy, Babs, Christine and Big Al would meet at Christine's house and discuss yarns and designs. They were all enthusiastic, but Christine was by far the most technically expert and, for the first time, she found that others looked to her for advice. Candy couldn't knit, Babs was quick, but careless, and Big Al, though his giant fingers were astonishingly delicate with the yarn and needles, was too slow for anything but the simplest work.

But Candy had big ideas for the knitting coven. She had a friend, a fellow student from her course, who had opened a little shop. Handmade knitwear could be a real earner, with quite a simple pattern selling at £60 or more. Deducting 20 per cent for the friend, another 20 for the cost of the yarn and other overheads, that still left half to be divided equally between the designer (Candy, of course) and the workforce – or, in this case, as it happened, Christine.

At first, Jack had resented it, making fun of her friends and her little sideline. But then the money had started to come in – only a few pounds at first, but then more, as the patterns grew more ambitious and the yarns more unusual. Now Candy experimented with combination yarns, with Lurex and rubber and silk fibres twisted into the wool. They were harder to knit with, beyond the skills of Babs or Big Al, but sometimes the results were dramatic, and a finished garment might sell for £80 or even £100.

Gradually, Christine's role in the knitting coven expanded still further. She no longer used the basic patterns, leaving the simple designs to Babs, and the deliveries – increasingly frequent now – to Big Al. Instead, she worked with the special yarns and, as the money continued to come in, began to take commissions on non-knitwear items. Occasional pieces of modern dance wear, performance gear, fancy dress. Some of it was quite unusual – the trousers with the mysterious flap, for instance – but Candy assured her that this was where the real money was. After a single payment of over £200 for a leather gladiator skirt with studded harness for a theatre performance of *Julius Caesar*, Christine found herself having to agree. After that, Candy suggested that they went into business together, with the friend as a sleeping partner, each owning a third. A lawyer drew up the papers. Christine protested that she didn't need a partnership; after all, Babs and Big Al were paid by the hour. But Candy wanted everything to be scrupulously fair.

'It's only right, darling,' she said, when Christine had mentioned her doubts. 'After all, you do so much of the work.' This touched Christine, who knew herself to be so much less intelligent or attractive than her friend and who often felt embarrassed at her own inadequacy. Candy deserved better, she thought; it was proof of her sweet nature that she never mentioned it.

It was at this point that Jack stopped complaining. Christine had a hobby room of her own now in which she kept the leather-adapted industrial sewing machine for her special work, and she spent most evenings in there, listening to the radio as she worked, while Jack spent increasing amounts of time at the health club. For, unlike Christine, Jack had not let himself go and had retained an impressive level of fitness.

This sometimes troubled Christine. It wasn't that she didn't trust her husband, she told herself, but three hours at the health club every night did seem a little excessive. She wondered if he was having an affair, then felt guilty for even considering it. Jack was very much a man's man – his reaction to the knitting coven showed it – and he needed male company from time to time. She was lucky, she told herself. He was cheerful, devoted and made no unreasonable sexual demands (though he might try once in a while, she thought; there was such a thing as being too chivalrous). No, she was lucky to have him, she repeated to herself. Perhaps he deserved better.

Still, thought Christine, sometimes it was a relief to know that Jack was safely out of the house when she worked on her special commissions. He had never made any secret of his dislike for Candy, and his contempt for Big Al, too, was thinly veiled. Besides, he had a limited knowledge of specialist leatherwork – you don't get much exposure to that kind of thing in retail management – and she knew that if he caught sight of her current order list, he would certainly make one of his sarcastic comments. True, it was a peculiar collection, but someone was paying over £300 for the lot, so there had to be a market for it somewhere.

Once more, she considered the trousers. Good-quality leather, black, thirty-two waist, decorative insert. The purpose of the back flap still eluded her – perhaps some kind of a tool pocket, she thought, though, honestly, you'd think they'd want a bit more protection if they're going to be working with equipment. She hoped she hadn't got it wrong, but it wasn't the first pair she'd made and the customers had never complained. Besides, she had given up on trying to improve patterns since she had inadvertently ruined a whole underwear commission (a conceptual dance company, Candy had said) by introducing a reinforced gusset to the basic design. Candy had been rather nasty about it, she remembered, saying, 'For God's sake, Christine, if we'd wanted gussets we'd have bloody well asked for them.' So now she only did what she was told. Perhaps dancers needed more ventilation – you know, down there – she thought. In that case, a reinforced gusset might cause all kinds of unexpected problems. No wonder Candy had been annoyed.

All the same, she thought, a most unusual pair of trousers. The black tutu was normal enough, she supposed, and the corset seemed designed to go with it somehow, though she couldn't work out how. It was stiffly boned (she'd used heavy-duty nylon slats) and laced up at the back, something like the one her grandmother used to wear, though obviously her grandmother's wasn't made of leather. Perhaps it was for someone with a slipped disc, thought Christine, though you'd expect them to do that kind of thing on the National Health. And what was this thing? Not a hat, precisely. In fact, from this angle it looked more like a kind of mask, although how were you supposed to see anything if there weren't any eyeholes? Christine shook her head disapprovingly. These dance people could come up with some very strange ideas nowadays. What was wrong with a nice *Swan Lake*? Or a *Nutcracker*?

And yet, she thought, wasn't there something rather satisfying in working with these materials? The buttery leather, the silk, the studs, the gauze? She'd always liked working with her hands, but recently she had given more time to her craft than ever before, and it wasn't just because Jack was out of the house. No, she was enjoying the work – responding to it, somehow – far more than she ever had with knits and sweaters. And when she was working, she had begun to have the strangest thoughts – like waking dreams. She imagined herself wearing the strange garments, feeling their fabulous textures against her skin, maybe (she blinked at the thought), maybe even performing in them. And in these dreams her designs were not for dance wear, as Candy had told her, nor for back supports or Shakespeare or gardening, but for something else, something thrilling and mysterious and full of power. Hunched guiltily over her sewing machine, a tiny smile on her face, Christine dreamed, and in her dreams she was someone else – a tall, leather-clad someone with a purposeful stride, someone who never did as she was told, a woman of authority.

Some chance, she thought, as she boxed up the

finished clothing. She never so much as ordered a pizza without consulting Jack, never took any decision regarding the company without turning to Candy for advice. A natural follower, was Christine Jones, a disciple, a perpetual associate, a drone. There's no harm in that, she told herself, we can't all be movers and shakers. Still, the thought depressed her, as did the nagging certainty that somehow she was missing something; something obvious, like coming out of a bathroom with toilet paper stuck to your shoe and walking on, oblivious, while everyone laughs at you behind their hands.

It was eight o'clock when Christine delivered the box to Big Al's. As usual, he seemed to have been waiting for her to arrive, because he opened the door at once, his round face beaming with pleasure.

'Christine! I thought you might drop round this afternoon. Come on in and have a cuppa.'

She hesitated. 'I don't know, Al, Jack might be back any minute.'

Al's face fell and Christine felt sorry for him. 'Oh, all right, then, just a quick one.'

Big Al's house would have been small even for a man of normal size. For him, it was tiny and he blundered around in it like an oversized puppy in a Victorian doll's house. He made tea for Christine in a doll-sized china cup, holding the teapot handle between finger and thumb.

'Biscuit?'

'Al, I shouldn't.'

'Never mind that, chuck. Skinny doesn't suit you.'

Christine smiled and took a custard cream.

Al had a way of making her feel like china herself, in spite of her fourteen stone. And he wasn't a 'lard-bucket', as Jack cruelly called him; more like an overstuffed armchair, shapeless but comfortable.

'I see you're done with that order,' he said, nodding towards the box.

'Yes. You can deliver it tomorrow.'

'Right.'

Christine thought that Al was looking slightly uncomfortable. She wondered if he had seen the patterns and, if so, what he thought of them.

'Funny load of gear,' she said. 'Still, if people want to buy it . . .'

She noticed that Al was wearing the jumper she'd knitted for him last Christmas, the green one with the snowflakes.

'Suits you lovely,' she said.

He flushed a little. 'It's me favourite.'

Christine laughed. 'Jack won't wear them. Says they're naff.'

'Jack's a bloody fool.'

The reply came back so quickly that Christine could hardly believe she had heard it. Big Al never used 'language', as he put it, and in all the time she had known him, Christine had never heard him say a bad thing about anyone.

He was flushing very red now, as if aware of having overstepped a line. 'Sorry, chuck,' he said. 'Dunno what came over me.'

But Christine was looking at him, puzzled. 'Is something wrong?'

Al shook his head but would not meet her eyes.

'Al?'

Pause.

'Al?'

As he spoke, slowly at first, then with increasing confidence, Christine poured them both a second cup of tea. It was funny how it all made sense: Candy, who deserved better, Jack, who deserved better, herself, quick of fingers but desperately slow of mind, working on her sewing machine while her friend earned 33 per cent working on her husband. A nice living for both of them. Jack was the sleeping partner, the third owner of the business. There had never been a friend with a clothing shop, but instead, a website on the Internet, where both

Jack and Candy knew Christine would never venture.

'It isn't dance wear at all, is it?' said Christine when he had finished.

Big Al shook his head.

'Is it . . .' She cast about for a suitable word. 'Erotica? Is that what we're selling? Sex toys? Fantasy wear?'

Big Al did not need to reply. His face said it all.

Christine took another biscuit. Funny how calm she felt. She had imagined Jack's betrayal so many times, but had expected to feel something quite different if, or more likely when, it happened. Instead, she found herself thinking how nice Big Al's eyes were, how nice and how kind.

'Where are they now?' she said at last.

'Candy's,' said Big Al.

'All right,' said Christine. 'Let's go.'

It was almost nine when they arrived at Candy's place. The lights were on in the top bedroom and Christine walked straight in without ringing the bell, knowing that Candy never locked the doors. Big Al followed her, up the stairs and into the bedroom.

The sheets were scarlet silk; the walls, mostly mirrors. Christine noticed with some surprise that Candy had cellulite on her legs, in spite of all her dieting. Jack was lying on his front, like a man with a bad stomach ache. It was so long since Christine had seen him undressed that he looked like a stranger.

'Jesus, Christine . . .' He tried to sit up, but the handcuffs stopped him — at least she assumed they were handcuffs, under all that furry stuff. She'd always assumed that Jack wasn't really interested in sex. Now she realised that it was just sex with her that didn't appeal to him. The outfit he was wearing, as well as the variety of objects lined up on the dressing table, spoke of an imaginative and adventurous sexual career. 'Now listen to me . . .' he said.

'So that's what they're like on,' said Christine. 'Thirty-two waist, was it? I think you're more of a thirty-four.'

It was her handiwork, all right. She would have recognised them blindfold. Black leather, decorative insert, studded seam. And the flap, of course. Candy was staring at her, open-mouthed, in lace-up boots and a pair of those ventilated panties.

It was the cruellest kind of betrayal. Such a cliché — her husband and her best friend, feigning to dislike each other as they continued their liaison right under her nose — but given extra zest by this final act of deception. She thought of herself, sitting at her sewing machine, dreaming her little dreams.

Poor stupid Christine, thinks it's dance wear, wouldn't know a dildo if she saw one, while Jack and Candy played their games and laughed themselves sick at the thought of their own cleverness and perversity.

And strangely, Christine found that it was not the sexual betrayal that angered her most, but the fact that they had done it in her clothes – her clothes, upon which she had lavished such care. Imagine Christine in that! Ghost laughter from a darkened room. And how they must have laughed! Well, thought Christine, you know what they say. He who laughs last . . . And, suddenly, unexpectedly, she began to smile.

'Christine,' said Jack, 'I think we need to talk.'

But Christine was already turning away. And only Big Al, still standing in the doorway, could see her tiny dangerous smile.

She found the second pair of marabou handcuffs among the items on the dressing table, along with a digital camera and a thick roll of masking tape. It took Christine a few moments to figure out how to work the camera, but after that it proved absurdly easy. She shot the pair from various angles, occasionally stopping to readjust a fold of fabric or to smooth out a crease in the soft leather. They might have been professionals, she thought happily, and they looked so right together.

'I'm thinking I might branch out,' she said, putting the camera carefully into her pocket. 'My share in the company, and half of Jack's, of course, should give me a nice little sum to start off with.'

She looked down at her husband, red-faced and struggling on the bed. It felt quite nice, for a change, she thought, though she still couldn't entirely see the attraction of all that gear. Still, she pondered, you should try anything once.

'I'll probably run the business from an Internet site,' she said thoughtfully. 'After all, it's worked fine so far. And besides . . .' she levelled her smile at Candy and Jack as she worked to remove the tape which gagged them, '. . . it would be such a shame to waste all these photographs, wouldn't it?'

'You can't do this,' gasped Jack, outraged.

'I think I can,' said Christine.

'What? Alone?'

She looked at Big Al. 'Not quite,' she said.

Big Al stared at her as if he couldn't altogether grasp what she was saying. 'What?'

'Al and Christine's World of Leather. How does that sound to you?'

Al grinned and went scarlet. Then he hugged her,

his eyes shining. For a minute, Christine was content to be suffocated and to enjoy the luxurious sensation of being close to someone that big, someone who outweighed her. There was a sensuality to Al, in spite of – and perhaps because of – his size, a sense of texture which reminded her of nights spent in front of her patterns, but without the loneliness. It was a kind of revelation. She looked up and saw him looking down at her, his chocolate-brown eyes spangled with lights. Her heart was racing like a sewing machine.

With an effort, she disentangled herself from his embrace and turned to face the dressing table, knowing that they would have time later to luxuriate in each other and conscious of one last thing, one final loose end to be definitively tied.

'Are you two imbeciles going to let me go now?' said Jack, trying unsuccessfully to look dignified in marabou and black leather.

'Not just yet, dear,' said Christine, selecting an object from the dressing table and approaching the bed with a smile. She still wasn't quite sure what the object was, or indeed, quite how to use it. But she was sure she'd work it out somehow, now that she'd guessed what the trouser flap was for.

Say Cheese

Wendy Holden

'Isn't this *wonderful*?' smiled William Vine, lifting the glass of rosé to his lips and taking what seemed to his wife Diana a sip of rather exaggerated length. As he smacked his lips appreciatively, she winced. He was trying too hard again.

'Steady on, Dad,' giggled Bella. 'You'll be under the table if you knock it back like that.'

'And then we'd be stuck,' grinned Rory. 'You're the only one who speaks decent French.'

'Which is ridiculous, considering your hugely expensive education,' William shot back. Diana, about to join in, subsided at this last sentence. Bella and Rory's expensive education, or the end of the main phase of it, was the entire reason they were here.

Both had now left school and in the autumn both would go to university. They would be leaving home, flying the nest, starting new lives. This holiday, Diana was miserably aware, would almost certainly be the last they would spend together as a family and the knowledge had cast a shadow over her entire week. Not that she had said a word about it, and neither had anyone else. But she knew everyone else knew, and knew everyone else knew they knew, and that made for a certain amount of tension.

William, of course, had tried to ease it by being relentlessly over-obliging, which frankly drove Diana mad. While she kept up appearances when the children were around, the minute she and William were alone she wanted to rage and cry. And all he seemed to want to do was fuss about, eternally asking if she was all right or whether she required sunglasses, suncream or pills for her ever more frequent headaches.

It was if he were the mother and she the irritable, fragile father. The holiday seemed to be bringing out the worst in each of them. There was no escape, as there was at home and work. Underlining Diana's irritation was a growing terror that this was not the man she wanted to spend the rest of her life with when the children finally, inevitably, went. She could hardly remember the William she had married, but she had an idea he was less of a pushover and a good deal less pathetically eager to please.

They had done their best to conceal the tension from the children, silently agreeing that they wanted Rory and Bella, at least, to have happy memories of this last vacation together. Hence the strong emphasis on lengthy, companionable lunches and suppers like this one, at a favourite restaurant in a village in the hills behind Antibes, on the very last night of their holiday.

Diana now wished desperately they had not come back to Antibes. It had, in theory, seemed the perfect choice for the last hurrah they all knew the holiday to be, but the reality was too poignant. They had been so many times in the past as a family and knew almost every paving stone and certainly every bar. Practically every restaurant held memories – the one in the port where the chef had taken Bella for a tour of the restaurant and kitchen. The one on the ramparts where the owner had persuaded them to try Rory with a gherkin, on the grounds that all French babies loved them. Rory hated them. And this one most of all, under the arcades of an ancient square in a quiet and pretty village. Here they had celebrated endless family landmarks, and here they were celebrating another one now, Bella and Rory's graduation from home to undergraduates. And William and Diana's new role as empty nesters.

'To us,' William was saying now, raising his rosé glass and taking another deep swig. Hating him for his jollity, his determination, quite literally, to see the world through rose-tinted spectacles, Diana jerked her glass stiffly upwards and took a violent gulp. What else was there to do? What else would there be to do, from now on?

'Cheer up, Mum,' Rory urged as the food started to arrive. Diana smiled faintly, knowing her sensitive, adored son had an inkling of her feelings. She must pull herself together and not cling. Another pressure of this holiday was the thought she was auditioning for a role in the future lives of her children. It was vital that they took away positive memories of this last lengthy period of exposure to one another. Otherwise, future contact would be merely dutiful, which she could not bear to contemplate.

'Ooh, yummy,' Bella enthused as her favourite starter, grilled peppers with anchovy sauce, arrived. Watching her raise her fork, Diana blinked away the tears at the memory of Bella at two, sitting up at the table on a pile of cushions, raising the heavy grown-up fork with difficulty and tasting this dish for the very first time.

'I remember you eating that for the very first time, Bella,' William grinned. 'Just here, at this very table. You were sitting on about four cushions, in a grown-up chair . . .'

'Was I, Dad?' Bella looked enchanted. Diana stabbed her stuffed courgette flowers, wondering why she felt so angry. It was, after all, William's memory as well as hers. But how dare he talk about it so easily, with such apparent enjoyment?

'It's as delicious as ever,' William beamed, tucking into his own favourite starter, grilled courgette slices with tarragon cream sauce. 'How's yours, darling?'

'Fine,' Diana muttered through gritted teeth, watching Rory with his fish soup. As he always had done, he was loading the little croutons with garlic mayonnaise and sprinkling them with grated Gruyère before sending them as a flotilla on what was quite literally the wine-dark sea. The restaurant had always slugged quantities of alcohol into its fish soup, one reason for Rory's preference.

'We should get someone to take a photograph of us all together,' Bella suggested suddenly, stopping short of adding why. 'I mean, it's such a lovely evening,' she continued lamely.

'Great idea,' William agreed enthusiastically, banging his fork down as he lunged for Diana's handbag. 'The camera's got a timer. All we have to do is find something to put it on.' He looked around him critically. 'Actually, all the surfaces at the right height are rather too near or too far. We'd better ask somebody.'

Bella giggled. 'Bags you do it, Dad.'

Rory nodded in agreement. 'Go for it, Dad.'

'William smiled thoughtfully. 'Funny, isn't it?' he said. 'I've been asked to take pictures for scores of people over the years, but this is the very first time I've had to ask anyone to do it for me.'

'You don't need to,' Diana said with an acid tinge to her voice. 'I'll take it. Of the three of you.' There they were, all chatting and smiling together, while she sat on the edge of the group, left out and grumpy. She may as well make herself useful.

There was a chorus of dismay, as of course Diana had meant there to be. 'But, Mum, you can't. We need all four of us in the picture,' Bella protested, stopping short of explaining why.

'In which case,' William concluded, 'we need to find someone.'

'But not just anybody,' Bella added quickly, as a brooding youth holding a cigarette in the contemptuous curl of his lip sloped by.

'Because this is a very special picture,' Rory added, as a young family walked past, a slim woman with a tall, dark-haired man, carrying one beautiful toddler each. As her eyes filled, Diana looked away.

The table, which stood in the shade of an arcaded passage just outside the restaurant, was an excellent vantage point for people-watching. This, beside the food and the general beauty of the place, was why the restaurant had been so popular with the Vines for so many years.

'We need to find the right person,' William said, as his and Diana's next courses arrived. 'Perhaps Marco,' he added, as the waiter they had known, it seemed, almost as long as they had known themselves, retreated back to the restaurant to fetch the rest of the food.

'I don't think so, Dad,' Bella objected. 'He's incredibly busy – just look at how full the place is. He'll just shoot it in a second. We want someone who'll spend two seconds, at least.'

'Blimey.' Rory looked at his sister. 'I didn't realise we were talking Mario Testino here.' But there was affection in his mocking and his mother, listening, loved them both for caring so much. The fact that the picture was important meant the holiday was important and that they were all important to each other. But it was true that the choice of photographer was important too.

'What about her?' she suggested as an old lady laboured past.

'Mu-um,' chorused the children. 'Look how thick her glasses are,' hissed Bella. 'She's obviously practically blind, poor old love.'

'I've had enough of this,' William announced, placing his knife and fork on the tablecloth. 'It's taking over the entire evening and interfering with my food. Which, at a restaurant like this, is a criminal waste.' Diana sat up slightly. William taking charge, and in a slightly testy manner at that!

'We will ask the very next person who goes by to take the picture,' William instructed.

'You mean you will,' Rory reminded him.

Naturally, once this course of action had been decided, no one passed the Vines' table for what seemed like an eternity.

'Probably everyone's gone to bed,' Bella lamented. 'It is starting to get dark, after all. Why don't we just ask Marco?'

'Because we won't,' William stated, passing her a piece of cheese on the blade of a knife. 'Now just taste this Camembert. It's absolutely perfect.'

The cheese had disappeared into Bella's mouth by the time the next person passed their table, but this didn't stop her choking on it suddenly. As Rory banged his sister on the back, Diana and William craned to see, in the gathering twilight, who it was.

An old, old man, William noted with disappointment. A man so ancient, so bent, so dry and dusty-looking that he seemed to predate photography entirely. No doubt he had never even seen a camera like theirs before, bog standard though it was, an unremarkable piece of Japanese technology suitable for universal use and more or less universal images.

'No, Dad,' hissed Rory while Bella giggled. 'You can't . . .'

Diana watched as William dabbed his mouth with a napkin and rose hurriedly to his feet. Chewing hastily, he waved the camera at the old stranger. '*Monsieur! Est-ce que je peux vous demander si c'est possible que . . .*'

The old man stopped. In the candlelight from the table, his eyes looked shocked and frightened. '*Mais monsieur, c'est impossible, je ne peux pas . . .*'

It was as William had thought. The old chap had never operated as much as a Box Brownie before. Yet something drove William on to insist, to try and push the clearly reluctant old man into doing what they wanted. Aware of the children watching, aware even more of Diana's cool and sceptical gaze, it suddenly seemed absolutely mandatory that he forced the old boy to bend to his will, to prove his authority. It was ridiculous, but it felt like a test.

What was almost as ridiculous was the distinct impression, which could not possibly have been the case, that the old man was doing the same, only in the opposite direction. His determination not to take the picture felt as violent as William's determination that he would. '*Mais, Monsieur*,' William half pleaded, half commanded, waving the camera at the old man who seemed to shrink before it like a vampire before a crucifix.

Speaking in rapid French, William set out the reasons for wanting this pictorial record. It was a beautiful evening. A beautiful restaurant. A beautiful village. The old man shrugged. Finally William, desperate, explained that it was the last night of what was probably their last family holiday together ever. Daylight was about to fade. It was special, unrepeatable moment. It would mean so much if only . . .

William had not meant to confess this. He hoped the rest of the family had not understood that he had vocalised the forbidden undercurrent of the entire past week. But, oddly enough, it seemed to have done the trick. The old man regarded him with a stare that was suddenly unnervingly bright and steady. Then, slowly, wordlessly, he reached out a wrinkled old hand for the camera. As William passed it over, Bella and Rory murmured appreciatively. Diana, meanwhile, gazed at her husband with what approached admiration. She had no idea he could be so persistent. So commanding. And in French, too. Perhaps there was a point to William, after all.

The old man lifted the camera and looked through the lens for an inordinately long time. 'Probably never seen one before,' Bella giggled in a whisper.

Eventually, the old man pressed the shutter and handed the camera back. The family said their thanks and goodbyes. But the old man didn't leave. Standing on the ancient cobbles in the gathering twilight, he fished in the small black bag he carried with him and brought out, to everyone's surprise, a camera of his own. Without saying anything, almost before the Vines could blink, he had clutched it to his eye, snapped a number of times then disappeared into the gathering gloom.

'He took a picture of us,' Diana said in surprise.

'Probably stolen our souls,' chuckled Rory.

'Very odd,' said William.

The pudding arrived.

'Isn't this wonderful?' smiled William, raising the glass of champagne to his lips. It was a year later and Diana, a mere few inches away across the cream-draped table of one of the most exclusive bars on the Riviera, raised her Bellini in its crystal glass and smiled.

'It is wonderful,' she said. That they were coming for a holiday to the glamorous Hôtel les Vagues on the Cap d'Antibes was a secret William had kept from her until the very last minute. He had claimed the subterfuge was because she wouldn't want to go without the children, but in fact it was the best possible way to return – in dazzling style – and he knew it. He seemed to have such confidence these days, such a sure touch.

'What a year it's been,' William remarked, helping himself to an olive. 'Rory successfully through his first-year exams at medical school, Bella successfully through her first-year law ones . . .'

'To our children.' As she sipped, Diana blinked away tears of pride.

William looked at her warmly. 'And to us,' he said

softly, reaching for her hand over the table. 'Our first year alone together for almost twenty years. And I've loved every minute of it.'

'Me too,' Diana said, her eyes welling up again.

'I remembered why I married you,' William added.

Diana nodded, her throat too full to speak. She could hardly bear to think, twelve months ago, that she had been entertaining thoughts of leaving him. But things had changed, and changed even before they returned home last year. Something had precipitated it, although now she could not remember what it was.

'Because I always beat you at Scrabble,' William was saying now.

'Ha ha.'

Diana looked at the sun slipping into the sea behind the mountains east of Cannes. 'What shall we do tomorrow?' she asked.

'You decide,' William instructed lazily.

Diana considered. 'I'd quite like to go to an exhibition of some sort, I think. There are quite a few on in the town.'

William looked doubtful. 'So long as it's not conceptual art.' He was, Diana realised, still recovering from the one she had persuaded him to go to six months ago, where the artist had stuck crushed baked-bean cans all over the canvases. Some of which still had the beans in them.

'What about this one?' Diana suggested the next day when they had completed their daily stroll round the market. She was standing in front of the entrance to the town's château, beside a poster announcing an exhibition by someone called Venet. 'It looks quite interesting,' she added. 'It says here he's one of France's great documentary photographers. A sort of Gaudier-Brzeska type.'

'Fine,' said William, who liked photographs so long as they were of people.

They went in. The exhibition was a retrospective, of the photographer's earliest works up to the present day. William and Diana admired shots of fifties Paris, sixties St Tropez, seventies London, eighties New York.

'Oh, how interesting,' Diana said, reading the English half of the display boards. 'Apparently poor Venet had the most awful photographer's block in the mid-eighties. He just gave up taking pictures. Until recently, when he just suddenly started again.'

'I'm sure that's me,' William joked, pointing at a tiny head in a crowd coming over London Bridge in a composition entitled 'City Commuters, London, 1975'. Diana, who was disappearing into the next room, looked back and smiled.

A second later, she was back. 'My God!' she hissed to her husband. 'There really is a picture of you. Of all of us. In the next room. Come and look.'

'Don't be ridiculous . . .' William was starting to say, but before she could finish the sentence he was next door and looking at an enormous blown-up image that he knew very well. Himself, Diana, Bella and Rory, sitting at a table in a village restaurant in the sunlit evening. The image was suffused with soft light, and had the epic quality of a golden memory, with all the romance and regret that implied. *Last Family Holiday*, read the label. An additional note added that this was the picture that had broken the great master's block.

William gave a long, low whistle. 'That old chap . . . the one in the village . . . the one we thought had never even held a camera before . . .'

'Was Venet!' Diana added. 'Yes, well, he did have his own camera if you remember. He whipped it out and took another of us afterwards with it. We thought it was odd at the time.'

Diana peered at the label again. For more than twenty years, it said, Venet had carried a camera around with him, but only on this night had he been persuaded to use it. The result had been a flood of

creativity and a return to form, followed by a surpassing of it. The rest of the room was filled with the
surpassing recent images, none of which Diana and
William thought so good as the one of them.

'We always said that that picture he took was the
best on the reel, and how unexpected that was,' Diana
murmured, once the shock had started to subside.

'*We* broke his photographer's block,' William said
wonderingly, still staring at the picture.

Yes, and he broke our marriage block, Diana
thought, having finally remembered what it was that
had, a year ago, forced the realisation her husband
was liveable with after all.

'How incredible, that you should have chosen him,'
Diana breathed in wonder.

William grinned and squeezed her hand. 'Oh, I
always knew how to pick them.'

Trouble in Paradise

Cathy Kelly

Clare Reid's birthday loomed. Not any old birthday, mind: but a significant one. In the leafy suburbs of Paradise Road, a winding cul-de-sac lined with houses of every variety, it was the sort of birthday which beloved husbands normally celebrated with a trip abroad (two nights on the Orient Express, then a week at a palazzo in Venice: Ella and Marcus, who lived in Paradise Villa) or a long weekend away in London (Fiona and Rick, Sorrento Cottage).

For such a birthday, grown-up children would club together to buy jewellery; friends would discuss whether a big surprise party was in order; and girlfriends from the book club would plan a night out in a wine bar where cocktails would be ordered with glee and everyone would discuss how fifty was the new forty.

Except that none of Clare's neighbours in Paradise Road knew quite what to do for her significant birthday. Because she and her husband of twenty-five years had just split up.

When he'd left their pretty detached house on the south-facing side of Paradise Road, Dan Reid had taken his fishing rods, his half of the furniture and everyone's expectations of precisely how Clare's fiftieth should be celebrated.

Even worse, Clare was keeping her great pain and suffering to herself. Still clear-eyed and serene, not a dark hair in her sleekly elegant knot out of place, she still smiled at people as she headed off to work in her little silver Golf, and hadn't been seen sobbing in desperation outside the supermarket.

'Honestly, it's better this way,' she told Elizabeth serenely when Elizabeth spotted Clare putting out the bins and had run downstairs and across the road in her nightie to say hello, that she'd heard the news and *if there was anything she could do* . . .

'Thank you, Elizabeth,' Clare had added, smiling. This had taken Elizabeth aback – *smiling* when your husband had just left you? 'You're so kind and I appreciate it but honestly,' Clare had patted

Elizabeth's bare arm at this point, 'it really is better this way.'

'*Better this way!*' demanded Elizabeth, who'd known Clare and Dan for fifteen years of chatting idly at the school gates. 'Better for whom? I daresay he's run off with some bimbo half her age. It's the male menopause, isn't it? Dump the poor first wife for a trophy blonde with a French manicure and a degree in male manipulation.'

Elizabeth, who'd reached the dreaded fifty a whole seven years ago, shook her head in temper, although her artfully streaked blonde hair was glued into place with hairspray and not a strand stirred. 'I hope Clare takes him for every penny he's got!'

Naturally, Elizabeth didn't say this to Clare. She said it at the book club where discussions on Anita Shreve's themes had been wilfully abandoned for detailed analysis on Clare, Dan, what to do about poor Clare's impending birthday, and *what must the children think.*

Thankfully, the Reid children had both left home and therefore were not around to witness the horrific break-up, the shattering of plates and whatever terrible things that must be going on behind the solid doors of the Reid household.

Hanna, the elder of the two, was studying science

in Cork, while Steve had left home only last year and was studying surfing on Bondi and had a girlfriend named Roxie, of all things. Roxie sounded like the sort of person with a belly ring, a tattoo and a tendency to wear navel-skimming tops and flip-flops, but these flaws were now immaterial in the grand scheme of things. Their parents had split up and the Reid children must be devastated.

The mothers among the book club thought of their own children and how age was no barrier to worrying about a six-foot rugby player when you could remember him as a six pound baby with a piercing cry and eyes that pleaded for Mummy.

'Typical, isn't it? Clearly Dan only stayed with Clare for the children,' said Fiona with a shiver. Fiona lived in the rounded cul-de-sac part of Paradise Road in an ugly 1960s bungalow that had resisted all attempts to make it look outwardly modern. She'd often envied Clare Reid's lovely house with the climbing rose that draped itself fragrantly over the porch.

She didn't envy poor Clare now. Fiona was in her late forties and Matt, her youngest, would be eighteen soon. He was currently planning a gap-year trip instead of burying himself in books for the forthcoming state exams. It didn't seem to matter how often she chided him about surfing websites for the best beaches in Thailand, he still hadn't touched a textbook.

Now, Fiona suddenly imagined how quiet and tidy the house would be with him gone. She'd have plenty of time to read the book club choices but wondered how she would really feel when the weight of silence hung around the house every day, with no Matt ambling in at odd hours wondering if his jeans were washed.

It wasn't as if Arthur was around much either. *Work* was his perennial excuse. Could work be the be-all and end-all of her husband's existence, Fiona thought. What about her? Didn't she count for something too?

'I think it's awful for a man to march off into the sunset as soon as the kids are old enough to fend for themselves. It's an insult, isn't it?' she said now. 'Like saying you don't mean anything and he only stayed until the children were old enough not to care. And just two months before her fiftieth birthday too. It's callous, that's what it is. Poor Clare.'

The book club went silent. This was the stuff of tragedy, just as heart-rending and real as anything they'd ever read about. And so sudden.

It was the very suddenness that shocked them all.

One minute, you had your life planned out for you. The next, your husband had run off with some gold-digger who could overlook age, male-pattern bald-ness and a paunch, for the heady lure of a lucrative milk carton packaging business and the latest S-class Mercedes.

'I wonder, did Clare notice Dan change when he started seeing this other woman?' Elizabeth said thoughtfully. 'You know, like they say in magazines, if he was coming home late, losing weight, making lots of whispery phone calls and saying he was working all the hours . . .'

The other ten members of the book club turned to look at her.

'I was just wondering?' Elizabeth said hastily. 'Right: the book. Who wants to go first?'

The Paradise Road Book Club had been Elizabeth's idea initially and had been running for two years. In that time, the eleven women had had enjoyable dalliances with the classics, lots of fun with contemporary literature and a few argument-laden nights over whether *The Da Vinci Code* was fabulously compulsive or not.

Not, insisted Patricia, a former English teacher, who kept her Booker, Orange and Whitbread prize-winners in a well-dusted line in the hall where everyone would see them.

Compulsive, illuminating and *true,* argued Fiona, who'd gone to a convent where the head nun had been heavily involved in Opus Dei and so keen on finding new recruits that it was considered dangerous to be alone in a room with her in case you were indoctrinated and had your mind wiped or whatever it was they did.

Elizabeth was a Jane Austen fan, favouring *Mansfield Park* as the ultimate bedtime reading and the Colin Firth version of *Pride and Prejudice* as her all-time favourite television viewing.

It was the combination of clear-sighted social comment she loved, along with the suggestion of closely reined-in passion restricted by the social mores of the time.

Clare Reid had been in the book club for the first year and then had gently bowed out, saying she had somewhere else to be on Monday evenings and although she loved the book club, it would have to go.

Nobody had thought much about her leaving then. Clare was an illustrator who often worked to difficult deadlines. But now, they all began seeing other, more sinister reasons behind her departure – that she couldn't cope with a social, chatty group of friends at a time when her personal life was in flux. That had to be it. Think of how hard it would be to pretend everything was all right between her and Dan when she knew it wasn't.

When that night's book club was over, everyone tidied up and checked the rota to see in whose house the next meeting would be held. Inevitably, the conversation slipped back to the Reid family.

'We've got to do something for Clare's birthday,' said Elizabeth with determination. 'She's our friend, one of us. We should make her birthday go with a bang, even if her lying, cheating husband won't. It's only six weeks away – any suggestions?'

'Perhaps we ought to talk to her first,' Mildred said doubtfully. Mildred was the newest member of the book club, having only recently moved on to Paradise Road with her sister, Winifred, and their pugs, Tristan and Isolde.

Mildred loved books and had eclectic tastes, but her absolute favourite novels were historical romances with strong, fierce warriors who tamed a gentle maiden's heart, killed all her foes and carried her off to bed as if she was as light as a feather. Of course, she didn't say this at the book club, not even when it was her turn to pick, because they might look down on her, mightn't they?

'No, let's not say anything to Clare,' Fiona insisted.

'Think of how hard it must be for her . . . everyone knowing he's gone. She probably thinks we all knew anyway. The wife's always the last one to know. She's embarrassed, imagining her husband with this other woman. Let's take her somewhere wonderful for a night out and we'll keep it a surprise.'

A night away in a small hotel where there were spa facilities was the plan. The book club would each pay their own way and pay for Clare too. They'd tell her a few days before. After all, it wasn't as if Clare appeared to have many pressing engagements these days.

'She goes out on Monday nights,' said Gloria, the club busybody and a woman who felt that people didn't take the whole neighbourhood watch scheme seriously enough.

Everyone listened, shocked, as Gloria recounted how she'd discovered that if she stood halfway up her stairs, she could see Clare's gate. From her vantage point, and with her opera glasses on, Gloria had seen Clare coming home one night with red eyes, a pale face and a tissue in her hand.

'Bet she'd been round Dan's love nest sobbing her heart out,' she sniffed.

'I might cry if my husband left me,' said Elizabeth sharply.

'I was only saying –' began Gloria.

'We're supposed to be her friends and friends rally round in time of need,' shot back Elizabeth. It would have been nice to have been in Clare's confidence and hear all about her counselling at first hand, but really, Gloria took the biscuit. Support was what Clare needed: not surveillance.

As Clare's birthday drew near, Fiona and Elizabeth checked on hotels where the club could enjoy the whole spa experience. They couldn't spend too much money but they wanted somewhere where Clare would feel pampered.

Fiona enjoyed the research. She liked taking charge: it felt good, invigorating. It was a mistake to wallow in self-pity and see what life would bring, instead of going out and getting it yourself. She didn't want to be like Clare Reid.

She booked a table at the local Italian restaurant and took her surprised husband Arthur out to dinner.

'What's this about?' said Arthur as they sat with menus in front of them and an opened bottle of wine.

'It's about us,' said Fiona. 'We've been talking in the book club –'

'All you do is gossip at that club,' smiled Arthur.

'– we've been talking about how when the children leave home, lots of people discover that they don't want to be married any more,' Fiona went on as if he hadn't interrupted. 'I wondered what you thought about that – should you have an affair or will I? Or should we make a stab at actually being a couple again? Any thoughts?'

Arthur needed the waitress to bring him some water because a bit of wine went down the wrong way. By the time they went home that night, Fiona felt better than she had in a long time. Arthur wasn't interested in an affair, it turned out. And he'd got quite a shock when Fiona had mentioned the possibility to him.

'I love you,' he blurted out, for once not caring that people might overhear in the busy restaurant.

'Great,' said Fiona, smiling back. 'Hopefully, you'll stop treating our home like a hotel then, and talk to me as if we're in love instead of talking to me like the hotel housekeeeper.'

Elizabeth phoned her grown-up daughter, Mia.

'Do you think your father's happy?' Elizabeth asked, when they'd gone through the usual spiel about Mia's job, how she'd left her latest boyfriend and what she was going to do about the holiday to Greece she'd booked for two.

'Happy? I don't know, Mum,' said Mia, startled.

'Happy with me, I meant,' Elizabeth went on.

'I think he can be grumpy, unappreciative and hopeless at showing his feelings,' Mia said, thinking that seeing as how her mother was asking, she might as well tell the truth.

'You know the way people look at their parents and can see that they should never have got married,' Elizabeth went on. 'Do you think that?'

'What's brought this on?'

'Lovely Clare Reid's husband has left her, for another woman, we think, and you know what, I was wondering if she was better off without him,' her mother replied candidly.

'Wow, you don't normally talk like this, Mum.'

'No,' agreed Elizabeth. 'It's just that Clare has set me thinking.'

'Dad doesn't appreciate you, if that's what you're asking' Mia said quickly. 'Hey, I've had an idea. I've got a spare ticket to Greece for next month. Why don't you come with me? Let Dad see how lonely it is to be grumpy and unappreciative on his own without you.'

Elizabeth began to cry. 'You're a great daughter,' she said. 'I'm not going to end up like poor Clare Reid, am I?'

The day before her birthday, Clare Reid was

surprised to be asked at the last minute to a coffee morning at Elizabeth's house across the road.

'Yes, I can come,' she told Elizabeth, 'but I'm wearing my ancient jeans and a shabby old sweatshirt. I'm hardly dressed for socialising.'

'Don't worry about that,' Elizabeth said warmly. 'It's you we want to see.'

Before she left for Elizabeth's, Clare looked around the house she loved and thought how lucky she was to be starting a new life. She was leaving in a week, so today would give her the chance to say au revoir to the women in the book club. She hoped they'd understand when she told them and not think she was being horrendously selfish.

It wasn't easy being selfish, actually, not after a lifetime of looking after other people. Women looked after people: it was that simple. They put their own needs after other people's. And she'd done that. She'd cooked, cleaned, worked part-time, stood in the freezing cold at football matches.

'I know it's the right decision but I don't know how to tell Dan,' she'd said to the counsellor she'd been seeing every second Monday night for the past year.

The counsellor refolded her arms and said nothing.

'OK, I do know how I can tell him,' Clare agreed. 'I have to tell him that I want some time out of our marriage, that I don't want to hurt him but that I'll hurt both of us inevitably if I'm not honest now. If he doesn't want to wait for me, that's his choice, but my choice is to travel the world on my own for a year and find out who I really am under all the roles I take on: wife, mum, chief bottle-washer.'

'Well done,' said the counsellor. 'I couldn't have put it better myself.'

When the kids had finally left home, Clare had taken stock of her life. For years, she'd needed Dan so much. But need was surprisingly reversible. Once she'd realised that life was very different now – no children to consider and a grown-up to share her life with – she'd realised she could change the rules. After all, she was only answerable to herself.

'Just take care,' Hanna had told her mother.

'I'll join you in India,' said Steve in delight. 'Roxie and me were thinking of going to India anyway, and it'll be cool to hook up with you.

'I wish it wasn't like this,' Dan said helplessly. 'I don't understand . . .'

'I know and I'm sorry, but I can't make you understand,' Clare said. 'I still love you but I've got to do this.'

Across the road in Elizabeth's house, the book club surveyed their efforts. The details of the night away in the hotel were on the coffee table, and everyone had bought something along as a mini-gift for Clare, although there were two copies of *Fear the Fear and Do It Anyway*.

Clare took one look at it all and burst into tears.

'You're so kind,' she said, hugging everyone in turn. 'This will be a lovely way to send me off on my trip, and I'll tell you all about that in a minute, but first, I've got a favour to ask.'

The Paradise Road Book Club leaned forward in one enthusiastic group. They would do anything, anything. This was what sisterhood was about. They had the names of lawyers with ice running through their veins; mediators' names; willing shoulders ready to be cried on . . .'

'I'm going away for a year and while I'm away, I'm going to be renting out the house. A lovely couple are taking it for the whole year and I told the wife all about the book club and how gorgeous you all are, and she'd love to join. What do you think? Will you take her on?'

Loose Change

Andrea Levy

I am not in the habit of making friends of strangers. I'm a Londoner. Not even little grey-haired old ladies passing comment on the weather can shame a response from me. I'm a Londoner – aloof sweats from my pores. But I was in a bit of a predicament; my period was two days early and I was caught unprepared.

I'd just gone into the National Portrait Gallery to get out of the cold. It had begun to feel, as I'd walked through the bleak streets, like acid was being thrown at my exposed skin. My fingers were numb searching for change for the tampon machine in my purse; I barely felt the pull of the zip against them. But I didn't have any.

I was forced to ask in a loud voice in this small lavatory, 'Has anyone got three twenty-pence pieces?' Everyone seemed to leave the place at once – all of them Londoners, I was sure of it. Only she was left – fixing her hair in the mirror.

'Do you have change?' She turned round slowly as I held out a ten-pound note. She had the most spectacular eyebrows. I could see the erect lines of black hair, like magnetised iron filings, tumbling across her eyes and almost joining above her nose. I must have been staring to remember them so clearly. She had wide black eyes and a round face with such a solid jawline that she looked to have taken a gentle whack from Tom and Jerry's cartoon frying pan. She dug into the pocket of her jacket and pulled out a bulging handful of money. It was coppers mostly. Some of it tinkled on to the floor. But she had change – too much – I didn't want a bag full of the stuff myself. 'Have you a five-pound note as well?' I asked.

She dropped the coins on to the basin area, spreading them out into the soapy puddles of water that were lying there. Then she said, 'You look?' She had an accent but I couldn't tell then where it was from; I thought maybe Spain.

'Is this all you've got?' I asked. She nodded. 'Well, look, let me just take this . . .' I picked three soggy coins out of the pile. 'I'll get some change in the shop and give you them back.' Her gaze was as keen as a cat with a string. 'Do you understand – only I don't want all those coins?'

'Yes,' she said softly.

I was grateful. I took the money. But when I emerged from the cubicle the girl and her handful of change were gone.

I found her again staring at the portrait of Darcey Bussell. Her head was inclining from one side to the other as if the painting were a dress she might soon try on for size. I approached her about the money but she just said, 'This is a good picture.' Was it my explanation left dangling or the fact that she liked the dreadful painting that caused my mouth to gape?

'Really, you like it?' I said.

'She doesn't look real. It looks like . . .' Her eyelids fluttered sleepily as she searched for the right word. 'A dream.'

That particular picture always reminded me of the doodles girls drew in their rough books at school.

'You don't like?' she asked. I shrugged. 'You show me the one you like,' she said.

As I mentioned before, I'm not in the habit of making friends of strangers, but there was something about this girl. Her eyes were encircled with dark shadows, so even when she smiled – introducing herself cheerfully as Laylor – they remained as mournful as a glum kid at a party. I took this fraternisation as defeat but I had to introduce her to a better portrait.

Alan Bennett with his mysterious little brown bag didn't impress her at all. She preferred the photograph of Beckham. Germaine Greer made her top lip curl and as for A. S. Byatt, she laughed out loud: 'This is child make this?'

We were almost making a scene. Laylor couldn't keep her voice down and people were beginning to watch us. I wanted to be released from my obligation. 'Look, let me buy us both a cup of tea,' I said, 'Then I can give you back your money.'

She brought out her handful of change again as we sat down at a table – eagerly passing it across to me to take some for the tea.

'No, I'll get this,' I said. Her money jangled like a win on a slot machine as she tipped it back into her pocket. I pushed over the twenty-pences I owed her. She began playing with them on the table top – pushing one around the other two in a figure of eight.

Suddenly she leaned towards me as if there were a conspiracy between us and said, 'I like art.' With that announcement a light briefly came on in those dull eyes to reveal that she was no more than eighteen. A student perhaps.

'Where are you from?' I asked.

'Uzbekistan,' she said.

Was that the Balkans? I wasn't sure. 'Where is that?'

She licked her finger, then with great concentration drew an outline on to the table top. 'This is Uzbekistan,' she said. She licked her finger again to carefully plop a wet dot on to the map, saying, 'And I come from here – Tashkent.'

'And where is all this?' I said, indicating the area around the little map with its slowly evaporating borders and town. She screwed up her face as if to say nowhere.

'Are you on holiday?' I asked.

She nodded.

'How long are you here for?'

Leaning her elbows on the table she took a sip of her tea. 'Ehh, it is bitter!' she shouted. 'Put some sugar in it,' I said, pushing the sugar sachets towards her.

She was reluctant. 'Is for free?' she asked.

'Yes, take one.'

The sugar spilled as she clumsily opened the packet. I laughed it off but she, with the focus of a prayer, put her cup up to the edge of the table and swept the sugar into it with the side of her hand. The rest of the detritus that was on the table top fell into the tea as well. Some crumbs, a tiny scrap of paper and a curly black hair floated on the surface of her drink. I felt sick as she put the cup back to her mouth.

'Pour that one away, I'll get you another one.'

Just as I said that, a young boy arrived at our table and stood legs astride before her. He pushed down the hood on his padded coat. His head was curious – flat as a cardboard cut-out – with hair stuck to his sweaty forehead in black curlicues. And his face was as doggedly determined as two fists raised. They began talking in whatever language it was they spoke. Laylor's tone pleading – the boy's, aggrieved. Laylor took the money from her pocket and held it up to him. She slapped his hand away when he tried to wrest all the coins from her palm. Then, as abruptly as he had appeared, he left. Laylor called something after him. Everyone turned to stare at her, except the boy who just carried on.

'Who was that?'

With the teacup resting on her lip, she said, 'My brother. He want to know where we sleep tonight.'

'Oh yes, where's that?' I was rummaging through

the contents of my bag for a tissue, so it was casually asked.

'It's square we have slept before.'

'Which hotel is it?' I thought of the Russell Hotel, that was on a square – uniformed attendants, bed-turning-down facilities, old-world style.

She was picking the curly black hair off her tongue when she said, 'No hotel, just the square.'

It was then I began to notice things I had not seen before; dirt under each of her chipped fingernails, the collar of her blouse crumpled and unironed, a tiny cut on her cheek, a fringe that looked to have been cut with blunt nail clippers. I found a tissue and used it to wipe my sweating palms.

'How do you mean just in the square?'

'We sleep out in the square,' she said. It was so simple she spread her hands to suggest the lie of her bed.

'Outside?'

She nodded.

'Tonight?'

'Yes.'

The memory of the bitter cold still tingled at my fingertips as I said, 'Why?'

It took her no more than two breaths to tell me the story. She and her brother had had to leave their country, Uzbekistan, when their parents – who were journalists – were arrested. It was arranged very quickly – friends of their parents acquired passports for them and put them on to a plane. They had been in England for three days but they knew no one here. This country was just a safe place. Now all the money they had could be lifted in the palm of a hand to a stranger in a toilet. So they were sleeping rough – in the shelter of a square, covered in blankets, on top of some cardboard.

At the next table a woman was complaining loudly that there was too much froth on her coffee. Her companion was relating the miserable tale of her daughter's attempt to get into publishing. What did they think about the strange girl sitting opposite me? Nothing. Only I knew what a menacing place Laylor's world had become.

She'd lost a tooth. I noticed the ugly gap when she smiled at me saying, 'I love London.'

She had sought me out – sifted me from the crowd. This young woman was desperate for help. She'd even cunningly made me obliged to her.

'I have picture of Tower Bridge at home on wall although I have not seen yet.'

But why me? I had my son to think of. Why pick on a single mother with a young son? We haven't got the time. Those two women at the next table, with their matching handbags and shoes, they did nothing but lunch. Why hadn't she approached them instead?

'From little girl, I always want to see it . . .' she went on.

I didn't know anything about the people in her situation. Didn't they have to go somewhere? Croydon was it? Couldn't she have gone to the police? Or some charity? My life was hard enough without this stranger tramping through it. She smelt of mildewed washing. Imagine her dragging that awful stink into my kitchen. Cupping her filthy hands around my bone china. Smearing my white linen. Her big face with its pantomime eyebrows leering over my son. Slumping on to my sofa and kicking off her muddy boots as she yanked me down into her particular hell. How would I ever get rid of her?

'You know where is Tower Bridge?'

Perhaps there was something tender-hearted in my face.

When my grandma first came to England from the Caribbean she lived through days as lonely and cold as an open grave. The story she told all her grand-children was about the stranger who woke her while she was sleeping in a doorway and offered her a warm bed for the night. It was this act of benevolence that kept my grandmother alive. She was convinced of it. Her Good Samaritan.

'Is something wrong?' the girl asked.

Now my grandmother talks with passion about scrounging refugees; those asylum seekers who can't even speak the language, storming the country and making it difficult for her and everyone else.

'Last week . . .' she began, her voice quivering, 'I was in home.' This was embarrassing. I couldn't turn the other way, the girl was staring straight at me. 'That day, Friday,' she went on, 'I cooked fish for my mother and brother.' The whites of her eyes were becoming soft and pink; she was going to cry. 'This day Friday I am here in London,' she said. 'And I worry I will not see my mother again.'

Only a savage would turn away when it was merely kindness that was needed.

I resolved to help her. I had three warm bedrooms, one of them empty. I would make her dinner. Fried chicken or maybe poached fish in wine. I would run her a bath filled with bubbles. Wrap her in thick towels heated on a rail. I would then hunt out some warm clothes and after I had put my son to bed I would make her cocoa. We would sit and talk. I would let her tell me all that she had been through. Wipe her tears and assure her that she was now safe.

I would phone a colleague from school and ask him for advice. Then in the morning I would take Laylor to wherever she needed to go. And before we said goodbye I would press my phone number into her hand.

All Laylor's grandchildren would know my name.

Her nose was running with snot. She pulled down the sleeve of her jacket to drag it across her face and said, 'I must find my brother.'

I didn't have any more tissues. 'I'll get you something to wipe your nose.' I said. I got up from the table. She watched me, frowning; the tiny hairs of her eyebrows locking together like Velcro. I walked to the counter where serviettes were lying in a neat pile. I picked up four. Then, standing straight, I walked on. Not back to Laylor but up the stairs to the exit. I pushed through the revolving doors and threw myself into the cold.

Orbiting

Kate Long

It was always the three of us, Cassie, Viv and me. I say always; actually I can date our coming-together from 7 September 1973. It is eight fifteen in the morning and we are standing at the bus stop, stiff in our brand new school uniforms. We each have an oversized briefcase and an anxious expression, and our initial bond is forged by fear.

Certainly we are not much alike. There's Cassie, tall, holds herself well, will go on to score top A levels, read medicine at university and become a GP. She is already buzzing with energy and ideas, destined to be a prefect and run FemSoc.

Viv, next to her, is beautiful and exotic. Even on this first day you can see the little signs of rebellion –

a leather wristband under her cuff, her top button undone beneath the tie – that will become the defining aspect of her personality. Viv will get thrown out of the sixth form and won't care. She will travel the world and buy ethnic art, run a successful gallery. Her mission in life will be to shake the Establishment.

And me? All I'm aiming to do at school is keep my head down. I am then what I am now; not tall not short, not pretty not plain, not clever not stupid, and these days you can add into the mix that I'm neither young nor old. Forever in the middle, which is a position that suits, most of the time.

But it has lasted, this friendship which began at the bus stop, all the way through school and what came after. When I had my pre-wedding crisis, when Viv was away in Paris and suicidal with homesickness, when Cassie's husband left her for his mistress, and a whole lot more grief besides. We have, as the song says, shared the hard times and the good.

Till now.

Now Cassie hates Viv, and wants me never to see her again. If I carry on speaking to Viv, Cassie will have nothing more to do with me, she says. She wants me to choose between them.

It begins with a furious lunchtime phone call – no, it begins further back than that.

I come home from work one day to find a Royal Mail card through the door. I have a parcel to pick up. Jamie goes to the sorting office for me because he's getting petrol anyway, and comes back with a box of Jo Malone bath oils. I can smell the scent before I get the wrapper off.

'What's this in aid of?' asks Jamie, worried in case he's missed some important anniversary. At least I assume this is what he's concerned about, not that I have a secret admirer, anything so crazy.

'I don't know,' I tell him, rooting for the tag through the nest of scented wadding.

It turns out to be from Viv. *Just because*, *X X X*, she has written, which throws me into a panic because the last time she sent lavish gifts was when she thought she had cancer and wanted to let us know what we'd meant to her. I got a brooch, and Cassie a David Inshaw print. I still wear that brooch, which is Victorian and in the shape of a bee.

I ring her at once. 'What's the matter?'

'Only that everything's completely utterly bloody wonderful,' she trills. I can hear the grin down the wire. It makes me smile too. 'Oh, Jo. I'm in love. It's the real thing. At last.'

'That's great,' I say, and mean it. Viv has not been lucky with romance. Over the years she's met a whole succession of rats and wasters, and on the rare occasions she has found a decent guy, she's become bored with him. Viv's self-destruct button, Cassie calls it. 'So when can we meet him?'

'As soon as Cassie gets back from the States we'll all meet up for lunch. She suggested Eaton's because they don't rush you there and we can have a good old chat.'

And I realise that I'm second on the list again, the second one to be told. It should not matter, I am forty-four not fourteen. Of course it doesn't matter.

'Look forward to it,' I tell her.

The next week is a busy one. I have to take some textbooks up to York that Michael forgot when he left this term. They're so heavy it's cheaper to drive over there than to post them. 'Feeble excuse,' smiles Jamie. 'You just want to see him again.' Which is true. I miss my son.

It's also a hectic period at work, and we have builders coming every day to give quotes on the extension, and there's Jamie's birthday to organise. Before I know it, Cassie is back in the country and phoning up, agog.

'This new man of Viv's, what do you reckon?'

'I don't know much about him,' I say. 'Other than that he's the Real Thing.'

'Yes, I got that impression from her emails. You wouldn't think someone as gorgeous as Viv would have to join a dating agency, though, would you?'

This detail I didn't know. 'Oh, come on, there's no stigma attached to agencies now. It's the modern time-saving way for today's multitasking professional. You ought to look into it yourself.'

'Ha ha. I've told you, I've had enough of men and their emotional clutter. Some of us enjoy our own company,' she says, pretending to be offended although I know she isn't. She is off men, though; hasn't looked at anyone since her husband walked out. Viv calls it Cassie's Survival Strategy.

That evening I am thoughtful. 'What's up?' asks Jamie. 'You look a bit sad.'

I'm not sad, I'm remembering one day at school when Cassie was absent with flu and Viv had managed to blag a date with an upper-sixth boy. 'He has his own car!' she'd hissed, dragging me out of the line of students filing into the hall, and marching me round the corner to the toilets. She sat in between two sinks and gave me a frame-by-frame account of the way she'd chatted him up. Then the door opened and the deputy head came in and tore a strip off us for truanting assembly. But even this was a daft thrill, with Viv winking away and pulling faces in the background, so that I'd laughed and we'd both ended up with a detention, which we'd done together and afterwards gone for a coffee in town. It had been nice to have Viv to myself. Although I missed Cassie, obviously.

'Men don't really have Best Friends, do they?'

Jamie shakes his head. 'We have hobbies. Much less bother.'

The trouble with three, I think to myself, is that there's always one person who's slightly on the outside, one person whose orbit is a little wider than the others'. And that's me.

Then the phone rings again and it's Michael to ask do I know his NHS number because he needs to register with a university dentist, and I forget about the girls and our respective tracks because I have to go hunt out his card.

Lunch with the Real Thing (Mark) has Viv hopping with nerves. 'Try not to scare him off,' she says before he arrives.

'Would we?' Cassie rolls her eyes.

I say: 'I couldn't scare anyone if I tried.'

Just then he walks into the restaurant and we all three turn and stare because he is gorgeous. I wonder if Cassie is revising her decision about never dating.

They make a spectacularly handsome couple. Mark has the same gypsy colouring as Viv, the same white teeth. His mother's French-Algerian, he can speak four languages, he travels a lot. His nails are immaculate and he wears an expensive watch. Viv has done well, she's glowing.

'I've heard all about you,' he says. 'The three musketeers.'

'Three wise monkeys.'

'Three amigos.'

'Three stooges.'

We're all laughing. Viv has told him all about her past so he knows about ours too. 'You dash to each other's rescue at times of crisis, I've heard.'

'They saved me,' I tell him. 'I was almost a runaway bride. But they caught a train up from London and talked me through it, and I realised it was only the wedding *day* I was scared of, not the being married.'

I don't tell him that it was Viv that had me on the verge of bolting in the first place. She and Cassie had been sharing a flat in Highgate, and when I got her funny postcard telling me about the latest mad party they'd crashed I suddenly wanted out of the predictable, even though I did love Jamie. Still do.

Mark is gazing at me as though I'm fascinating.

'It'll be our silver wedding anniversary next year,' I add.

'That's good,' he says. 'And you flew out to Viv when she was down and out in Paris?'

'I went,' says Cassie. 'You were too heavily pregnant, weren't you, Jo?'

I nod.

'But you sent me loads of funny letters and cards,' says Viv. 'That made a huge difference.'

'I was thinking about you all the time.'

'Not while you were giving birth.'

'No.'

'Sometimes,' says Mark, 'there are things that take priority over friendship.' He takes Viv's hand. 'Occasionally.'

We all sense her thrill. My fingers tingle in sympathy.

In the toilets I ask Cassie what she thinks.

'He's very smooth,' she says, in a way that annoys me slightly. Why does she have to be so suspicious? But then I've never been abandoned by my husband. It's easy for me to assume the best of a man.

I grimace at myself in the mirror. 'You know I still feel bad I never made it to Paris that time. I always feel I let her down.'

'Don't beat yourself up, there's no need.'

'No, I should have been there.'

The dryer is going so I don't hear what she's saying at first. Then the noise shuts off and she goes, '– it wouldn't have been appropriate.'

'Why ever not?'

Cassie comes over and lowers her voice. I can tell she is a little drunk. 'It just wouldn't.'

'But why?'

'Because – Viv was pregnant and she didn't want to be.'

I can't believe my ears. Viv pregnant? 'So what happened?'

'What do you think happened? It was upsetting but it was something she had to do. I went with her, I looked after her, she got through OK.'

They've kept this secret from me all these years. Cassie sees my mortification, and at once puts her arm around me. 'Sorry, Jo. She made me swear not to tell anyone, not even you, because afterwards she just wanted to forget it. Anyway, she would have told you if you'd been there. It was bad timing all round, that's all.'

Back in the restaurant Viv is explaining to Mark how I booked a weekend at a spa for the three of us after Cassie's divorce came through. 'My brilliant mates,' she says. 'What would I do without them?' In my mind I can hear Jamie: *Come on, it happened eighteen years ago. I don't see why you girls have to know everything about each other's private lives anyway.*

'A toast.' Cassie is holding her glass in the air. 'To moving forward.'

'Cheers,' I say.

It's only a few days after this I get the call that tips our dynamic upside down.

Cassie is so angry she can hardly get the question out. 'Did you know Mark was married?'

'No way! Did Viv?'

'Yes! That's the point. That's why I'm so bloody livid.'

It takes me a while to catch on. Does she know Mark's wife? But no, it's the principle that's upsetting her.

'It's, it's *unsisterly*,' she continues. 'When Colm left me for that other woman it was the worst time ever. It was such a betrayal. Honestly, Jo, I wanted to die.'

'I remember.'

'And I thought then, what kind of woman does that, takes someone else's husband? Huh? What kind of –' She breaks off as though there aren't the words. 'I never thought Viv, of all people, would behave like that,' she manages at last. 'It's brought everything back.'

'There might be extenuating circumstances,' I say cautiously. 'We ought to hear Viv's side.'

'Like hell we should,' Cassie snaps. 'I don't want to listen to her selfish excuses. I don't want to hear from her at all.'

'She's your friend.'

'Was my friend. She's not the person I thought she was. It's clear I didn't know her at all.' A pause. I sense what's coming next. 'Well? Don't you think it's an appalling way to behave? Jo?'

'I need to speak to Viv,' I tell her.

So I do.

'I love him,' Viv says simply. 'I've never met anyone like him. I've never felt this way before. When Fate presents you with an opportunity like that, you have to take it, you have to. Because otherwise you'd spend the rest of your life hating yourself. How would you feel without Jamie by your side?'

'That's not the same,' I argue.

'It is in terms of love. He's the one for you; Mark's the one for me. I'm sorry about what happened to Cassie's marriage but that's not my fault. She shouldn't be imposing her experience on to my relationship because it's got nothing to do with her.

Unless you've been in this situation you can't possibly understand.'

'What about Mark's wife?'

'She doesn't love him any more.'

'So they'll be getting a divorce?'

'It could be on the cards.'

I want to believe her. 'Can't you wait till he sorts himself out, Viv? That would be better for everyone, surely. Do it all above board.'

'Don't tell me,' she cries, 'to walk away from this one chance, Jo. All these years I've been waiting. And you don't know what tomorrow holds, how much time any of us has left. I have to take this chance of happiness while it's here. My whole heart is telling me to. There are no rules where love's concerned. Please, try to explain to Cassie because she won't talk to me any more.'

I put down the receiver feeling like a wet rag.

'Girlfriend trouble?' says Jamie, handing me a cup of coffee. He stands and watches me as I sip.

'You wouldn't ever be unfaithful to me, would you?' I ask, knowing it is a stupid question.

'Haven't got the time or energy,' he says.

Now best mate to both of them, I still find myself stuck in the middle.

'Have you seen Viv lately?' asks Cassie, lips pursed in disapproval.

'I don't know how you can still speak to Cass after the things she's accused me of,' says Viv.

If I could get away with it I'd pretend exclusive loyalty to each, but I'm no good at lying. Anyway, for all they're cross with me, each of them needs me on her side.

'You're in demand these days,' remarks Jamie, as I put my coat on ready for another coffee-and-counselling session. 'Oh, don't forget to pick up some Grolsch for Michael if you're going past the supermarket. You don't want him to think we've forgotten what he likes.'

Unbelievably, it had slipped my mind that my son is home this weekend; I don't admit that, though. 'It's on my list.'

I grab my car keys and go.

When the phone rings after ten on a Sunday night I know it's trouble.

'Can you get over here?' sobs Viv. She's verging on hysterical. 'Now?'

'My God, what's happened?'

'He's dumped me, Jo. It's over.'

'I'm there.'

I almost clip the gatepost in my haste to get the car out. When I arrive at Viv's, the front door is open so I go straight through, terrified at what I might find. She's kneeling in the middle of the room, her hair in disarray, her make-up down her face. 'What am I going to do?' she keeps asking me.

Her mistake was, she says, to issue an ultimatum. Now the relationship was established, she wanted to see more of him; he maintained that was impossible. She threatened to call his wife and tell her everything unless he made more space in his schedule. 'I had to try something, Jo,' she wails. The stratagem backfired. He took fright, and finished the affair. 'He was the One,' she says over and over.

The doorbell rings. I jump a mile but Viv barely stirs.

'Viv?'

'I called Cassie,' she says from between splayed fingers, and her voice sounds very small. 'You don't mind, do you?'

'Of course not!' I don't, either. I go and let her in.

'Viv's pretty upset –' I begin, anxious in case Cassie thinks this is the time to deliver the *I told you so* line, which of course she has every right to do. She shakes her head at me, pushes past and there's no hesitation; she walks straight over and embraces Viv, kneels down and shushes and rocks her, stroking her hair as though she was a little girl.

I stand there for a moment then I go through to the kitchen and put the kettle on. We can have a whisky coffee, it'll do us all good. After a while I creep back and look round the door. They are still crouched on the carpet. Viv has her head on Cassie's shoulder.

I step back; sad for Viv, that life can be such a bitch, but relieved we're back together.

Happy to be on the outside orbit again.

Too Good to be True

Santa Montefiore

When Celestia Somersby moved into Old Lodge, the sleepy, insular village of Westcotton was roused to wakefulness by a blazing curiosity. It wasn't that they hadn't witnessed the arrival of strangers, though, being a small, remote town on the Devonshire coast there was little to entice people; it was because Celestia Somersby was a woman of mystery. 'She's very beautiful,' commented Betty Knight, standing back to admire the expanding flower display she was arranging in the nave of the little church. Vivien Pratt screwed up her nose and leaned on her broom.

'In a severe way,' she replied with a snort. 'I don't think that black she wears is very becoming. Makes her look pale and drawn. Older, too,' she added and there was an ill-disguised timbre of pleasure in her voice, for she was sixty-five and looked it.

'You can't deny she's elegant, though. I used to wear long skirts with boots like that when I was young,' said Betty with a sigh.

'It's not your age, dear,' said Vivien, passing her reptilian eyes up and down Betty's squat build. 'It's your girth. You shouldn't indulge so. I'm not this thin by nature but by abstinence, Betty. Jesus taught us that, and *he* was thin, wasn't he? No cream buns and pies from Edith's Pantry for him, just the odd fish and crust of bread after the five thousand had troughed.'

'Do you think she's a divorcee?' Betty pulled her stomach in then let it out with a wheeze as a wilting lily diverted her attention.

'She wears a ring, you know. I saw it. Though there's been no sign of a man. Must be divorced, otherwise why would she look so sad?'

'If Cyril gave me a divorce, I wouldn't look sad. I'd be positively gleeful. Thirty years of sitting about like a fat walrus. I'd be more than happy to roll him back into the sea.'

'You'd be lost, dear, have no illusions. That woman's a walking tragedy; you can see it on her face. A smile would do much for that sallow complexion.'

Vivien didn't bother to reflect on her own smile, lost long ago with her sense of fun.

'She hasn't said so much as a hello to anyone. Just lots of sightings, though no one seems to know what she does or why she's come. There, I think Reverend Jollie will appreciate my effort this week. I do love spring, don't you? Still, she'll come to church on Sunday, I'm sure. We can all get a good look at her then.'

'My dear, if she hasn't had the decency to introduce herself by Sunday, I shall think her very rude indeed. She shan't be welcome here.'

'That's not for you to say, Vivien. This is God's house.'

'Then I shan't invite her back for tea. She'll know she's caused offence then, won't she?' *And she'll know who calls the shots around here, too.*

By Sunday the whole village was whispering about the enigmatic Celestia Somersby. She had wandered into Agatha Tingle's shop and bought a basket of provisions, infuriating the docile shopkeeper by hiding her features beneath a black sunhat and dark glasses. She had said nothing, just paid, handing the older woman crisp pound notes with long white fingers. Agatha gossiped with Betty and Vivien over tea in Edith's Pantry, dissecting every detail, from the goods she had bought to the strange old-fashioned buckled shoes she wore on her feet, while Vivien sipped weak tea and Betty bit into a large slice of chocolate cake. What they didn't know, however, was that Fitzroy Merridale had seen her down on the beach, walking wistfully with her feet in the surf, her long black dress billowing about her ankles, the chiffon scarf tied around her hat flapping like the wings of a bat and that there, in the roaring wind and the crashing of waves, he had lost his heart. It had been a wonderful moment. An awakening from somewhere dull into somewhere bright and full of possibilities.

Since that exquisite sighting, Fitzroy had been able to think of little else but Celestia Somersby. He had sat in the Four Codgers pub and listened to the mutters of speculation. Some said that she was divorced, others that she had murdered her husband. He believed none of it and took pleasure from the fact that she hadn't deigned to speak to any of them, because he knew instinctively that she would talk to him. After all, he was one of the few in town her age. Westcotton was an old people's town. He had only moved there to write, having found no inspiration in London. He was also bold. Why, he mused, was it up to her to approach them? Surely as the newcomer *they* should make the gesture and welcome *her* into their midst. He sat in the pew, on the cold hard seat of ancient wood, and looked about him: Agatha, Betty, Vivien, Edith and a gaggle of other grandmothers in feathered hats and pastel dresses. Their husbands fat and weathered or thin and dominated. A few young couples with fidgeting children, following in the deep, stodgy footsteps of their parents. There was nothing for Celestia Somersby here. Why had she come?

When Reverend Jollie stepped into the nave, his long gowns disguising a belly full of Edith's scones, the disappointment that was felt by every member of his congregation caused the very air in the church to drop. Betty glanced warily at her flowers, afraid that the lilies would wilt too, for everyone had hoped to get a proper look at Celestia Somersby. She had not come.

Reverend Jollie was aware of their frustration because it reflected his own. He had indulged in fantasies of a more godly nature than Fitzroy Merridale, envisaging her confessing her sins, of which there were many, on to his chest. He was appalled at his own weakness, for since Celestia Somersby had arrived in Westcotton he had wished he were Catholic.

With a heavy sigh he raised his palms to the sky and addressed the sheep in his flock like the good shepherd that he was. 'Welcome, friends . . .' Just when his enthusiasm was on the point of stalling, the large doors of the church opened with a deep groan. At once the air was charged with expectation. Reverend Jollie watched his congregation turn their heads to face the entrance now gaping open like the toothless yawn of an old man. Fitzroy Merridale's heart stopped for a second as did his breath, suspended between anticipation and disappointment, willing it to be her. He craned his neck past Cyril Knight's thick shoulders and saw, to his delight, the slim, hesitant figure he had dreamed about since seeing her walking barefoot up the beach. She remained there for what seemed like a very long while, her arms outstretched on either side, her gloved hands holding the doors open. She wore black and her white face and neck glowed luminous beneath the veil that was pinned to her hat. Only her crimson lips and the pink apples of her cheeks retained their colour. With a purposeful stride she walked up the aisle, passing the many pairs of eyes that strained for a better view of her face. To Reverend Jollie's astonishment she knelt before him, for he still stood in front of the altar, and crossed herself, inclining her head as Catholics do. He experienced a frisson of excitement, then let out a controlled, though staggered, breath. She smiled, a small but unmistakable smile, before turning and walking back down the aisle to a seat at the back. Fitzroy grinned with admiration. What a cool, confident display that was and how dignified. He had noticed her slim ankles and the high heels on those old-fashioned buckled shoes. He wondered what she looked like with her hair down, cascading over naked shoulders.

Fitzroy wasn't the only man in the church unable to concentrate on the service, even Reverend Jollie flustered over the sermon like an overexcited girl, anticipating communion when she would at last raise her veil and cast her dark eyes to him in submission. He was to be disappointed, however, for although she knelt before him she did not raise her veil nor her eyes, which remained lowered and demure.

'Well!' huffed Vivien once the service was over and they were all standing about in the sunshine. 'She might have introduced herself. What does she have to hide? I wonder. I shall not invite her to tea.'

'I don't think she'll mind,' said Betty with a laugh. 'She doesn't look the type for tea. Much too common for her, I suspect, as are we.'

'Oh, for goodness' sake, Betty. You talk such nonsense. Your father might have been a plumber but mine, my dear, was the son of a gentleman.'

Betty raised her eyebrows cynically. She knew better than to argue with Vivien Pratt.

Fitzroy had noticed Celestia leave during the blessing and had slipped out behind her. As she walked briskly down the path towards the green he hurried after her. 'Miss Somersby,' he said, catching her up. 'May I introduce myself?' She continued to walk until they were out of sight of the church. Only then did she turn. He was surprised at her small stature for her charisma gave the impression that she was taller. She did not lift her veil, but he saw her eyes shining behind it. 'My name is Fitzroy Merridale. I want to welcome you to Westcotton.'

'Thank you.' Her voice was soft and deep like brown suede. He noticed she looked around furtively.

'May I accompany you home?' he asked. She nodded and proceeded to walk across the green. 'I don't imagine you know anyone here.'

'That is why I have moved,' she said and her words weighed heavily with significance.

'I see,' he replied, intrigued. 'I hope you don't mind me approaching you. You just seem so . . . alone.'

'I am alone,' she said, then sighed. 'It is nice to talk to someone.' Fitzroy felt his insides flutter as if they were filled with bubbles.

'I'm a bit of a loner myself. I'm trying to write a novel, but it's not really working. I live in a cottage by the sea. I saw you the other day, walking along the beach.' He was sure she smiled beneath her veil. Encouraged, he continued. 'You had taken your shoes off and your feet were in the water. It must have been cold.'

'I didn't notice,' she replied.

'Well, I live near there. It's meant to fill me with inspiration, but I just stare out at a void. You inspired me, though.'

She stopped and looked up at him. 'Did I?'

'Yes, you gave me an idea for a story.' He felt himself blush and put his hands in his pockets. 'I've already begun.'

She stared at him a long moment then walked on. 'Why don't you come back for tea? It's not much, but it's home.'

The house was pretty, with tall ceilings and sash windows overlooking a large garden surrounded by lime trees. Once inside the wall that encircled the property, they were entirely alone. Fitzroy followed her into the house. He watched as she took off her hat in front of a gilt mirror in the hall. She unpinned her hair so that it fell in dark waves over her shoulders and down her back. Then she slipped off her gloves and unbuttoned her coat with delicate white fingers. When she turned to him he was struck by the surprisingly pale colour of her eyes. Like water in a tropical sea. Her mouth twisted once again into a small smile and he felt the colour rise in his cheeks. She was more beautiful than he had imagined.

He followed her into the sitting room where a fire smouldered in the grate. There was a piano upon which large church candles were placed in clusters. The melted wax revealed that they were often lit. 'Do you play?' he asked.

'Of course,' she said and sat down on the stool. As she launched into an emotive solo, her face was suddenly darkened by some unspoken sadness.

'Play something happy,' he asked.

She raised those strange pale eyes to him and shook her head. 'I'm afraid I can't play what is not in my heart.'

'Then don't play,' he said impulsively. 'Please don't play if it makes you sad.' Once again she smiled but this time it was the sort of smile one gives in the face of a beautiful sunset. A smile tinged with sorrow. She got up from the stool and walked up to him. The look in her eyes was intense. He turned away.

She raised her hand and ran it down his cheek. 'You're a sensitive man,' she said and then she kissed him. He didn't pull away or question his good fortune, but wrapped her in his arms and pressed his lips to hers. He breathed in the scent of her skin, warm and sweet like the smell of bluebells, and closed his eyes.

Suddenly she pushed him away. 'You must go!' she said hastily, shaking her head as if ashamed of what had come over her.

'But, Celestia!' he pleaded.

'Not here. Not here, Fitzroy. I can't. It's wrong.' She staggered back and leaned against the piano, her hand pressed against her forehead.

'What's wrong? Are you married?'

'No.'

'Are you divorced?'

'No.'

'Are you a widow?'

She stared at him with frightened eyes and hurried into the hall. 'You must go!'

'Will we meet again?'

'There's a cave on the beach, you know the one. I'll meet you there tomorrow at noon. Don't breathe a word to anyone!' Fitzroy promised then departed. The door closed behind him and he was left bewildered. If she had been mysterious before, she was even more mysterious now.

The next day Fitzroy went down to the beach and waited for her in the cave. He waited and waited but she did not come. When finally he was on the point of leaving she hurried in through the narrow entrance and fell into his arms. 'I'm sorry,' she breathed, kissing him fervently. 'Forgive me!' He did not bother to ask why she was late. He did not care. He had her in his arms and was happy.

The following weeks passed in the same manner. They met in the cave and she was always late. But he had learned to wait for her. They didn't talk much and every time they parted he felt he knew her less than before. In the evenings he went to the Four Codgers and listened to the talk. The rumours had grown. They called her the Black Widow and were certain she had killed her husband. Maybe one, perhaps more. Fitzroy sat smiling to himself. He knew her better than any of them.

At the end of May, when the air was filled with the sugary scent of summer, Fitzroy invited her back to his cottage. 'I want to make love to you,' he said. At first she was hesitant, as if betraying another or breaking a vow, but then overcome with desire she agreed. In the amber light of evening he unburdened her of the black clothes she wore, unwrapping her slowly as if she were a precious gift. Her skin was soft and creamy and blushing with youth. *You are too vibrant a woman to be subdued by black*, he thought as he kissed her flesh. Then he noticed a scar on her chest. It was pale, barely visible. It was the texture that made it stand out. Afraid of wounding her, he said nothing. After they had made love they lay entwined, engulfed by an unsettling mixture of joy and sorrow, as if instinctively aware of the transience of their affair.

Then one night in the Four Codgers, Fitzroy heard them talk of another man. One who came and left her house in a car. He was dark, in his late forties. He never stayed for long. Fitzroy was consumed with jealousy. He marched over to Old Lodge and knocked on the door. When she did not open it he pounded with his fists. 'Who is he?' he bellowed into the night air. Before walking away he noticed a brief flash of light from upstairs and the hasty drawing of a curtain.

The following morning there was a furore on the beach. Policemen and onlookers and dozens of people he did not recognise. When he approached, Vivien Pratt drew him aside. 'Don't,' she said, shaking her head. 'It's that woman. Celestia Somersby. She's dead.'

'Dead?' he gasped, feeling his world unravel about him.

'Drowned.' Then she hissed. 'They say it's suicide. I'm not so sure. Might have been murder.'

Celestia Somersby, or Jane Hardwick as she was really called, was not buried in Westcotton. Fitzroy found her brother sorting through her things at Old Lodge. 'She was a Londoner at heart,' he said sadly. 'She was once an actress. A good actress too, before the accident. After that she was too frightened of the stage to continue. She turned her life into a drama. Moving from place to place where no one knew her. Where she could be anyone she wanted to be so long as she was playing a role.'

'Why did she kill herself?' Fitzroy asked and the pain must have echoed up from the hollowness in his heart. Her brother looked at him for a long moment then smiled compassionately.

'She fooled you too, didn't she?' He sighed and picked up her photograph. 'She died, my friend, because she couldn't sustain that bizarre life for ever.

She wanted to be Celestia but Jane was always one step behind her. I think she preferred to die dramatically than live modestly.'

'But I loved her.'

'No, you didn't. You loved someone who didn't exist. Even she had lost sight of who she really was. But in a way she got what she wanted. A dramatic life and a dramatic death and she will live on as Celestia in your memory and in the memory of the others who gave her their hearts. Only I will remember her as Jane but she never cared much for me. I was a constant reminder of the truth and she cared little for that.'

Love's Labours

Elizabeth Noble

The cup of tea someone had handed her had gone cold. She'd barely taken a sip. She was alone in the corridor, but nurses in green outfits, with white plastic clogs, passed her periodically, pushing open the white doors and disappearing through them.

There were only chairs in this place. No out of date magazines depicting long-over trends. No drink dispenser. No leaflets extolling the virtues of giving up cigarettes, or cutting down on salt, or meeting other people with twins. The people who waited in this corridor couldn't be distracted, even if they wanted to be.

Staring at the doors as they opened briefly, she thought she could see her daughter through them. A

different girl each time they swung. The four-year-
old, in long white socks, walking reluctantly away
from her, hand in hand with a teacher, on her first day
at school, looking at her over one hunched shoulder,
trying not to cry. The awkward teenager, feigning
disinterest in her, turning belligerently towards her
friends; the eighteen-year-old, waving optimistically
as she left her at university for her first term, away
from home, away from her.

Life had kept taking her away. Making me leave
her.

Only she'd been the one walking away, four
months ago. Sitting here now it seemed so stupid. So
futile and pointless. All that wasted time, posturing
about something ridiculous.

Emma had always had lousy taste in boyfriends.
That was what she had said to her. It was a joke
between them at first. Emma said she was a cliché.
The mother who never thought anyone was good
enough for her little girl. When she was older, and it
wasn't so funny, she accused her of being bitter, being
a man hater. She didn't hate men. In her darker
moments she'd blamed herself. There'd been no
suitable role model in the home, thanks to her own
marriage falling apart before Emma could walk. Mind
you, even if he'd been in the home, Emma's father

would have been no example to follow. He was handsome, and funny. But he was selfish and manipulative and bullying. He'd never hit her – she wouldn't have stood for that (she promised herself), but he hectored. And criticised. His wit was his weapon, and he used it on her almost every day. Her parents had loved him. He was attentive to her mother, and with her father always achieved the desired balance of respect and blokiness. She shouldn't have married him. That was so clear to her now, that she never understood why it hadn't been then.

And there hadn't been anyone since. Not really. When Emma was small she'd hidden behind motherhood. By the time Emma was old enough to understand, she'd forgotten how to do it. How to flirt, or just be interesting to a man. She didn't hate men. She was frightened of them. Not that she ever admitted that, to anyone. It was easier, in the end, to be on her own. No risk, and no effort and no chance of being hurt.

They'd had fun. They'd been a team. She'd never understood the other mothers at the school gates, the ones who had moaned about their children. Emma was her best friend, not some onerous responsibility she'd been saddled with, like those other women sometimes made it sound.

The hardest part was letting Emma make her own way. Her own mistakes and her own choices. She applied the clarity that had been missing from her own view of her husband to Emma's boyfriends. She'd applied it to Chris. She didn't like his five o'clock shadow. She knew it was what young people did. Or rather, didn't. They didn't shave. It made him look grubby and lazy. He wore his fingernails long, because he played the guitar, but she didn't like them either. She didn't like the thought of his nails scratching Emma's flesh, or his stubble sandpapering her cheeks. Emma said she'd made up her mind about him the minute she'd laid eyes on him, like she'd always done.

'What's he done wrong, mum?'

He hadn't done anything wrong. But his demeanour let her know that he didn't care what she thought about him. That was enough.

Emma had tried. She'd had Chris round for dinner, but her mother had picked arguments about stupid, unimportant things. In the garden, afterwards, smoking a cigarette, Chris had shaken his head. 'She's got issues, your mother.'

She'd told Emma she wanted her to have a career, have opportunities. Not to tie herself down so young. Emma said she could do all that and still have Chris.

That it wasn't a straight choice – one thing or the other. 'If you didn't do that stuff, Mum, that's your problem. Not mine.'

Months had passed, and things had become more difficult. She grew to dread him coming. Emma was changing. There was something new and defiant in her tone now.

'I'm not giving this one up because he doesn't fit your idea of what I need, mum. I'm not.'

It was the same tone when she'd told her she was pregnant. So much for not being tied down, she'd thought, with a hollow laugh. News like that shouldn't be delivered that way. She'd imagined crying instant, easy tears of joy, touching a still-flat belly reverently. Not wanting to slap her.

She'd gone round that day, the day Emma had told her, four months ago, because she hadn't slept all the previous night. She'd lain there and argued with herself. If you believed, if *she* believed, that Emma was making a big mistake, moving in with Chris, didn't she have a duty to tell her? Wasn't it a mother's job, to say so? To risk it? Strange, that two people should come together, both with momentous things to say, neither expecting what agenda the other one has.

If Emma had told her about the baby she was

expecting first . . . If she had answered the door and held open her arms, and told her about the child the right way, what would she have done with what she had come to say? Where would she have put the words?

But Emma had left her with no choice, hadn't she? She'd gone first, told her what a mistake she was making, giving her life to Chris, told her she knew – in her heart, in her uterus – that he was wrong for her. How could she do anything else after she'd told her she was pregnant, but walk away?

But how had she stayed away? Sitting here now, waiting, it was hard to comprehend, and even harder to forgive herself. She'd expected Emma to call her, to come round. The first day, the first weekend, the first week. She hadn't. And some stupid pride had kicked in, so she didn't make the first move either, and the weeks passed. She would never have that time back again.

Emma *had* called, though, eventually, when the twinges turned into pains. The baby was coming early. Emma had been late. Fourteen days late. In a hot, airless August. It was cold now. The 'phone had rung during *EastEnders*. She might not have answered it, not during *EastEnders*. Except that she knew, or she hoped. She wasn't sure which. The voice said, 'Mum?' The tone was altogether different and new.

The drive to where Emma and Chris lived took half an hour. The roads were icy. Radio Four drove her mad. The other stations played happy tunes she wasn't ready to listen to. She poked impatiently at the channel button, and then turned it off altogether. She knew she was driving too fast. Once she passed a police car, driving the other way, and was afraid that he would turn around and follow her, but he rounded a bend and disappeared from her rear-view mirror.

Turned out, they both needed her. Chris answered the door, and his face was grateful. He looked so young. She went in, past him, pulling off her coat and her gloves.

'Have you called for an ambulance?'

'She won't let me. She says it'll be hours yet. I called the midwife. She'll be here in a bit.'

'But it's too early.'

'I know. She's afraid of the hospital, I think.' He rubbed his hair. 'She's been sick. Three or four times. I didn't know she'd be sick.'

She'd been sick, too, when Emma was coming. Sick with fear, she imagined. She remembered repeatedly walking around the flat they'd lived in when they were married, very fast, like a rat in a run.

Kitchen to bedroom. Bathroom to living room. Kitchen. Throwing up in every sink she'd passed. She felt she would have to concentrate more on the pain if she wasn't moving.

When she went into the bedroom, Emma smiled at her. It didn't matter any more, what had been said between them. Everything had shrunk back, and the only thing that mattered was what was happening in that room, right then. Emma was on her knees, leaning over the bed. She had some electrical contraption attached to the small of her back, and she was moving her pelvis round in circles, moaning softly.

When Emma was coming, and she'd been admitted, they wanted her to lie down on the bed, on her back. Emma's father had said he was going to find a cup of tea, 'or something'. That he'd be right back.

But he'd missed it. She always knew he'd missed it on purpose. She hadn't minded. She'd been lost in something, towards the end. She'd gone to some- where he couldn't have come with her. And then, when she'd pushed Emma out, it was just the two of them. A sticky, warm, damson-coloured baby, squirming and screaming on her belly, legs juddering and arms shaking wildly. When he'd tentatively poked his head around the door, already murmuring apology, she'd almost forgotten that he was meant to be with her.

Chris knelt on the other side of the bed, facing Emma, and she reached out her arms towards him. Their hands entwined in the middle of the mattress, and with each contraction, she rocked backwards, and he held her hands, so that his arms were pulled straight, stretched out in front of him. Her eyes – wide with fear – never left his.

'Mum.'

Instinctively she knelt down next to Chris, and he released one of Emma's hands. She reached for her daughter. She wished Emma could push the pain through her tight fingers, into her. They stayed like that, barely speaking, for almost an hour, until the midwife came. Her knees touched Chris's.

Once, Emma said, 'I'm sorry.' She shushed her like an infant. 'No, no. Never mind. I'm sorry. I'm sorry. It doesn't matter now. I'm here. We're here.' She didn't have to make herself say it.

On the mantelpiece behind Emma were two photographs, in wide black frames. Emma aged about seven. Not about seven. Exactly seven. Her birthday. Sitting on her lap in the park. She remembered it being taken. She had her arms around her daughter, fingers splayed to pull her close, and they were both laughing, Emma's head pushed back into her shoulder. In the other picture, Chris cradled her growing bump from behind. They stood in autumn leaves, on one of those impossibly blue days. She was leaning on him exactly the same way, and smiling happily.

When the midwife arrived, with her erratic, curly hair, and her unthreatening non-uniform, she asked them to wait outside while she examined Emma, and they both felt affronted. She had seen it on his face as she felt it cross her own. Emma smiled at them. 'It's fine. Go and have a drink, for God's sake.'

Chris switched the kettle on, and put teabags with tags and strings into mugs on the kitchen table.

'Sugar?'

'Please. One.'

'I love her, you know.'

'I know.'

'Do you?'

'I didn't. Didn't know. Until now.'

He shrugged.

'You never asked me. If I loved her. Or gave me a chance to show you.'

'I know.' She felt foolish.

He was stirring the milk in when the midwife came into the room. She was dialling her mobile, and she spoke to them, quickly and quietly, while they listened to the rings, before the hospital answered.

Only one person in the ambulance with the midwife. Chris touched her hand, very lightly. 'You go with her. I'll bring the car. Her bag and stuff – she'll need them.'

She couldn't have driven. She watched him unlock the car door and climb inside, and then the ambulance doors slammed shut.

Emma couldn't sit down. They laughed about that; grim, desperate laughing.

'I am going to be okay, aren't I mum?'

All the questions, over all the years. All the things she had been able to make right, to fix. And now she didn't know.

'Of course you are.'

This was 2006. Of course she would be all right. She shivered. Emma would be okay. But she didn't know about the baby.

'I'm glad you're here.'

'Me too, sweetheart.'

She wanted to say that she'd been wrong about Chris. She wanted to confess her stupidity and her failings and ask for forgiveness, but now wasn't the time. Her beautiful daughter, bent double, balancing on the floor of an ambulance, on her way to face God knew what, sought out her eyes with her own, and whispered, 'I know.'

Only her partner would be allowed into the operating theatre, they said. They didn't know whether they would be able to get the baby out. They might have to do an operation, if the baby became too distressed. They would need to be fast. The nurse had looked at her apologetically, and briefly squeezed the top of her arm. She wanted her to say, 'Don't worry, she'll be fine.' But she didn't. She probably wasn't allowed to. They didn't know, did they? What she did say was, 'Tough, isn't it, being shut out when you've been through so much with them.' She meant tonight. She meant all of her life. And it was. Then she'd taken the 'partner' away, to get changed, and cleaned up, so that he could go in. That wasn't fair. He'd only been with her for a couple of years. She'd had her a lifetime. She wasn't ready to step aside for him. Not out there, and certainly not in here. But it wasn't her decision, was it? It was hospital policy. She tried to stand still, but internally, a sort of momentum was building up – it made her want to swing her arms, hop from foot to foot, rock wildly on her heels. Just move her neck on the top of her spine, backwards and forwards. But she clenched her fists and concentrated on making herself be still.

He looked strange, unfamiliar in his scrubs. The hat wasn't on straight, and one rogue ear stuck out. She felt a strong urge to tuck it back inside, but she kept her hands down by her side. His eyes implored her. She put her arm around his shoulder. 'Go and be with her. Tell her I'm right here. Tell her I love her.'

'I can't go.'

'You have to go. You'll be all right. I'll be right here.'

'I'm sorry you can't come in.'

'It's as it should be. She needs you.'

She needs both of us.

At last, the doors gave one last swing. He was here. The mask was around his neck. He was pulling off the hat with one hand, holding it while he rubbed his hair. He was always doing that, rubbing his hair. He looked like Stan Laurel.

He was shaking his head.

Everything and nothing marauded through her head, and she jumped to her feet. Fear wouldn't let her sit still. He was shaking his head. That meant . . . she couldn't say out loud what that meant, not even out loud in her head. She wanted to back away from him. She wanted to stop him getting close enough to speak to her, as though if it wasn't articulated it couldn't be true, it couldn't be so.

He was in front of her now, though. For the first time in that long, long night and day, she noticed that he was clean-shaven. And he was white with shock, and he was smiling, his eyes brimming with tears.

'She's here. She's fine. They're both fine.' His voice cracked with the last sentence, and his shoulders dropped, and it was the easiest and the best thing to do, to put her arms around him and hold him.

Emma's hair was tangled and she reached up to smooth it back from her damp, flushed face. The gown she wore had come loose and it was slipping off one shoulder. Her left hand was bandaged, a plastic cannula protruding, attaching her to a drip beside the bed. The baby was barely visible inside a mound of yellow cotton blankets that lay against her right arm. A tea cosy hat covered most of her little head, and slipped down across her brow, and her tiny hands were tucked away. She looked up at them both, standing together at the door, looking at her, and her own daughter, and she smiled, beckoning them over to the bed, and gently lifting the yellow bundle in their direction.

The Problem with Oliver

Maggie O'Farrell

Fionnuala leans against the cold, salt-saturated planks of the great wooden wall that bisects the beach and pulls the cuffs of her jumper down over her hands. The sun is still bright behind the fast-moving, piled clouds, but a stiff, persistent breeze is blowing off the restless, pebble-raking sea.

She looks up at the clouds: cumulonimbus, cirrostratus, altostratus, altocumulus. She squeezes her eyes shut, trying to visualise that page in her geography notes. It is exactly seven and three-quarter weeks to her first A-level exam and the thought of it makes terror curdle inside her like old milk.

Fionnuala opens her eyes again and feels a momentary surprise at seeing the beach, the sky, the pebbles, the wet driftwood and a man in a red cagoule with his trousers rolled up, hauling a yelling child after him. She glances at her watch. Four thirty. If she isn't home in twenty minutes, there will be questions about why her orchestra practice overran. Where is he?

She shifts her school bag to the other shoulder, her thoughts slipping sideways on to their usual track, a track that runs always parallel to whatever she's doing: if she has seven and three-quarter weeks and three subjects, that gives her roughly two weeks and three and a third days for each. But if she takes one day off per week, then . . .

Suddenly he's there, right in front of her and he is cupping his freezing hands around her face and his lips are icy and rigid with cold and she is wrapped inside his big coat and the sea breeze is whipping her hair into his, so that she can't tell whose hair is whose. And her mind has slipped sideways again but this time she is just thinking: Oliver, Oliver.

Three streets away, Grainne raises her head from her bench. She glances at the locked and bolted door of the kiln. She massages her neck with two of her knuckles, then looks out of the window. The cat is inching along the wall, body held low, eyes fixed on a finch that's pecking at some crumbs. Grainne picks up a clay-heavy cloth and hurls it at the window. It thunks against the pane, scaring the bird into sudden, vocal flight. The cat stares in at her, swishing its tail like a lash.

Oliver is full of excuses: he was late out of class, the bus was delayed, the traffic terrible. He doesn't go to the local school, like Fionnuala, but a private school outside Southwold.

'How long have we got?'

'Not long.' She looks at her watch and pulls a face. 'About fifteen minutes.'

He sighs and his arms loosen around her. 'Finn,' he begins (when he'd first asked her name, she'd swallowed the last two syllables – it was less embarrassing and that way he could never find out that she was named after a mythological princess who was turned into a swan), 'I don't really know why we have to . . . carry on being this . . . this secretive. It seems kind of . . . weird. I mean, she can't be that bad, can she?'

This was the only disadvantage of him going to a different, out-of-town school. Everyone at the comprehensive knew that her mother was the mad Irish potter. Heard the one about the dyslexic Irish devil-worshipper? Sold his soul to Santa. Heard the one about the Irish turkey? It was looking forward to Christmas.

Fionnuala grimaces. 'No, she is. You don't know her.' She doesn't say that her mother has a contempt for Englishmen equalled only by her feelings towards weak tea and amoebic dysentery. She tries to joke: 'How can I tell her I've got a boyfriend called Oliver?'

He frowns, slightly hurt. 'What?'

'Well,' she says slowly. Jesus, does she have to spell it out for him? 'Irish people sometimes have a bit of a problem with that name.'

'How come?'

'You know.' Please know. 'Cromwell and all that.' She looks at his face, flushed and perplexed, close to hers. Can he really not know? Really, really? Do you know nothing about history, she wants to say, nothing at all? Then hears the question, shouted, in her mother's voice. 'Never mind,' she says.

When she pushes open the front door, a familiar smell hits her: the pungent chemicals of glazing, the chalky dampness of clay. When she was little, she used to wish her house smelt like other people's – of roast dinners, fresh bread and furniture polish.

'Hello,' she shouts as she wipes her feet, seeing, in a slight panic, sand spraying up from the mat. 'Hello?'

Then her mother is coming round the door from

the kitchen, her shirt studded with clots of dried clay, her arms grey to the elbows.

She is laughing. 'Do you know,' she is saying, 'I just had an out-of-body experience!'

Fionnuala eyes her. Has she been smoking? 'What?'

'An out-of-body experience,' she repeats. 'My first ever. I looked out of the window and I saw you coming along the pavement and do you know for a split second I thought, what am I doing out there? Why am I walking along the road?' She laughs again, looking closely at her, as if willing Fionnuala to understand. 'And then I realised it was you and I was me, in here, in the house.'

Fionnuala lets her bag slump to the floor. Her mother is mad. It's official. They don't even look alike – not any more. Not since Fionnuala started straightening her hair. 'What are you talking about?' she mutters, furious. 'How could you think I was you?' She pushes past her mother, into the kitchen. 'Anyway, I'm surprised you could see anything, through that stupid tree.'

The tree is a big bone of contention, not only between Fionnuala and her mother, but between her mother and the neighbours, the council, the tourist board – anyone and everyone. Her mother refuses to cut it or trim it or even touch it. Because it's a hawthorn tree and folklore has it that the fairies live in hawthorn trees and that they will wreak a terrible revenge on you if you damage their home. Irish folklore, of course.

Fionnuala once made the mistake of explaining this to a girl at school, who then told the whole class and soon people she didn't even know were shouting after her, 'How's the leprechaun tree?'

She looks out at the immense black-branched tree, which now covers their entire house, making it a tiny Sleeping Beauty's palace. 'Oh, please cut it, Mum,' she begs suddenly. 'Please. You don't even believe in fairies.'

'Do I not?' her mother says with that slow smile so that Fionnuala knows she's trying to annoy her. 'You can't underestimate them. They're not like your sissy English fairies. These are the great, indigenous tribes of Ireland who were driven underground by the invading Celts.'

'What are they doing in Suffolk, then?' Fionnuala mutters, reaching for the kettle.

'How was orchestra?' Grainne asks her daughter.

'All right.' Fionnuala bumps the kettle against the tap, making a loud clashing noise.

'What were you playing?'

'Um . . .' The water thunders into the metal bottom of the kettle. 'A bit of Elgar. And . . . some Britten.'

As Fionnuala turns round, Grainne sees her glance towards the beach hut key, hanging on a nail beside the back door. The hut belongs to a friend of hers in London – Grainne keeps the key for her here.

'So,' she says, picking at the clay ingrained under her fingernails. 'Do you have work to do tonight?'

'Uh-huh.' Again, Grainne sees her glance at the key, as if measuring the distance between it and her.

'Revising, is it?'

'Yeah.' Fionnuala slinks sideways and escapes from the room, forgetting the boiling kettle which is filling the air with steam.

Fionnuala has a literature test paper spread out on her desk. She is timing herself. Her alarm clock says she's been at this forty-five minutes but she's only on question two. How can that be?

She hunches closer to the block of foolscap and reads the question again: *Orwell's overriding theme is the individual caught in a hostile social mechanism. Discuss.* Fionnuala sees her pen moving: *Orwell's overriding theme*, she begins.

Then she stops.

Why had she said that to Oliver? That she could get the key to the beach hut for tomorrow? She must be mad. Does she want to . . . does she want that? She's ridiculously old not to have done it, judging by the standards of most of the people at school, but her mother has always warned her against it. Don't give them what they want, she yells, it'll save you a lot of trouble later on. Grainne had been younger than she is now when she'd had her and had to move to England to get away from the fury of her family.

'Fionnuala!' The sound of her mother's voice knifing into the silence makes her jump. 'Dinner!'

In the kitchen, her mother is dropping rippled, damp lettuce leaves on to two plates. Fionnuala seizes her left wrist. 'For Chrissake, Mum, you could have washed your hands.' Everything her mother cooks tastes of clay.

'Sorry, love. Forgot.' She splits the baked potatoes in two and slaps a yellow wedge of butter into their pale, steaming innards. 'Want to see what I made today?'

'OK,' Fionnuala says grudgingly, picking up the plates.

In the studio, Grainne uncovers a tray of Celtic crosses, wall plaques, paperweights, key fobs, pendants. Her daughter looks them over, expressionless, forking potato into her mouth.

'The usual stuff for the Yanks and the Brits,'

Grainne says. 'Eiresatz – it keeps a roof over our heads.' She whips the cover off the second tray: deep-sided bowls, curved like boat hulks, swarming with tiny three-dimensional figures.

When Fionnuala was a child, she'd loved Grainne's chunky, faceless homunculi. Grainne made her an entire house of them, complete with their own minuscule beds, cups, plates and bath. Grainne wonders for a moment where it got to.

Must be in the attic somewhere.

Fionnuala stretches out a finger and touches two embracing figures, poised on the circular brink of a bowl. Grainne watches her. Sometimes Fionnuala is so like she was at that age it makes Grainne suspicious that someone somewhere is playing a joke on them, making time loop round twice.

'I like them,' her daughter says, removing her hand. 'Will you sell them?'

'Don't know yet.' Grainne gets up quickly, covering the paperweights. Fionnuala wanders out of the room.

Before Grainne covers the bowls, she touches the embracing figures herself, once, and very lightly, finding a place where the imprint of her own thumb lies.

Fionnuala stands in the kitchen, aghast. The key is

gone. The hook where it hangs, where it always hangs, is empty. There's even a whitish shadow of the key on the wallpaper, like a photo negative. Fionnuala puts down her plate with a crash. Her pulse is clicking painfully in her neck. Her mother. Her bloody mother. How does she do that? How on earth . . .

At the sound of her mother coming along the passage behind her, Fionnuala bolts from the kitchen, into the hall and out through the front door. She hears her mother's voice, calling, 'Where in God's name are you going?'

The night is damp and stormy, the pavements slicked with wet, the sound of the sea crashing through the gaps in the buildings. Fionnuala runs the length of their road, her breath ragged and laboured. At the lighthouse, she turns left into a narrow winding street. She yanks open the phone box and steps in. She shivers inside her school shirt, the ends of her hair dripping water to the floor, to her shoulders, to the phone as she dials. Fury, or the cold, is making her shake so that she can't seem to hit the right numbers.

'Oliver? Listen, it's all off. Tomorrow's off. She knows.'

Back at the house, the windows are all burning with light. Fionnuala kicks off her sodden shoes at the door and thuds up the stairs, into her room. She knows she needs to sink on to her bed and cry – she just needs to. But as her body hits the crocheted cover her mother made for her when she was a baby, she feels the hard crinkle of paper. Fionnuala shifts her weight, pushing the damp skeins of hair away from her eyes. It's an envelope. Red, squarish. Her name in her mother's handwriting. She rips it open with the edge of her finger. A brass key drops out, on to the bed. And a note: *Bring him back for tea some afternoon. I'd like to meet him. I might even make a cake.*

Fionnuala stands and goes over to the window. The house is empty, she realises, her mother gone – somewhere. She looks out into the street. The dark, twisted branches of the hawthorn tree tap-tap against the side of the house, as if wanting to come in.

Life Begins at Forty

Patricia Scanlan

'So you're absolutely sure that you don't want a surprise party for your fortieth?' Liz, my older sister, laughs as we sit sipping vanilla coffee in the trendy new café off Griffith Avenue.

'I'm positive.' I grimace. 'It's bad enough being forty without having to make a song and dance about it in public.'

'Life begins at forty, honey,' she says airily, as our tikka wraps and salads arrive. 'Look at me, a half a stone heavier, eyesight failing, grey hair multiplying at a rate of knots, everything going south and do I care?'

'That's because you've given up. You've gone all Zen-like with all that meditation stuff you do. Well, I intend to fight ageing tooth and nail.'

'You do that, Amy,' Liz soothes, munching on a crouton.

I'm dreading forty.

I'm thirty-nine years, eleven months, two days and forty minutes old. I've a husband, Steve, eight-year-old twin daughters, Millie and Kate, all much loved. My work as an office administrator in a busy consultant's clinic is varied and satisfying. Life is good.

'Well, we have to have some sort of a celebration now that you're joining the club. I told Steve I'd try and find out what you'd *really* like to do. Will we have a girls' night in Wicklow?' Liz asks.

'Don't you mean ladies' or women's night?' I say drily. 'Girls we ain't.'

'Oh, get over it. We all had to go through it, wait until you're my age. If you think forty is bad, try forty-five.' My sister is unsympathetic to my trauma. Still, she's treating me to lunch and trying to help my darling husband, who knows my feelings about turning forty, organise some sort of birthday treat. I shouldn't be so ungracious.

We finish our wraps and order more coffee and a selection of cream cakes. It's my last fling, I promise myself. I've got to stop this comfort eating.

I bite into a creamy éclair pushing away the

thoughts of calories and cellulite and all those other horrible, guilt-inducing words that are starting to become part of my vocabulary.

'We could go to Rugatino's for a slap-up and stay the night in the cottage quaffing champers in front of the fire. No children and no husbands,' my sister suggests enthusiastically.

'Sounds blissful,' I agree. 'I'd love to get down to Wicklow for a few days. But do you think it would be a bit mean leaving Steve and the twins out of it?'

'Leave it to me. We'll have our girls' day and night on the Friday and Steve and the girls and Bill and my lot can come down on Saturday. We can have a barbecue if the weather is dry.'

I laugh. Only Liz could suggest a barbie at the end of February.

'The kids would love that. We can wrap up and drink hot ports on the deck. Jennie's all on for it,' Liz continues. Jennie is Liz's sister-in-law and she's a dote. She owns the cottage next door to Liz's. We're like a little tribe in the small development of holiday cottages where we all decamp for weekends and holidays.

'You're on,' I say, enjoying the frisson of anticipation my sister's plan generates. What could be nicer than a long, brisk walk on the beach and then to sit on the deck of our small beachside haven listening to the roar of the surf with family and dear friends, easing myself into my new decade?

'Great. That's that organised. I'd say Mum and Dad will be happy enough not to have to travel from Cork, especially if the weather's bad. We can have them to stay at Easter and have an excuse for another cake. It's so helpful of you to make organising your birthday so simple.' Liz is clearly relieved that I've taken the hassle-free birthday route.

'Paula won't be too happy that I'm not having a big bash.' I lick the last bit of cream off my fingers. Paula is my sister-in-law. She's married to Steve's brother, Tom. She's a selfish, lazy cow, to put it mildly.

'And how *are* the Freeloaders?' Liz queries as she pays the bill and shrugs into her coat.

I giggle. Liz shoots from the hip and always has. She's constantly telling me that I let Paula walk all over me and that I should draw my boundaries. I know she's right. I'm just not good at that sort of thing. But it's getting beyond a joke at this stage. Freeloaders is not far wrong when describing my in-laws. You know the type . . . the ones that arrive with one arm as long as the other, eat and drink you out of house and home and, half the times, buzz off without even doing the washing-up. My in-laws, Paula, Tom, and brats, Roger, Barry and Carla, could give masterclasses in freeloading.

When Steve and I bought our small holiday cottage in Brittas Bay six years ago we certainly didn't envisage an invasion for two weeks every summer of the in-laws from hell. But that's what's happened. Paula, Tom and Co. have come to see it as *their* cottage too.

They started arriving for weekends, unannounced, the first year. In the beginning it was fun. We all had young children. It was nice for the cousins to play together but it started becoming a habit, and Steve and I were doing all the shopping, cooking and housework.

Then Paula started bringing the kids down for a couple of days during the summer holidays, and that was when I should have stepped in and nipped it in the bud. But I'm no good at being assertive. It's a huge personality flaw and I hate myself for my wimpishness.

Of course I plan all the things I'm going to say, like:

'Paula, I don't mind you coming the odd weekend with the kids but my holidays are the only decent time I have with the girls and I want to be able to concentrate on them.'

Or: *'Paula, we really don't have the space, especially as*

the children are getting older.' This is not an excuse. We only have two bedrooms in the cottage and when the Keegans arrive, my pair end up on camp beds in the sitting room.

I keep saying I'm going to do something about it, but all I do is moan to Liz about it. I know she's sick of me. She'd have no problem putting the skids under Paula.

Steve is ambivalent about it. He feels we're lucky to have a holiday home and should share our good fortune. I wouldn't mind so much if she pulled her weight, but honestly, Paula is so lazy that I end up doing everything while she chills out on the deck reading and drinking wine and I just feel *soooo* resentful because it's my holiday too. Her kids are allowed to run riot and the poor twins invariably get into trouble, when it's Carla and the boys I should be shouting at.

It's all right for Steve to be so magnanimous. It's not his holiday that's ruined. We split our hols so that the girls can have the maximum time at the beach. Paula regularly arrives for my two weeks. I feel my husband should back me up and speak to his brother about it, but he doesn't want to cause bad feeling.

'What about *my* bad feelings?' I ask resentfully, every summer, as I prepare to go back to work after another ruined holiday. It's the one issue that causes conflict between us and I'm weary of it.

This year, *definitely*, I'm putting an end to it, I decide as I emerge from the café into a howling gale that whips my hair around my face and reddens my cheeks with its icy, stinging fingers. We don't linger. Liz has to pick up my twins and her youngest boy from school and I've to get back to work. I'm so lucky to have her. If it weren't for Liz I'd have had second thoughts about staying at work once the girls were too old for the crèche. She's like a second mother to them. Paula would never offer to help out if you were in a fix. She's one of life's great Me, Me, Me's and that's probably why I feel so resentful.

The Keegans go on a foreign holiday every year. Paula and her girlfriends jet off to Boston or New York for pre-Christmas shopping weekends. She's never once asked me to join them. And she always had some excuse on the rare occasions when I asked her to mind the twins when they were younger. I stopped asking but it took me a long time to realise that Steve and I were being used.

I know it's childish and silly but part of me is glad that I'm not having a big party just so that I don't have to invite them. What is it about the Keegans? They press all my buttons and bring out the worst in me.

Fortunately, I'm so busy when I get back to work, I forget all about my in-laws and they are far from my mind for the next couple of weeks until I get a call from Paula a few days before my birthday.

'Hi, Amy,' she trills. My heart sinks to my boots. The only time Paula rings is when she wants to moan or has something to boast about.

'So!' she demands. 'What are you doing for the big Four 0? Is Steve bringing you away? Tom took me to Prague for mine.' We're sick of hearing about the trip to Prague.

'No, it's going to be very low-key,' I say off-handedly. If she gets wind of the weekend in Wicklow I wouldn't put it past her to muscle in, so I say nothing.

'Oh come on, no party, or even a meal out?' Paula is incredulous.

'Just a cake with the kids. It's all I want, honestly. You know me, I hate fuss.'

'But it's your fortieth,' she protests. 'Steve should push the boat out.'

'I didn't say he wasn't, Paula!' I can't keep the edge of exasperation out of my voice. 'Look, I'm up to my eyes here today. I'll catch you again,' I fib.

'Oh . . . oh! OK, I'll pop a card in the post for you then.' She's clearly disappointed.

'Lovely,' I say insincerely. 'Bye, thanks for ringing.'

Phew! I think as I hang up. Then I start to worry. What if she hears of my night out with the girls in Wicklow? I resolve to warn them not to mention it to her if they see her in the summer. Bad humour envelops me. So what if I'm having a girls' night. It's none of her business. Why can't I just deal with it and say it to her straight out?

I try and forget about it, but it niggles and I bring up the subject with Liz that evening. 'Am I being a wagon? Should I invite her?' I grumble.

'Absolutely *not*!' Liz is emphatic. 'We are not spending our precious night listening to her twittering on about her new conservatory or her trip to New York and all the rest of it. Forget it.'

'Fine,' I capitulate happily, glad of my sister's authoritative stance. I don't feel such a heel.

My birthday dawns, dark and windy. I'm smothered with hugs and kisses from the girls and Steve's gift of a sapphire-and-diamond pendant brings gasps of appreciation from his three women.

'I thought it would match your eyes,' he says, a tad bashfully. 'You can change it if you don't like it.'

'It's gorgeous, Steve, I love it.' I'm thrilled with his thoughtful gift and kiss him soundly, much to the girls' delight.

'Oohhh . . . kissy-kissy!!' squeals Kate. Steve laughs but I can tell he's pleased that I love it.

'We helped Dad pick it,' Millie assures me, slipping an arm around my neck.

'I couldn't have got a nicer present,' I tell her, basking in the joy of being so loved and cherished.

'Auntie Liz has a surprise for you so you've to be dressed by eight o'clock,' Kate informs me gleefully. I know Liz has something up her sleeve. She's told me to be ready to leave early. This is great, I think happily as I stand under the bracing spray of the shower while my darlings make pancakes for breakfast. Forty's not so bad after all.

'Where are we going?' I ask an hour later as Liz heads for Wicklow via the East Link.

'You'll see,' she replies smugly and it's only when we take the slip road to Enniskerry that comprehension dawns.

'Are we going to Powerscourt Springs?'

'You bet we are. Happy birthday, little sister. I hope you're all prepared for a day of blissful pampering. I sure am. Jennie's meeting us there.'

A day at a luxurious health spa with the girls. What more could I want? Forty is getting better by the second.

It is the most perfect day. I'm massaged,

manicured, pedicured and pampered to within an inch of my life and then, as the sun begins to turn the Wicklow Hills pink and gold, chauffeured to dinner at a riverside restaurant and forced to drink gallons of champagne. Later snuggled in warm dressing gowns in front of a blazing fire, listening to the roar of the sea, we watch a DVD of *Sex and the City*. It's the best birthday I've ever had.

It's lovely to see the girls tumbling out of the car and galloping across the dunes the next day. A brisk walk in the bracing, salty air, the waves pounding against the shore, diminishes our hangovers. We adults laugh and joke as the kids investigate the treasure troves to be found among the rocks. I feel really happy and contented and look forward to our barbecue later on.

'Oh no! It's that gang!' Kate scowls as recognition dawns when we see figures approaching along the beach.

I don't believe it. It was too good to last. Paula is waving gaily and I hear Liz curse under her breath.

'Hey, you guys, better late than never,' Tom declares expansively.

I look at Steve. He's not best pleased.

'Steve told me you'd all gone to Powerscourt Springs. You never let on,' Paula accuses, eyes beady flints behind the smile as she falls into place beside Jennie, Liz and myself.

'I didn't know,' I manage weakly.

'It was a surprise. My treat,' Liz informs her curtly.

'Oh! I could have joined you last night,' she persists.

This is too much. Since when do I have to start telling Madame Paula my every move?

'We were having a girls' night,' I hear myself say. 'I guess we didn't get to New York, like you and your friends. But Wicklow suits us fine.'

She inhales sharply and Liz flashes me an approving glance.

I don't care any more. I've had enough. I'm forty and it's time to draw a line in the sand. Literally.

'Um . . . right. Well, Steve mentioned you were coming down for the weekend. I rang to wish you happy birthday, you see. We thought we'd come and give you your present.'

'That's very kind, Paula. It's a bit of a trek up and down in the one day just to give me a present. It could have waited.' I'm feeling reckless now. She's not getting away with it this time.

'*Oh!*' She stares at me, not sure how to react. 'We brought the sleeping bags, we can doss on the floor,' she ventures.

I draw a breath. I can sense Liz and Jennie waiting for my response. Bill is collecting periwinkles with the kids while Tom and Steve skim stones along the waves. Gulls circle and squeal. My lovely day is ruined.

Do it, do it, a voice urges.

I swallow, hard. And then I think, to hell with her. She's not my friend and never has been. She's just someone I have to put up with.

'Actually, Paula.' I come to a stop and eyeball her. 'I've been meaning to say this for a while. The cottage really is too small for all of us and I don't like putting the girls out of their beds. It's not fair. And while we're on the subject, if you don't mind, this year and from now on, I'd like to spend my holidays alone with the girls. Our time is precious and that two weeks I have off in the summer is the only decent chunk of time I get to spend with them. There are nice, reasonably priced hotels and B&Bs in the area. I'm sure you can find somewhere cheap'n'cheerful to stay. And to be honest I'd prefer if you would give me advance notice if you're calling, it just makes life easier for me in case we've made plans and so on.' I'm on a roll.

Paula lowers her gaze first. Two ruby spots stain her cheeks. 'I see,' she says tightly, thin-lipped. 'Fair enough.' She can't hide her shock.

'Great, that's sorted. Let's go and put the kettle on,' I suggest brightly. I'm exhilarated. I've done it. I've said my piece. I can't believe it.

'Well done, Amy,' Liz murmurs as we pour steaming tea into mugs ten minutes later. Paula is chatting to Jennie on the deck; her brittle tones carry in on the breeze. 'She's raging,' Liz chuckles.

I start laughing too. 'I don't care. She's had it coming for a long time.'

'When the Keegans get up to go, let them go,' I whisper to Steve. 'I've had a word with Paula. Sorted things.'

'Right,' he agrees. 'If that's what you want.'

'It is. My present to myself.' I smile at him. He hugs me supportively.

They leave an hour later.

I'm free.

Roll on summer.

The Shape of Ladies

Alexander McCall Smith

Mma Ramotswe, sole begetter and proprietrix of the No. 1 Ladies' Detective Agency, Botswana's only detective agency for the problems of ladies (and others), was sitting in her office, drinking a cup of redbush tea. It was her fourth cup of bush tea that day, but that did not matter. She could drink six or even seven cups if she wished, as bush tea contained no caffeine and was said to be rather good for you. So she was never affected by those worries which coffee drinkers had about having too much caffeine, or which tea drinkers had about their teeth being turned brown by all the tannin in their favourite brew.

Mma Makutsi, her assistant, had recently started to drink ordinary tea again, and had to watch how many cups she consumed during the day, or she would find difficulty in sleeping at night. And Mma Makutsi was also worried that too much tea might not help her complexion, which was a difficult one.

'I have heard that drinks like coffee and tea may not be good for the skin,' she remarked to Mma Ramotswe. 'Perhaps I should stop drinking them.'

'I have heard that too, Mma,' said Mma Ramotswe. 'But you cannot stop everything that you like just for the sake of looking good. That is the trouble with these fashionable ladies who starve themselves in order to stay thin. What's the point of that? Why be hungry and unhappy when you could just as easily be full of good food and happy?'

'You are right, Mma,' said Mma Makutsi. 'I have heard such ladies described as fashion victims. That is very sad, isn't it.'

Mma Ramotswe nodded. 'It is much better to be traditionally built. Traditionally built people are always happier. Have you noticed that, Mma Makutsi? Have you seen how miserable those thin people look most of the time, and just how contented traditionally built people look?'

Mma Makutsi looked out of the window. Outside the office, in the heat of the day, the acacia trees looked drained of life and energy. Under the relentless hammer of the midday sun, nature seemed to be browbeaten into submission, afraid to move, torpid. On a branch of one of the trees a grey lourie, known as the go-away bird because of its cry, perched half concealed by the foliage. Mma Makutsi watched the bird, and thought. One never saw traditionally built birds, she reflected; such birds, if they existed, would be unable to get off the ground to escape their predators. A traditionally built bird would not last long.

She turned to Mma Ramotswe. 'Of course what you say is right, Mma,' she began. 'But do you not think that you might be saying that because you cannot lose weight? Would you say the same thing if you were not traditionally built yourself?'

There was a silence in the room – a silence which was suddenly broken by the plaintive cry outside of the go-away bird. It was as if the bird himself had heard this remark and wished to refute it.

Mma Ramotswe stared at Mma Makutsi, who dropped her gaze. The younger woman had been wanting to say something like that for some time now, whenever Mma Ramotswe started to go on about the advantages of being traditionally built, but perhaps she should not have said it. Mma Ramotswe was such a kind woman, who was always courteous to others, and Mma Makutsi now remembered the numerous acts of kindness which she herself had been shown by her employer. The first of these had been Mma Ramotswe's taking her on as a secretary, when there was not really enough work to justify such a post – even in the case of somebody who had got 97 per cent in the final examinations of the Botswana Secretarial College.

'I'm sorry, Mma Ramotswe,' she began, stumbling over the words in her embarrassment. 'I had not . . . I had not thought before I started –'

Mma Ramotswe cut her short. 'Don't worry, Mma. What you said is true enough, I think. Maybe I do go on a bit about the advantages of being traditionally built. But I don't think that it's because I couldn't lose weight. Of course I could lose weight.'

Mma Makutsi had not intended to show surprise, but her eyes widened nonetheless. 'Could you, Mma?' she asked. 'Are you sure about that?'

'Of course I could,' said Mma Ramotswe. 'If I wanted to. But I'm not sure if I want to, you see. I am not going to be intimidated into going on one of these diets. Why should I? I am happy as I am. You know that.'

Mma Makutsi smiled. 'Oh, I know that, Mma,' she said. 'But you know it's not just a question of happiness. It's also a question of health.'

Mma Ramotswe took a sip of her bush tea. 'I am very healthy,' she said firmly. 'And this bush tea keeps me that way.'

'So we'll never know whether you have the will-power or not,' muttered Mma Makutsi, almost under her breath.

Mma Makutsi had not intended this remark to have any particular effect. In fact, she had more or less made it to herself. But it did not go unnoticed by Mma Ramotswe, who put her teacup down on the desk with a sudden thud.

'If you need me to show you that, Mma,' she said, 'then I shall be very happy to go on a diet and settle the matter.'

'Oh, please don't . . .' began Mma Makutsi. But her protest was waved away by Mma Ramotswe.

'I have made up my mind, Mma Makutsi,' she said. 'So I suggest that we get on with some work. The matter is now closed.'

Mma Ramotswe drove home in her tiny white van, back down Tlokweng Road and into the area of town known as the Village. She drove past Mrs Moffat's house, with its great jacaranda tree that shaded the house and half the garden. She slowed down, seeing her friend in her garden watering her vegetables, and waved. Mrs Moffat waved back, and Mma Ramotswe noticed for the first time that her friend was not at all traditionally built. What was her secret? she wondered. She seemed to enjoy cake well enough; when they met for tea there was always some cake on the table. But how many pieces did she eat? wondered Mma Ramotswe. Did she ever take a second piece, or did she stop at one? She tried to remember the last time she had had tea with Mrs Moffat. They had sat out on the veranda and talked and there had been four pieces of cake on a plate in front of them. She remembered that cake, which had been covered with a delicious lemon icing, and she could see Mrs Moffat offering her a second piece, and she remembered taking it. Then she recalled licking the icing off the tips of her fingers and being offered yet another piece. And she had accepted. Yes, she had; the memory was coming back clearly now. So that answered that: she had eaten three pieces of cake to Mrs Moffat's single piece. Perhaps that provided the answer to the question which she had asked in the first place. Mrs Moffat was not traditionally built because she usually only ate one piece of cake. Traditionally built people ate at least three pieces.

When she arrived home, she went straight into the

kitchen. It was half past five, and this was the time that she liked to sit on her veranda, a cup of tea in hand, and observe the ending of the day. On the road outside her house, which was normally quiet, there would be a few passing cars as people made their way back home. She recognised many of these cars – the large red car that belonged to the man who worked for the diamond company; the sleek black car of the woman who had a beauty salon in one of the hotels; the car that belonged to her neighbour, who had those unpleasant yellow dogs that liked to bark at night. That last car was not a car she would have liked to travel in, with its windows covered with marks where the dogs had pressed their moist noses against the glass.

She watched the cars, and the passers-by, people walking home on foot – a man whistling a tune she half recognised; a young boy shuffling along, scuffing his shoes in the dirt at the side of the road, who looked up and saw her through the hedge and looked away quickly, as if expecting some reproach. She smiled; she would not reprimand a young boy in public these days, at least not in Gaborone, although adults would do that quite readily in the villages. *It takes a whole village to raise a child*, people said, and Mma Ramotswe agreed. But things had changed in town, and people were less ready to remind children of what they should do and what they should not do. That was bad. How could children grow up knowing what to do if adults were not there to tell them? Mma Ramotswe shook her head.

Her tea finished, she stood up and made her way back into the kitchen. There was a meal to be prepared now, and she opened the fridge door to take out the small parcel of beef that she had bought the previous day from the supermarket at the beginning of the Tlokweng Road. It was good Botswana beef, they had said, and the thought of it made her mouth water. This was fine, grass-fed beef, from the land that she knew so well, from cattle which might have belonged to people she knew, or their cousins, or somebody with whom she could easily establish some form of contact. For that is what Botswana was like. Everybody would know somebody who knew somebody else; nobody could be a stranger, no matter how hard he tried.

She took the beef out of the packet and put it on a chopping board. The meat was tender and light red; it would make a very fine stew once she had added onions to it, and some carrots too. And then there would be some mashed potatoes, which the children, the two adopted orphans, loved to eat. Puso, the boy, especially liked potatoes prepared in that way. He would make a little hill of the potatoes and create a dam at the top, a dam filled with rich, heavy gravy. Mma Ramotswe smiled at the thought. Boys were like that – they never stopped playing. Just like men.

It was hungry work making the stew and the smell of the meat being browned in her large blackened saucepan made her stomach seem to knock at her ribs. Yes, she would enjoy the stew too, and would perhaps have two helpings – there was certainly enough for that. But then she stopped. Her diet had begun, and she had told herself she would have only a very small portion of stew and no potatoes at all. It was a terrible thought. Perhaps the diet should begin tomorrow, after breakfast. Perhaps it should begin at the end of the week, once she had given herself time to get used to the idea of being hungry. Perhaps . . .

At the table, seated with Mr J. L. B. Matekoni and the children, Mma Ramotswe took the lid off the pot in which the stew had been brought from the kitchen. Immediately a rich, tempting smell filled the air, making Mr J. L. B. Matekoni lean forward with anticipation.

'This smells very good,' he said, rubbing his hands together. 'I have been working very hard all day and am looking forward to this good meal you have made, Mma Ramotswe.'

Mma Ramotswe looked at him and frowned. 'I have been working hard all day too,' she snapped. 'There is not just one person in this house who works hard.'

Mr J. L. B. Matekoni looked up in surprise. It was unlike Mma Ramotswe to snap at him, and yet her response to his innocent comment had been distinctly short. 'I'm sorry,' he said, mildly. 'I know that you work hard, Mma Ramotswe. Everybody knows that.'

Mma Ramotswe said nothing, but concentrated on ladling out helpings of the stew and vegetables that went with it. She gave Mr J. L. B. Matekoni a particularly large portion, and she also gave generous helpings to Puso and his sister, Motheleli. But when it came to her own turn, she gave herself only a very small amount, barely enough to cover one corner of the plate.

'Are you not hungry tonight?' asked Mr J. L. B. Matekoni. 'This stew is very good, Mma Ramotswe. You should have some more.'

'No thank you, Rra,' said Mma Ramotswe. She tried to make her voice sound normal, but it came out sounding irritated, as if she were cross with Mr J. L. B. Matekoni for even raising the issue. He said nothing further. Women were sometimes inexplicably moody, he had observed, and this was an example of that. And the best thing to do in such circumstances was to be completely quiet. Resistance was useless; all men knew that.

Over the next two days, although she cooked good meals for the household, Mma Ramotswe ate very little. At work, when Mma Makutsi took two large doughnuts out of a greasy paper bag and offered one to her, Mma Ramotswe merely shook her head curtly.

'Then I shall have to eat it myself,' said Mma Makutsi, laying it carefully on a piece of scrap paper at the side of her desk. 'I don't mind eating two doughnuts.'

Mma Ramotswe looked across the room at the doughnut. It was a very fine doughnut, and she would dearly have loved to have savoured it with the cup of bush tea that was before her on the desk, but she had made the decision to go on a diet and she was determined to go ahead with it. After all, this was not just a question of weight; it was a question of willpower.

After a few minutes, Mma Makutsi reached out for the second doughnut and sunk her teeth into a corner of it, closing her eyes with delight as she did so. Mma

Ramotswe watched, and for a few moment her upper lip trembled – not enough to be seen by Mma Makutsi, had her eyes been open at the time, but enough to be felt by Mma Ramotswe herself, who struggled to control it.

'I wish you wouldn't sit there and eat doughnuts all day,' she said testily. 'It doesn't give a very good impression to the clients. They don't expect the people who are meant to be working on their cases to be sitting around eating doughnuts.'

Mma Makutsi opened her eyes. 'But we have no clients at the moment,' she said, through a mouthful of doughnut. 'No clients at all.' As she spoke, a few crumbs of doughnut escaped from her lips and shot forwards on to the desk. She reached for them and stuffed them back into her mouth.

It was very clear to Mma Makutsi what the problem was. The new diet of Mma Ramotswe's was making her feel so hungry and uncomfortable that she was snapping at people for the slightest thing. And the thought occurred to her: if this is the way that Mma Ramotswe was when she was on the way to being thin, then one could only imagine how difficult she would be once she reached her goal. She would be impossible to work with, sitting there being short with anybody who said or did anything.

At lunch break, when Mma Ramotswe went off shopping by herself, Mma Makutsi wandered out of the office and into the workshop of Tlokweng Road Speedy Motors, the business with which they shared premises. Mr J. L. B. Matekoni, spanner in hand, was standing over an exposed car engine, talking to one of the apprentices. Mma Makutsi drew him aside.

'Have you noticed how touchy Mma Ramotswe has been over the last few days?' she asked.

Mr J. L. B. Matekoni put the spanner down on an upturned oil drum. 'Oh yes, Mma,' he sighed. 'She has been very cross with the world. It is most unlike her. And she seems to have lost her appetite too.'

Mma Makutsi laughed. 'I don't think that she has lost her appetite,' she said. 'I think that her appetite is still there.'

'Then why is she not eating?' asked Mr J. L. B. Matekoni. 'Is she ill, do you think?'

'She is dieting,' said Mma Makutsi. 'She wants to become thin.'

Mr J. L. B. Matekoni stared at Mma Makutsi. 'But she cannot!' he exclaimed. 'I did not want to marry a thin lady. I wanted a nice, plump lady. She cannot do this.'

Mma Makutsi thought for a moment. An idea was coming to her as to how she might deal with this, and she leaned forward and grasped Mr J. L. B. Matekoni's arm as she explained to him what she might do to bring Mma Ramotswe to her senses. He listened, and nodded. It seemed to him to be a good plan, a clever plan – just what one might expect from an intelligent woman like Mma Makutsi, with her large round spectacles.

Once Mma Ramotswe had come back from her shopping and had settled back at her desk, Mma Makutsi looked across the room and addressed her.

'I was talking to Mr J. L. B. Matekoni at lunchtime,' she said. 'And he told me that he is very unhappy.'

Mma Ramotswe raised an eyebrow. 'Why should he be unhappy?' she asked. 'The garage is doing well.'

'It's nothing to do with that,' said Mma Makutsi. 'He's worried that you will become thin. He knows that you are a strong-willed person and that it will be easy for you to lose weight, but he does not want that to happen. He thinks that traditionally built ladies are far more beautiful.'

Mma Ramotswe looked down at her hands, which were folded over her lap. 'Is that really what he thinks?' she asked.

'Yes,' said Mma Makutsi. 'That is what he thinks.'

Mma Ramotswe unfolded her hands. 'Perhaps . . .' she began.

She did not finish the sentence. Mma Makutsi had now taken out the bag of doughnuts which the apprentice had been sent off to buy after her lunch-time conversation with Mr J. L. B. Matekoni. She rose to her feet and brought the bag over to the other woman.

Mma Ramotswe stared into the bag.

'Oh well,' she said.

The Problem of Men

Alexander McCall Smith

Precious Ramotswe, more generally known as Mma Ramotswe, was the founder and owner of the No. 1 Ladies' Detective Agency, Botswana's only detective agency for the solution of the problems of ladies – and of others. It was a Friday morning, and she was sitting in her office with her assistant Mma Makutsi, reflecting on a particularly difficult case in which she had been involved. Outside, the sun was high in the sky, beating down on the green canopy of the acacia trees; and the air was still. It was not a day to do very much, other than to think.

It was not that the case in question had involved any particularly difficult inquiries; it had really been quite a simple matter. It was the emotional aspects of it all that had proved to be so demanding. It was so hard to break the news to a client that her husband had been unfaithful, and yet that was the result of so many investigations. And there was that poor, nervous woman, sitting in the client's chair, watching Mma Ramotswe with her wide eyes and receiving the tawdry details of what they had seen. Each sentence seemed to fall like a hammer blow upon her, and at one point Mma Ramotswe had stopped and wondered whether she shouldn't just say: 'Of course, we could be wrong about all this. Maybe the young woman we saw him with was a cousin or somebody like that.' But she knew that she could not do so, and so she had persisted and watched the woman's world collapse about her.

'That was a very hard thing to do, Mma Makutsi,' said Mma Ramotswe as they sat and drank their morning cup of redbush tea.

'It is never easy to give such news,' agreed Mma Makutsi. 'But then she probably knew all along that her husband was behaving badly. That was why she came to see us in the first place.'

'She was hoping that we would set her mind at rest,' said Mma Ramotswe. 'And we have just made her unhappy.'

For a few moments nothing was said. Then Mma

Ramotswe broke the silence. 'But it is never easy for women,' she said. 'If you are a man, then you can behave as you like. If you are tired of one lady, you can find another. That just isn't fair, is it, Mma?'

Mma Makutsi nodded in agreement. 'Men think that this is the way the world should be,' she said. 'They think that it is right that everything should be suited to them.'

'It is very bad,' said Mma Ramotswe. 'And women let them get away with it.'

'But what can we do?' asked Mma Makutsi. 'It is not easy to change things. There is not very much we can do.'

Mma Ramotswe had to agree. Mma Makutsi was right – things were not easily changed, and yet she was not sure that she agreed with her view that nothing could be done. She would have to think of something, as that evening she had been invited to speak to the Ladies' Club of Gaborone on the subject of 'The Problem of Men' and she could hardly talk about a problem without offering a solution. And yet what was one to do about men? Mma Makutsi apparently had no suggestions, and she herself was far from certain.

At home that evening, as she prepared the evening meal for Mr J. L. B. Matekoni and the two foster-children, Mma Ramotswe's mind was still on the talk that she was due to give. She now rather regretted agreeing to do it; it would have been easy to say no, it would have been easy to claim to be too busy – and she was, was she not? There was a lot to do in the office and she had a house to run and her husband, Mr J. L. B. Matekoni, to look after. It would have been perfectly proper to claim to have too much to do.

But she had agreed, and that was all there was to it. One of the things that she believed very strongly in was keeping one's word. Her late father, that great man, Mr Obed Ramotswe, had stressed to her that if you made a promise, then you had to keep it, no matter what. He had never let her down – not once – and she had never known him to let anybody else down either. That was because he believed in the old Botswana values, for which there was no substitute, no matter what modern people said.

Around the table that evening, although the children were talkative enough, and although Mr J. L. B. Matekoni had something to say on the subject of a difficult car repair he had been attempting that day, Mma Ramotswe was largely silent.

'Are you worried about something?' asked Mr J. L. B. Matekoni. 'You are not saying much.'

'I have nothing much to say,' said Mma Ramotswe. 'Perhaps I shall have more to say tomorrow, but tonight I have very little to say.'

She realised that she had not answered his question about being worried, but she did not want to talk about her speaking engagement, even with Mr J. L. B. Matekoni.

After they had finished the meal, he stood up and announced that he and the children would wash up the dishes. Then he saw her to her tiny white van, which was parked outside, and opened the door for her.

'You must not be nervous about speaking to these ladies,' he said, confidentially. 'I am sure that you will speak very well. I am sure of that.'

She looked at him. 'I do not know what to say,' she confessed. 'That is my problem. I do not know what to say.'

'What is the subject of your talk?' asked Mr J. L. B. Matekoni. 'Perhaps I can give you some ideas.'

She thought quickly. How could she tell him that she was talking about the problem of men? No man would understand what that was about; indeed Mr J. L. B. Matekoni might feel that he was somehow part of the problem.

'It is about women's business,' said Mma

Ramotswe lightly. 'This Ladies' Club likes to talk about all sorts of things that concern ladies.'

Mr J. L. B. Matekoni nodded. 'So they have invited you because you are a lady detective?' he asked.

'I think so,' said Mma Ramotswe.

'So that is what you are going to talk about,' concluded Mr J. L. B Matekoni. 'You are going to talk about how a lady goes about being a detective.'

Mma Ramotswe was silent. That was not true, but perhaps she did not need to say anything more.

'Well,' went on Mr J. L. B. Matekoni, 'you will have a lot to talk about. You have a lot of experience now. You can tell them about some of your cases.'

Yes, thought Mma Ramotswe. That's exactly what I can do. I can tell them about some of my cases and the men I have encountered in them. I can tell them about the bad behaviour of men. The ladies will be interested in that.

She drove the tiny white van down Zebra Drive and out on to the road that led to the technical college. The Ladies' Club was meeting in a room at the college, as they were expecting a large turnout and they needed somewhere larger than their usual small church hall.

'Many of the ladies have strong views on this subject,' the organiser had said to her. 'There will be many ladies at your talk, Mma.'

And indeed by the time that Mma Ramotswe arrived at the college, it was clear that the organiser had been right. As she stood outside the lecture room, talking to the other woman, people were still arriving. And from inside the room there emanated that hum of conversation that suggests a large crowd.

'There are many, many people here,' said the organiser. 'You are our most popular speaker this year. We are very pleased that you have come to talk to us.'

'How long would you like me to talk for?' asked Mma Ramotswe. She had imagined that twenty minutes might be about right. That would enable her to say something and yet leave time for questions.

'About two hours,' said the organiser. 'We will start at eight o'clock and you should finish by ten.'

Mma Ramotswe gasped. 'I cannot do that,' she said. 'I have never spoken for two hours before. I cannot speak that long.'

'Well, one hour then,' said the organiser. 'One hour will be enough.'

'No,' said Mma Ramotswe. 'I cannot talk for one hour. I am far too busy to talk for one hour. I shall talk for half an hour.'

The organiser opened her mouth to say something but thought better of it and nodded her assent. 'We should go in now,' she said. 'The ladies are waiting.'

Mma Ramotswe took a deep breath and followed her into the room. Inside, seated on folding wooden chairs, were ten rows of ladies. Many of them were engaged in conversation with those around them, but when Mma Ramotswe entered the room the hubbub died down. They looked expectantly at Mma Ramotswe. So this was the famous lady detective! So this was the founder of the No. 1 Ladies' Detective Agency!

The organiser clapped her hands together. 'Ladies! You are welcome to the meeting, which is going to begin right now. And we are very lucky, are we not, to have a very important speaker tonight, Precious Ramotswe. This lady is the only lady detective in Botswana and so we are all waiting very eagerly to hear what she has to say.'

At this, several members of the audience uttered sounds of general agreement which the organiser acknowledged with a nod of her head.

'But you have not come to hear me, ladies,' went on the organiser. 'I have many things to say on the subject of tonight's talk, but you have not come to hear my views on this issue. It is Mma Ramotswe whom you have come to hear. Is that not so?'

Again there were murmurs of agreement. 'So in that case,' said the organiser, 'I shall ask Mma Ramotswe to speak to you. And the subject of her talk is an important one. It is "The Problem with Men".'

'No,' said Mma Ramotswe. 'It is "The Problem *of* Men".'

The organiser looked at her notes and then looked back at Mma Ramotswe. 'It says here that it is "The Problem *with* Men". But it is your talk, Mma, and I must not interfere. You can decide what your talk is to be called.'

'"The Problem of Men",' said Mma Ramotswe firmly. 'That is the title of my talk.'

'That is fine then,' said the organiser. '"The Problem of Men". That is also an important topic. You must speak on it, Mma. The ladies did not come here to hear the two of us discussing the title. You are the one who must speak.'

'That is true,' said Mma Ramotswe. 'That is why I am trying to speak.'

'Then you must speak,' said the organiser. 'I have nothing further to say.'

'I shall begin then,' said Mma Ramotswe.

'Good,' said the organiser.

Mma Ramotswe took a step forward and placed her hands on the table which separated her from her audience. She looked out at the ladies.

'Good evening,' she said.

Several of the ladies returned her greeting. Others smiled, looking at Mma Ramotswe expectantly.

'Now,' said Mma Ramotswe, looking over the heads of her audience to those sitting in the back row. 'There are many ladies who wonder what is wrong with men. Ladies have been asking this question for many years and they have not yet found the answer. Sometimes there are ladies who think that they have found the answer, but when you ask them what this answer is, they cannot give it to you. That is the problem with this question. There is no answer.'

She paused. There was complete silence in the room, apart from a noise in one corner, where one of the ladies had dropped a purse on the floor and was struggling to recover it from under her chair.

Mma Ramotswe thought. She had imagined that she might talk about some of her cases, where men were shown to have behaved badly, but now that she came to order her thoughts, her mind seemed a complete blank. There were so many cases of this sort that they seemed to merge into one another. There was the case of the government man, who was arrogant and who had had to be taught a lesson of humility. There was the case of the man who had let a girl down as a young man, not much more than a boy really, and had then regretted it very much later on. At least he had tried to set things right later. There was the case of the man who was carrying on affairs with two ladies at the same time and who had been unmasked by some clever work on the part of Mma Makutsi. All of these cases were instances of masculine bad behaviour, and surely it would be easy to tell stories about that.

But then she stopped and she saw the face of Mr J. L. B. Matekoni, that great mechanic, who was capable of such kindness and who that very evening had offered to do the washing-up. She remembered how he had fixed her tiny white van for her even before they had become engaged to be married. She remembered the many acts of kindness that he had carried out for Mma Potokwani, the matron at the orphan farm. She remembered how he had fixed the water pump at the orphan farm time after time, nursing it back to health in circumstances when a lesser mechanic – and a lesser man – would have condemned it out of hand.

And then she thought of her father, of that great man, Obed Ramotswe, a miner who had scrimped and saved in order to build a future for her. He had taught her about the old Botswana values and told her of how he had met Seretse Khama himself, first President of Botswana and Paramount Chief. And of how he had shaken the hand of Khama when he had paid a visit to Mochudi. There was not a day, not one, when she did not think about her father, and of how she would love him to be able to see how well she had done and how happy she was with Mr J. L. B. Matekoni.

She looked at the audience. Two ladies in the front row were staring at her, and one was whispering to the other.

Mma Ramotswe began to speak again. 'I had come here tonight to talk about all the problems that men create for women. These problems are very big, and we all know what they are. We all know about the men who are violent, the men who are abusive, the men who spend all the family money on drink. We all know about those.'

The audience had become perfectly quiet. The

women in the front row who had been whispering to one another stopped now.

'But then,' said Mma Ramotswe, 'I have just been thinking about the good men that I know. And there are many good men. In fact, the more I think of it, the more I realise that there are maybe more good men than bad men. What do you think, ladies? Are there more good men than bad men?'

For a few moments nobody spoke. Then a woman at the back stood up and said: 'I think that there are many, many good men. And I think that even the men who do not seem so good have a good side to them, and that you can find that side if you look hard enough.'

'Yes,' said a woman from somewhere in the middle. 'What my sister has just said is right. There are many good men. I do not think that there is a problem with men.'

'Or a problem of men,' interjected Mma Ramotswe.

'No. Nor that.'

'So perhaps we should end the meeting on that note,' said Mma Ramotswe, sitting down on the chair behind the table.

The organiser stood up again and clapped her hands for silence:

'Ladies, this has been a very interesting evening,' she said. 'We have decided that we should not see men as a problem. That is a good decision to have reached, although it does not seem to have taken us a long time to reach it. In fact, we have reached it rather quickly.' She paused. 'But maybe we can come back to this subject some other day, and we can get another speaker.' This last remark was accompanied by a sideways glance at Mma Ramotswe, who just smiled.

That Monday, in the office of the No. 1 Ladies' Detective Agency, Mma Makutsi asked Mma Ramotswe how Friday's meeting had gone.

'Did you sort out the problem with men?' she enquired.

'*Of* men,' corrected Mma Ramotswe. 'No, we did not sort that out. In fact, we decided that . . .' She tailed off.

'Yes?' asked Mma Makutsi.

'You know, Mma Makutsi, not all men are a problem,' said Mma Ramotswe.

Mma Makutsi stared at her employer. 'Have you been weak, Mma? Were all those ladies weak?'

Mma Ramotswe did not say anything at first. She looked out of the window at the thorn tree behind the office. There were two grey doves on a branch of the tree, two faithful grey doves. They sat beside each other on their branch, dappled by the sun through the delicate leaves of the tree.

'It is time for more bush tea, I think,' said Mma Ramotswe.

A Kiss in the Tomatoes

Adriana Trigiani

I am so angry at my husband my face matches my bright red turtleneck sweater. My head looks like the stub end of a match. Lit. Thank goodness red is my colour because I've been angry for three days now, and it doesn't look like it's going to subside. In our annual spring Holiday Negotiations, as we call them when we're speaking, we decided that this running from one in-law's home to the other each Easter was wearing thin, so we decided to stay home. Well, we were going to stay home until my mother suffered an injury and we were lured back to Chicago on the first plane out of New York on Holy Thursday.

My husband had a notion that Mother was faking, because he called to check on her, and she was downright bubbly until she figured out it was him. I called Mother's best friend, Agnes Castlewood, who (despite two hearing aids, a cane and orthotic shoes with custom metal plates) gets around better than any other seventy-something in the Chicago-land area and therefore can be counted on in a crisis. All dear Agnes wants in return for her trouble is a dozen fresh bagels sent every so often from Bagels on the Square in Greenwich Village. This harmless payola keeps Agnes fairly honest about Mother's condition, well, it did until now. When I pressed Agnes about Mother's story it was full of holes. I believe Mother slipped Agnes a twenty because she was very vague about the nature of Mother's infirmity, only that she had 'taken a spill' and then, in a very wimpy voice kept saying, 'It's best if you come home immediately.' So we did.

It wasn't easy to pack up three boys, Aaron, eight, Emilio seven and James, five (known around here as James the First, because he was conceived the first time in my life that I did not use birth control), their stuff, their father and me on short notice. Alas, I did it, and while I'm wearing a heating pad on my lower back for a pulled muscle and an ice pack on my head for a throbbing migraine, I survived the taxi ride from Greenwich Village to La Guardia airport without killing anyone (driver included), which is a major feat in my state of mind.

My husband John Rockefeller (no relation) is a good, decent man who loves children and most of the time loves me. We've hit that wall though, you know The Wall, where we've been together fourteen years, married for ten, so we completely take one another for granted, where I will do anything (short of lose ten pounds, wear a bustier and giggle on cue) to pry a compliment out of him. I hate myself for being so shallow, for needing his approval, but it's not my fault. He started this when we were courting. He showered me with tingly kisses, compliments and inappropriate gifts. How I miss them! Now, I have to beg him to tell me I'm pretty, and believe me, a girl doesn't feel pretty when she has to fish for her lifelong lover to tell her so. However, this is not why I'm angry. I'm angry because he is right.

'Your mother has staged another drama,' John whispers softly from behind the door of Mother's kitchen.

'I know. But we're here now so let's roll with it. Hide the eggs.' I give my husband a basket of hard-boiled eggs dyed acid green, nuclear pink and tumour purple.

'We are here on false pretences,' he whispers loudly.

'I don't have a crystal ball. I couldn't tell she was absolutely fine from eight hundred miles away.'

'Agnes Castlewood is in cahoots with your mother.'

'It gives them something to do.'

'Why don't you confront your mother and tell her if she can't come to New York she has to wait until the summer to see the kids? Why can't you be honest?'

'Oh John. Please. She's old and she's . . . lonely.' For whatever reason, this revelation makes me burst into tears. The sound of my weeping brings my sons into the kitchen.

'What's wrong, Ma?' Tender Emilio circles his arms around my waist.

'What did you do, Daddy?' Defender Aaron looks at his father suspiciously.

'Did you cut yourself with a steak knife? Let me see the blood!' Devilish James runs to the sink for evidence.

'I'm fine.' I tell them reassuringly. 'Daddy's gonna hide the Easter eggs.'

'Where? Gram only has a dinky terrace and it's empty,' Aaron says.

'There's only a dead plant,' James points.

'He'll think of something,' I promise. I look at John. 'Right?' John doesn't answer, rather looks at me with such contempt you would think I had stolen his remote control during the Super Bowl or during the free night of the Playboy channel on cable.

'You can hide them in the hallway.' My mother's voice booms from the doorway. She raps her cane of the floor. Mother looks lovely. Her hair is done in a lovely blonde French horn. She wears a simple pink pantsuit with a crystal butterfly brooch the size of an SUV.

'What about the neighbours?' I ask her.

Mother often forgets she lives in a retirement village, which has more rules than James's nursery school which we call Cell block Eight.

'I don't care about them.'

'Mother, we don't want to cause any trouble.'

'John. Go hide the eggs,' Mother says firmly. 'And if anybody gives you any trouble, you tell them to see me.' John and the boys heed her tone and go. It dawns on me that everyone is afraid of Mother, which is probably why we're here. She goes to the refrigerator and opens it. 'Hmm.'

I peer into the empty fridge. 'I'll go to the store.'

Mother pulls money out of her sweater pocket, which I tuck back into it. 'Thank you. We need two roasting chickens, a dozen potatoes and some fresh broccoli. I made a pie yesterday.'

'It's a shame you don't plan things.' I give Mother a kiss.

Mother smiles. 'It's good to have you home.'

Biasco's Market has not changed since I was a girl. There is something reassuring about the orange-and-white-striped awnings, the door that jingles with the clank of an old cowbell when you open it, and the specials handwritten on a blackboard over the single register. (No computer screen here!) The smell of fresh coffee beans fills the air. I inhale, remembering how happy I was as a girl living in a city that felt safe and stayed the same, no matter how much time had passed.

The vegetable bins were my favourite spot, not because I'm a fan of legumes, but because long before they were popular, Mr Biasco put a misting machine that would spray intermittent fresh cold water over the bins to keep the lettuce from wilting. The fun of it was that you never knew when the mist would appear, and if you were standing under them, you'd get a good dousing. Now that I'm a thirty-six-year-old hag mother and in dire need of moisture, I stick my head under the mister and wait. A few seconds pass and then I hear the whirl, followed by the gurgle and then the whoosh of the mist. I'm hit with a good spritz.

'You're blocking the tomatoes,' a man's deep voice says from behind me. I turn around.

'Oh my God. Scott?'

'Hi, Annie.' His familiar face, with the wide smile and Italianate nose, is the same. His dimpled chin, like the lines around his eyes, seem deeper; of course, they would, he's twenty years older. He's actually more handsome than he was in high school, though there's none of the sandy hair he used to fuss over (it's gone, gone, gone), but his eyes are still as blue as Lake Michigan on a good day.

'What are you doing here?' I lean casually against the bin.

'Getting a ham. It's Easter.'

'Right, right. I'm getting . . .' Why can't I remember what I'm getting?

'What?'

'. . . dinner. Chickens.'

'That's not very festive.'

'I know. I'm just following orders. Mother . . .'

'My mom sees her at church. Says she's doing well.'

'Sort of. Well, I guess she is doing fine,' I smile brightly.

'You look good.'

'You're crazy.' I bury my face in my hands, hoping

I remembered to put on foundation before leaving the house. I didn't.

Scott pulls my hands away from my face. 'I mean it. How many kids you got?'

'Three boys.'

He checks me out a little too long and a little too closely. 'And you're still beautiful.'

Instead of letting the compliment sink in, the compliment that under normal circumstances I crave, fish for and would pay cold, hard cash for, is not fully heard, instead, I blush, giggle and talk so fast a passer-by mistakes me for an auctioneer. 'I'm just happy I'm not in a mental institution.'

Scott throws his head back and laughs, which gives me a moment to check *him* out. He's in great shape, though it's hard to tell specifics because he wears a flannel shirt (not tucked) and jeans that look how I feel (faded blue and baggy). 'You want to grab a cup of coffee?' he asks.

I think of my husband who is in the claustrophobic hallway of the retirement village cramming eggs into planters, in door jambs and into the pockets of Mother's neighbours who don't mind children and think, what a fine man he is, and then in an instant, 'screw him', I'm here, freshly misted and an old boyfriend still thinks I'm pretty, I deserve that cup of coffee. 'Yes, I'd love to have a cup of coffee . . . but I can't.' I explain the egg hunt and Mother and how I'm in a rush. 'It's one of the things I want to change about my life – I'm always rushing, I never . . . savour.'

'I get it.'

We look at each other with an understanding that only lifelong friends have, about who they are, where they come from, how everything has changed, and yet, in Biasco's Market, how nothing has changed. I don't need the cup of coffee and neither does he, we already know everything about each other without having a conversation. 'I know you get it,' I smile.

I turn to look for my cart, which has rolled away and lodged by the apples. It got away from me somehow.

'Annie?'

'Yes?'

Scott pulls me close and kisses me. It's been fourteen years and seven months since I kissed a man besides my husband, and it's like I'm thirteen years old again, I have no idea what I'm doing. His kiss feels permanent somehow, not new. It's as if this kiss in the tomatoes seals something off in me, and pushes me into a new place. The ticker tape in my head says, 'You're getting kissed! You're getting kissed!'

'Take care of yourself.' He says and goes.

I raise my hand to call after him, but no sound comes out of my mouth. I hear the whirl of the motor; with my hand in the air like a crossing guard, I am misted.

'Where are the chickens?' Mother asks as she unloads the groceries from the bag. 'What's this?' Mother lifts out a large bag of Milky Way candy bars, three heads of fresh broccoli, two pounds of pasta, a bottle of olive oil so expensive she gasps, two pounds of shrimp, two bottles of wine and a chocolate cake. 'Did you pick up the wrong bag?'

'Nope. They were out of chickens.'

'John took the boys to the park. The egg hunt was a bust.'

'I thought maybe it would be.'

'Did you see anyone at the market?' Mother asks.

'Do you remember Scott Tranowski?'

'I see his mother every Sunday in church.'

'He told me. Well, I saw him. He was there.'

'What's he up to?'

'Nothing much.' I put the shrimp in the refrigerator.

'He's divorced. Broke Miriam's heart.' Mother snaps the heads off the broccoli and puts them in a strainer. I don't know why this news lifts my spirits, but it does.

'Maaaa? Maaa?' I hear from the living room.

'I thought you said they went to the park.'

'Do you think a teeter-totter and a lame set of monkey bars is going to keep your little crew entertained?'

'Ma, Daddy gave all our eggs away at the park,' Aaron tells us.

'He did?'

John comes in with the empty basket. 'I gave up. There's no place to hide eggs in Chicago.' John leans over and kisses me. 'You look pretty,' he says without bribes or prompting, catching us both by surprise. 'Really pretty.'

'Thanks, honey.'

'What happened?' John surveys my face.

'She saw an old boyfriend.' Mother pipes up.

'Mother!'

'Well, you did. Don't worry, John. He's bald.'

'Bald? Then I won't worry. Annie doesn't like bald.'

The boys pull John back into the living room, where they start one of their World War III wrestling matches.

'I'm sorry I made you come all this way, Annie,' Mother says softly as she rinses the shrimp.

'I'm not.' I watch my husband and sons through the

door and feel that nice warm feeling that somebody likes me, and how convenient that I happen to be married to him.

Mother puts her arms around me. 'I . . . don't know. Sometimes I feel like time is ice in my hands. It's going away. And I miss you all so much.'

'Come to New York. I want you to live with us.'

'. . . No, no, I can't.'

'Please.'

'And put Agnes Castlewood out of job? I know you send her over here to spy on me.'

'OK, it's not spying. It's checking in.'

'Whatever you say.' Mother smiles. 'I'm sorry I made more out of my little fall than it was. I shouldn't take advantage of your good nature and make you worry for nothing.

'It's all right, Ma. Really. You're a little manipulative, but who isn't when they really want something?'

Mother smiles again. 'My days run together sometimes, unless I have something to look forward to. I've learned, though, not to get into a rut. Life is funny, it starts over and over and over again.'

'What do you mean?'

'Yesterday I was here alone, and it was going to be a crappy Easter, and today, here you all are, and it's going to be a glorious holiday.'

I put my arms around my mother and hold her. The boys laugh and carry on, and I can't help but think Mother is right. Life does start over and over again, and sometimes a kiss from an old boyfriend makes everything seem new again, or at the very least, reminds you that what you have is pretty terrific.

Tidings

Lynne Truss

Jane brushed some mince-pie crumbs from her purple jumper and adjusted her reading glasses. The wind was moaning in the chimney and the day drawing to its early December close. On her desk, her computer hummed and glowed. She patted it, fondly. What a marvellous time she'd had. How many years, just before Christmas, had she secretly fantasised about this moment? Well, quite a few, obviously, to judge by how happy she now was. Oh yes. God rest ye, merry gentlemen; let nothing you dismay. Bringing tidings of comfort and joy.

My dear Gerald, Caro, Zoe, Laura, Elvis and Pooh [she read],

Well, what a year you've had! Every year seems to be improve on the last in your household, if your four-page illustrated Wilsons Christmas Gazette is anything to go by!

Jane picked up the offending object and, with satisfaction, tore it into quarters.

Zoe's exams! Laura's success in the world speed-texting competition! Gerald becoming general manager (Eastern region)! My dears, I was quite exhausted just reading it. Do you know, yours was the fourth regular Christmas newsletter I received this year on the same day, and I hope you don't mind, I felt compelled – well, I know it's unconventional these days, but I just felt compelled to send you a personal reply!

Somehow I don't get round to writing and printing my own Christmas newsletters, you see. For one thing, I'm sure I could never master that wonderful breathless reporting style – or indeed imitate your enviable devil-may-care attitude to written English. But more importantly, there is a part of me that simply can't help thinking: isn't there something a bit self-important about writing an account of your family's year and sending it to people in lieu of personal Christmas greetings? Even if your 13-year-old daughter did come a glorious sixth in the regional qualifiers of a paltry bloody texting championship, don't you think a brief note mentioning how quickly time flies and wishing me a seasonal type of joy might be more in the spirit of Christmas?

Oh, Caro, how long is it now since we actually saw each other? It's been so many years, of course, but I know we spoke just after John left in 1997, because I vividly remember your saying how you had actually never liked him (so helpful!), and that it was wicked the way he had 'stolen my child-bearing years'. This was an aspect of the thing that had not occurred to me, actually – so well done, you! You were just about to suggest a supportive reunion, I think, when one of your lovely daughters demanded to use the phone, so you said goodbye ('Speak soon!'), and we never spoke again. I missed John very much at first, of course. How I felt the need of old friends! But I had started to get over it, as it happens, when I saw the following, in your newsletter the following Christmas:

MARCH. We hear sad news that Caro's old

friend Jane has been dumped by husband of 25 years. This brings Caro and Gerald closer together than ever. 'Jane is in our thoughts,' admits Gerald to young Zoe. 'It's possible she won't recover from this. Thank goodness we Wilsons all have each other.'

I couldn't help thinking, Caro, that when you sent me that particular edition of the Wilsons Christmas Gazette, you might have wielded a black marker (or even scissors) to considerate effect.

Anyway, here are a few thoughts on the latest newsletter.

1) There should be an apostrophe after 'Wilsons' on the masthead. Properly, it should read, 'The Wilsons' Christmas Gazette' because it belongs to you. A small thing, the plural possessive apostrophe, but I'm surprised the new passion for grammatical correctness should have passed you by!

2) Paragraph two: you say Zoe came top in her year for French, History and English. Now, this is odd, because when I checked with the school, they said Zoe was actually a 'middling' student

who might not get any GCSEs at all if she didn't stop hanging round the shopping precinct in the evenings with a boy called Wayne.

3) Paragraph six: Gerald's new job is in fact a demotion, isn't it? Rather unwise to attempt sleight of hand here.

4) The school sports picture. You have bungled the airbrushing of the large tattoo still clearly circling Laura's upper arm.

5) Concerning the 'glorious' holiday in Antigua: you see the person at the back of the group photo, sort of looking to the right in a big hat? Well, look closely and you'll see . . . it's me! Yes, I followed you to Antigua as I have followed you everywhere for the past five years, as it happens, because I hate you, Caro Wilson, you smug cow. I hate you and I hate in particular the way you send these four-page full-colour Christmas letters to people as though you were the Queen or somebody.

Oh dear, I didn't mean to reveal this much so quickly. Please forget I said any of that, and accept my very best wishes to you and yours. I enclose some book tokens for the girls, and an amusing volume called 'Adultery for Dummies' for Gerald, because I fear he hasn't read it. Now, if you're wondering what's been happening to me all these years (but why should you?), it's not an uninteresting story. For one thing, guess what, I've become quite rich! Fancy that! From dumped divorcee to self-made businesswoman in such a short time! In the autumn of 1998, you see, I met a handsome and ambitious young man called Jason at my step class and gave him a lift home. We became lovers instantly. He is quite gorgeous. After a six-month visit to Australia, we set up an advanced surveillance business (his idea), which has been incredibly successful. We have an office in Park Lane and a manor house in East Sussex. We have 25 operatives, hundreds of accounts and have been retained by several Gulf States, but the best thing is, Caro: I've had your entire family (even Elvis and Pooh!) under 24-hour intensive surveillance from the very start, just for the pleasure of establishing that your happy sing-song Christmas newsletters are full of complete and utter self-flattering rubbish.

Oh well. Season's greetings. Don't bother trying to find the cameras and microphones; if Mossad can't do it, I don't suppose you can.

Above all, Happy Christmas!
    With love,
    Jane

P.S. Don't be too hard on Gerald when you do
eventually find out. Men are such weaklings
where attractive younger women are concerned.

Jane folded the letter and placed it quickly in an
envelope. She felt quite hot. Blimey, had she gone too
far? She thought about it briefly and then decided no.
Caro deserved everything she got. With any luck, by
the end of Boxing Day, the Wilson house would be a
mass of upturned floorboards and ripped wallpaper as
the whole family searched for non-existent bugging
devices. Gerald would be out on his ear. Of course,
Jane had no idea whether Gerald had been unfaithful
to Caro. Nor had she ever foiled the best minds of
Mossad, or even contacted Zoe's school. She had just
decided that, while goodwill to all men at Christmas
is a very fine ideal, it doesn't have to extend to people
who send out thoughtlessly self-centred newsletters
telling you how fantastically clever the children are.
    She needed to work quickly, however. Mark would
be home soon from the garden centre in Swindon
with the Christmas tree, and he didn't share her

abomination of Christmas newsletters; also, he might be quite alarmed by the invention of Jason and the step class. So she must press on! The next letter she had painstakingly written in spidery ballpoint on lined paper. It had taken ages, but would be worth it. 'Oh yes,' she said, happily, as she shuffled its pages. 'This will put a spoke in *their* wheel.' She took another Christmas newsletter, tore it twice, and ceremoniously added its fragments to the pile.

Dear Jan, Barry, Jemima, Ben, Beatrice, Petra and Raffles,
Thank you so, so, SO MUCH for your adorable Christmas newsletter. You have no idea what it means to me every year to hear about your lovely holidays and all the successes of your beautiful children. You all seem to love each other very much – and the new house looks fabulous. Don't delay a moment longer in having that swimming pool built. You won't regret it. Did I not tell you I'd moved, by the way? Fortunately, the people who bought my house from the receivers have been terribly good about sending my post on to my Morecambe B&B.

I hope this won't sound too 'sad', Jan, but I feel I have to tell you. Hearing your bouncy family news once a year is just about the only thing keeping me going! Oh dear. I feel I know you all so intimately, you see, thanks to your newsletters – even though we last actually saw each other, Jan, when we were both 23! I've never met Barry or any of the children, and yet — oh, I'm going to get all emotional now! – I love them as though they were my own. Truly, I do. When little Beatrice was born, I was actually on the verge of saying goodbye to this cruel world! I had the pills lined up and everything. But the news of her birth, and your happiness, gave me such hope. You ARE happy, aren't you? You are really, really, really happy? If I thought you were in any way making your family life sound more loving and ecstatic than it really was – well, I don't know what I'd do!

So, a very happy Christmas to you – and please, please KEEP SENDING THESE LOVELY LETTERS. Perhaps you could send them MONTHLY? Or even ONCE A WEEK. Perhaps you could set up a Freefone number for me to call in the middle of the night and listen to your voices. Trust me, it means everything to me – EVERYTHING – that you so generously include me in your happy, happy world. In fact, tell you what, Jan. This has honestly just occurred to me. Can I come and live with you? I feel I know you all SO WELL.

Best wishes,
Jane

Mark entered the room as she was signing the second letter with her left hand, to make it more wobbly.

'Hello, darling,' he said. 'Still beavering away at the correspondence? That computer's been on all day.'

'I know,' she said, smiling. 'I've been a bit creative.'

'Good for you,' he said. 'Cup of tea?'

'Love one.'

On his way to the kitchen, Mark spotted the small heap of torn-up Christmas newsletters and picked one up.

'You're wrong about these, you know, darling,' he said.

'Mm,' said Jane.

'There's no harm in them; they're just for information.'

'Yes?'

'It's natural to lose touch with people.'

'Then you should write to them at Christmas and

ask them how they are, not send them a bloody bulletin!'

Jane's voice had risen. Mark gave up. His capacity for giving up immediately when challenged was one of the things Jane had first loved about him.

'Cup of tea, then?'

'Lovely.'

'More to do?'

'Just a couple.'

'All right.'

He left the room, and Jane returned to the computer. She frowned. Letter 3? She already couldn't remember Letter 3. But as it came out of the printer, she cheered up at once. Forget Letter 2. Letter 3 was a triumph.

Dear Mr and Mrs Johnson (or, if you will, Alison, Jamie, Flo, Lauren, Bosie, Buster and Bubbles),

I am writing in connection with the newsletter you sent to Mrs Jane Fellowes, who has moved from this address. Mistaking this to be post intended for myself, I opened the aforesaid correspondence and was already engaged in its perusal before I realised my mistake. But I felt compelled to read on. As a former inspector at

the Inland Revenue, I noticed that, under the
heading 'June', you admit to a 'windfall' from a
'mad aunt' and make several unwise admissions
concerning your decision not to declare it all to
'the taxman'. I am bound to inform you that I
have copied the evidence and forwarded it to the
relevant authorities. You will be hearing from
them after Christmas. In certain cases of brazen
tax evasion, incidentally, a custodial sentence
may be applied.

May I take the opportunity, however, of
congratulating you on a first-class production? I
am told by acquaintances that the 'Christmas
newsletter' is now an accepted feature of British
life and is sent quite indiscriminately to people in
one's address book without checking whether
they are still alive, still regard themselves as
'friends', and so on. Personally, I like to write a
brief note to people I have not seen for a long
time. I ask them how they are, give them selected
news that I am positive will interest them and
wish them a happy Christmas. I would not feel
comfortable sending them a published account
of my year, oh dear no! I would feel it was a trifle
one-way as a form of communication. I would
feel arrogant. But I have observed how family life

can distort people's ideas of their own importance, and of course I apologise for running on in this vein, especially when you are now facing criminal charges.

Season's greetings,

Yours sincerely

J.B. Funbury, Esq.

The evening was drawing in. Jane drew the curtains but didn't like to switch on the main lamps. It seemed important to this exercise that she completed it under the pool of light from the anglepoise. However, Mark came in immediately and snapped the switch.

'Don't sit in the dark, darling.'

'Was I? I didn't notice.'

'Here we are.' He produced a mug of tea from a tray, and a saucer with two mince pies. 'I see you've already started these,' he said.

'Needed to keep my strength up.'

'Want me to leave you alone?'

'Just for another few minutes.'

'OK.'

Jane felt a warm, internal-lunging feeling – like a strong tug – that she had only ever felt with Mark.

'I love you, Mark.'

'I know.'

'All right, then.'

He kissed the top of her head.

'All right, then,' he agreed.

'Nearly there,' she thought, but her balloon had been burst and she felt a twinge of misgiving. She printed Letter 4, the last one; it was to a family in Brighton. In this one she told them she had been studying, alone, for some years, the writings of Nostradamus, and that by studying the numerology and other symbolisms of their newsletter, she had come to the conclusion that their hamster, Georgie, was the Antichrist. 'Does his fur swirl to the right or to the left?' she had asked urgently. 'Has he drawn blood yet?' And so on. She was particularly proud of the sentence: 'How do you account for the fact that, if you join together all appearances of the letter H on page three, you get an outline of a goat?' But suddenly, she felt she couldn't go through with it. It was all Mark's fault. Mark was such a saint. She looked at her letter with deep regret – and binned it. Every year she got to about this point in her scheme, and every year Mark's superior soul got in the way — it got in the way without him even trying.

'Mark!' He appeared at the door with a tea towel and a wet mug. 'Yes, darling?'

'Look, explain to me again about the Christmas

letters.' He came and put an arm around her. 'You've been writing those horrible replies again, haven't you?'

She pursed her lips in tacit admission.

'Tell me what you've written.'

'Well, I've done a person who's got a private detective agency and has been stalking the family for five years. Then I've got someone who is incredibly vulnerable and on the verge of suicide and the only thing keeping her going is their annual Christmas letter.'

Mark looked unimpressed. Jane's voice lowered, and she gabbled the rest.

'Then – then, well, I've got a tax inspector who's turned them in and a person who's worked out that their hamster is an agent of Satan.'

Wordlessly, Mark rolled his eyes, pursed his lips and got up.

'I've done a brilliant job,' Jane insisted. 'Mark, listen, *none of them will ever bother us again*.'

But as he left the room, she turned to her keyboard and started again.

Dear Everyone [she wrote],

   Isn't it awful that we don't see each other any more? The years pass, and all that happens is that we send each other vain hopes at Christmas that one day we'll meet. Children are born, grow up, get exams. Pets do funny things. We get new jobs, new partners, new houses. And once a year we contact each other – out of guilt perhaps, out of duty even, but mainly to show that friendship outlasts absence, and that we do still care about each other.

Look, can I just say I HATE family Christmas newsletters. Please don't send them to me any more. I can imagine they are fun to do. I can also imagine how, once so much effort has been put into their production, you feel it necessary to send them to everyone you've ever met. But I think the sending of greetings at Christmas is not about keeping virtual strangers up to date with your children's stellar achievements. It's not about news or showing off. It's about stopping for a minute to think about a person you haven't seen for a long time — and in return, perhaps, finding out that, for a similar fleeting moment, they also remembered you.

You will see I am not naming names, by the way. But a rather naughty hamster called Georgie will, I think, know who he is.

Thank you for reading this. Mark made me do it. He's much too nice for me. I hope to see you sometime and tell you about him in person.

Season's greetings,

God bless us, every one (even Georgie),

Jane

The Brooch

Penny Vincenzi

It was a very beautiful brooch. It was what used to be called paste, and now would be called diamanté, glittery and brilliant and in the shape of a full moon with two stars trailing off it on two slender threads. It was the sort of thing you could make stories up about, which Anna had when she was little, like the moon wearing the stars like a sort of sash or the stars were trying to get away from it. The brooch belonged to her grandmother, Bella, and was pinned to her large cushiony bosom and Anna would sit on her knee and play with it; later on she had been allowed to wear it, when they went to tea with her, and she would keep saying she wanted to go to the lavatory so she could pass the big mirror in the hall and admire it, pinned on to her cardigan, right in the middle of her small flat chest One day she thought, she would have wonderful bosoms like her grandmother and the brooch would show up much better. She had always known she would have the brooch; her grandmother had promised her that, adding quickly that Rachel, Anna's older sister, would have her pearls.

Rachel wasn't really in the least interested in either the brooch or the pearls, she was a tomboy and only cared about getting into the school teams and climbing trees like the boys, but she did mind that Anna was so clearly the favourite and so she used to make a great fuss and demand to be allowed to wear the brooch too. She didn't really want to but making Anna miserable made her feel a bit better.

Rachel wasn't pretty like Anna, who had fair curls and big blue eyes; she had dark straight hair, and brown eyes, and almost sallow skin, but she did much better at school, she was sharp and clever, and she wanted to be a doctor when she grew up.

The girls had never got on; their mother, Diana, often said they were fighting in their playpen.

Rachel had a sharp tongue and a quick temper, but her method of attack – usually a kick or a bite – was swift and swiftly over; Anna could bear a grudge for hours or even days, and she could hold her tears back until her mother was in earshot, and then suddenly wail and clutch her injury to get the maximum mileage from it. Rachel was almost always in trouble.

The only person who always stuck up for her was her Grandpa George. 'She's got such spirit,' he would say fondly. He was a bit suspicious of Anna and her wide blue eyes; 'we know all about her,' he would say winking at Rachel. 'Bit too good to be true, isn't she?' She adored him back; it made up for the fuss Grandmother Bella made of Anna.

In 1960, when Anna was seven and Rachel eight, Grandmother Bella died. It was a terrible shock; she was only fifty-eight. 'She's too young to die,' people kept saying, at the funeral. The girls thought this ridiculous; fifty-eight was terribly old. But the most shocked person – of course – was Grandpa George, who was ten years older than Bella and had not expected to have to endure a lonely old age.

For a long time he was broken-hearted; pining for his Bella in their big empty house. The only person able to comfort him was Rachel, and she would go over most Sundays to see him, taking him for walks, making him take her for drives, playing Scrabble with him (his favourite game) and usually winning, keeping him up to date with the new pop music. Everyone said how wonderful she was, which made

Anna very cross. Not only had she lost her grandmother, she had lost her role as star grandchild. She spent a lot of time sobbing loudly in her room whenever Rachel set off to visit Grandpa George.

One of the things that had happened, because of Grandmother Bella dying so young, was that she hadn't ever made a will.

'Not that it terribly mattered, she and Daddy shared everything,' Diana said sadly; but there was one thing that came to matter very much.

Grandpa George called Rachel into his study one day. 'Something for you,' he said, 'something I want you to have. It was Granny Bella's favourite and I know she'd want you to have it if she knew what a comfort you've been. Here, darling. With my love.'

And there it was, in a little box: the moon-and-stars brooch.

It was very difficult. Even Diana was upset.

'Anna was told she could have that brooch,' she said to Rachel. 'She's going to be broken-hearted.'

Which made Rachel cross. 'It's me that's cheered Grandpa up,' she said.

'I know, darling, but –'

'And he wants me to have it. It would be horrible to tell him he's got it wrong.'

Richard, their father, agreed. 'For God's sake,

Diana, Anna's only seven. She can have some other trinket.

I'll have a word with George.'

Which he did and Anna was duly given the seed-pearl necklace.

She was furious: so furious that for days she could hardly eat. It was so unfair. That brooch was hers: Granny Bella had promised her, Rachel didn't want it. She'd rather have a new hockey stick.

'I do want it,' said Rachel, 'I jolly well do. And Grandpa George wants me to have it. So just shut up about it. It's mine.'

She never wore it of course. But she would never lend it to Anna. As the girls grew up, into flower-power fashion, and thence the floaty romanticism of the seventies, Anna longed to have it, to pin it one of her Biba hats, or her Laura Ashley bodices, but Rachel just said no. It was hers, Grandpa George wanted her to have it. The only times she did wear it was for Grandpa George's visits and on the dreadful day of his funeral, when it seemed to help. Otherwise it stayed in her drawer, in its box. She took it with her when she went to Cambridge to study medicine.

Anna didn't go to university; she went to teacher training college. She said being a teacher would fit in better with having her own children. Rachel was very scornful and said it was a pathetic reason to choose a career.

Rachel was very successful with men. They came flocking to her door, from when she was about fifteen. Pretty, sweet-faced Anna did less well; in fact by the time she was twenty she still hadn't had a proper boyfriend.

'Rachel has sex appeal, as your mother used to call it,' said Richard smiling when Diana fretted over this. 'It's just something in her. Don't fuss. Anna will find Mr Right. Give her time.'

Rachel was in love. With someone from Cambridge, a very good-looking and charming someone, who seemed to like her, but had never asked her out. She was incensed; it had never happened to her before.

'It's exactly because you're not sure of him that you like him so much,' her mother said.

'It isn't!' cried Rachel in agony. 'He's the best-looking bloke in my year, in any year. And he's so funny and sexy. I know how Anna feels now. Never getting a man.'

'Rachel, be quiet,' said Diana sharply. But it was too late: Anna had heard her. She fled to her room in tears.

Two days later, a miracle happened. Two miracles

actually. The good-looking and charming someone, whose name was Lucas, asked Rachel to go to a big dinner party with him. And the same night, Anna was invited to the college Christmas ball by the one boy in her year she fancied.

'It's just too good to be true,' Diana said happily. Richard, who had taken to calling her Mrs Bennet, was very amused.

'You know what would look wonderful with that,' said Diana, as Rachel showed her the low-cut black velvet dress she planned to wear, 'Granny's brooch.'

Rachel rummaged in her drawer, found the box and pinned it on the dress, at its lowest point where it nestled, lighting up her cleavage. 'You're right,' she said.

Diana thought thankfully of the floaty chiffon creation that Anna was wearing; there was no way she'd want to wear anything sparkling in it. Only Anna did not want to wear it on the dress, but she had read an article in *Vogue* which said that the place for sparkle was in your hair. 'Ransack Granny's jewellery box,' it said and showed something very similar to the moon-and-stars brooch. Anna bought a couple of slides from Fenwick's, and they did look quite nice, but . . . She took a deep breath and asked Rachel, really very nicely, if she could possibly borrow the brooch. Rachel said no.

'You're so mean,' said Anna. 'It's not as if you're going to wear it.'

'I am actually,' said Rachel. 'Aren't I, Mummy?'

Diana nodded, rather unhappily. Rachel gave Anna a distinctly crushing smile.

'So sorry,' she said.

They quarrelled noisily for at least another half-hour before Anna gave up.

Anna left for the evening long before Rachel did; she looked lovely, they all agreed. Even Rachel said so.

'And those slides are perfect.'

'Well, they're all right,' said Anna.

'Isn't lover boy going to collect you?'

Anna flushed. 'No. He lives miles away. He's meeting me there.'

'I'll take you, darling,' said Richard.

'No, honestly, it's fine, lots of us are going to share a cab. I'm first pick-up . . .'

'Well, have a lovely time,' said Diana.

'I will. Thank you.'

And she was gone.

A howl of rage came from Rachel's bedroom half an hour later. The brooch wasn't in her drawer. It wasn't anywhere. They searched every corner of every room, including Anna's. Well, Rachel did.

'She's got it,' she said, tears of rage filling her eyes. 'Cow. She knows how much tonight matters. I hate her. I thought she looked funny, when she left. She couldn't wait to get out of the house. Bitch.'

'Rachel, darling –'

'Don't darling me. She must have it, she must. Oh God, there's the bell, is my mascara running, oh, I hate her so much.'

Rachel came down to Sunday breakfast pale and heavy-eyed. The evening had not been a success.

'It's your fault,' she said to a rather subdued Anna. 'I was so upset about the brooch, I couldn't think of anything else. I don't know how you could have done it, Anna, you really are a prize cow.'

'Rachel, I did not take the brooch.'

'Of course you did. Don't lie about it. And where is it now? Where have you hidden it?'

'I hate you,' said Anna suddenly, her voice heavy with emotion. 'I absolutely hate you.'

'And I hate you. You're pathetic; you're a liar as well as a thief. Anyway, how was your evening? Had your first kiss at last, have you? You must be the oldest virgin in the Home Counties.'

'Rachel!' said her father. 'Apologise to your sister at once. And don't talk in that disgusting way.'

'I won't apologise. Why should I? She took that brooch and ruined my evening.'

'That is so pathetic,' said Anna. 'It's just a wonderful excuse. You can't bring yourself to admit that someone just didn't fancy you for once. You're not just a tart you're totally arrogant.'

'I am not a tart.'

'You're a tart. And until you apologise, for what you said to me, I'm not going to speak to you.'

'Fine. That's fine by me. It'll be a relief. You never say anything remotely interesting anyway. No wonder men don't like you. You're just so boring. And desperate. It shows, you know, the way you flirt with everyone, even the milkman, everyone finds it really amusing –'

'Shut up,' shrieked Anna and fled from the room.

Diana was sure it would blow over; they were both upset, they often quarrelled. But this time was different and it didn't blow over; and they didn't forgive one another. The wounds were too deep; what had been said was too desperately personal and cruel.

The brooch was never found.

Six months later, Lucas suddenly invited Rachel out

to dinner in Cambridge; he said he'd suddenly realised what a treasure lay within his reach and, after a very token resistance, she forgave him. Within three months they were engaged and a year later married.

It was quite a big wedding; Rachel had no grown-up bridesmaids, just four small ones and four pageboys. It was a convenient reason for her not to have Anna, who wasn't deceived. Diana begged Rachel to rethink; 'It's a very public slap in the face, darling, and she'll be so upset.'

But Rachel wouldn't. 'After the things she said to me, I don't want her as my bridesmaid. All right?'

A year later, Anna was married; David, her husband-to-be, was extremely nice, if a little dull, a teacher at her infants school. Anna had several grown-up bridesmaids, but Rachel was out of the question, since she was married herself.

'And I don't like the idea of a matron of honour. Sorry, Rachel.'

In neither set of wedding photographs could a shot be found of the sisters together.

The two husbands didn't like each other much and had nothing in common; there was no need for them to meet except at family gatherings. The distance between the sisters grew.

Rachel had two boys; Anna three girls. Neither invited the other to be godmother.

Rachel continued to work; Anna stayed at home, and if they did meet, there were always references to the deprived children of working mothers, and the dullness of stay-at-home ones.

Diana struggled down the years to bring the girls together; she suggested joint holidays, gave lots of big birthdays parties, and of course there was always Christmas. But if Rachel was going to be with her parents, Anna seemed to have to spend it with David's. And the other way round.

Then there were holidays: Diana and Richard invited everyone to Tuscany; both families accepted, but at the last minute Lucas phoned and said Rachel wasn't well and couldn't come. Diana told him just to send the children, but he said it would be too much. 'We'll hopefully come out later. When Rachel's better.'

They never arrived.

When they got home, Anna phoned Rachel.

'I do hope you're better,' she said icily. 'I suppose you realise you broke Mummy's heart.'

'You're always so bloody dramatic, Anna. She was fine about it, Lucas said.'

'Oh really? You don't have a heart yourself, that's

your problem. You're a bitch, Rachel. Well, we had a much nicer time without you, I can tell you that.'

'Yes, it must have been so interesting, sitting at the dinner table, listening to David's views on education every night. I do wish we'd been there.'

Anna slammed the phone down.

Next summer Diana invited just the children to stay with her and Richard in a cottage they rented in Cornwall.

'They're all over five, and we can manage between us. I'd so like them to get to know one another.'

That holiday wasn't a success either; the children fought relentlessly and one dreadful day one of Rachel's boys pushed one of Anna's girls into a rock pool and her leg was so badly cut she had to have stitches.

'Like mother like son,' said Anna icily, when they both arrived to collect the children two days early. Rachel was so genuinely shocked her eyes filled with tears.

'I was about to apologise for him,' she said. 'He's very sorry too. But just forget it.'

'I wish I could,' said Anna.

It was Diana's sixty-fifth birthday and she was having a party. 'Three-line whip,' Richard said heavily as he phoned with the invitation. 'You're all to behave yourselves.'

He had aged a lot over the years; he looked nearer seventy himself. Rachel's sons were darkly handsome: the elder, seventeen-year-old Tom, extremely sexy. Anna's sixteen-year-old Lizzy, sweetly pretty. The two of them were found in one of the bedrooms towards the end of the party, both of them half undressed, Tom kissing Lizzy's breasts. No real harm was done; but the ensuing row was frightful, with both sets of parents hurling abuse at one another. Phrases like 'exactly what I would have expected' and 'not as innocent as she looks' – filled the air.

Diana, her evening ruined, went to bed in tears.

Richard died in 2000, just a week short of their golden wedding. His last words to his daughters were 'Please, you two. Make it up.'

Diana sat weeping silently at the funeral, with one girl at either side of her; after everyone had gone, she called the two of them into the drawing room.

'I don't think I could feel more unhappy,' she said, 'but I could face the future a little more easily if you two would be friends. This hostility was one of the things that wore Daddy out. I think it's time you grew up. Please try.'

'I'd like to,' said Rachel to Anna, when they were alone, 'but it's up to you really. You took the brooch. That's where it all began.'

'It began with you not believing me.'

The reconciliation never got off the ground.

Six months later, Diana put the house on the market; it sold very quickly, and she bought a pretty little Georgian cottage nearer the town.

A month later, the new owner rang her; he had had the floorboards taken up in one of the bedrooms and found something he thought might be valuable. 'It's a brooch. Lovely thing, sort of moon and stars.'

Diana called Rachel and told her. 'Do you remember,' she said, 'there was that wide gap between two of the boards near your bed, it created an awful draught. I was so glad to get it carpeted over. The brooch must have slipped down there, off your bed.'

'I remember,' said Rachel. Her voice was rather small. 'I'd better talk to Anna.'

Anna was very gracious. 'I was hardly blameless. I said some awful things to you as well.'

'Yes, you did.'

'Not that you were exactly polite.'

'Well, what did you expect?'

'Rachel,' said Anna wearily. 'It's time I told you the truth.'

'What truth?'

'I didn't need to take the brooch. I didn't go out that night.'

'Of course you went out. I saw you go. All dressed up.'

'Rachel, I went to the cinema. On my own. That boy phoned me and cancelled. Obviously he'd found something better to do. Or someone better to take. I couldn't face telling you. Or anyone. A date at last and it was cancelled. So I got the taxi to the station, got on a train to London where no one was likely to know me, and went to the latest Bond film. To this day I can't hear that music without feeling sick. Then I just went home again, said I'd had a lovely time and went to bed. And cried most of the night.'

Rachel stared at her; she was rather white.

'Oh my God,' she said, 'how awful. You should have told me. Long ago. What can I say, Anna, what can I do?'

'Nothing,' said Anna, smiling sweetly, 'really nothing. It's fine.'

'It's not fine. I feel dreadful. Well – look, whatever else, you must have the brooch now. Of course you must. I insist. Really –'

Anna drove home, the brooch in its box on the

passenger seat beside her. Every so often she smiled down at it.

Pity she had had to wait so long. But she had got it back at last. It had proved a very good hiding place for it. Very good indeed. And it had made her feel just a little better that awful night, knowing Rachel couldn't wear it either . . .

A message from
Breast Cancer Care:

Breast Cancer Care would like to thank all the wonderful writers who have contributed their entertaining stories to create this brilliant read. The funds raised from this book will help make a profound difference to the lives of people affected by breast cancer across the UK.

Every day, 100 people discover they have breast cancer. Breast Cancer Care is there for every one of them, 24 hours a day, seven days a week. Through our helpline, website forums and face to face activities we offer the chance to talk to someone who has 'been there' and has experienced breast cancer themselves. In addition, our highly specialised team provides all the latest knowledge and information through our website, helpline, booklets and factsheets that help people understand their diagnosis and the choices they have.

Each year Breast Cancer Care responds to more than two million requests for support and information about breast cancer or breast health concerns and every response is given free of charge.

If you or someone you know is going through breast cancer or has a breast health concern call the Breast Cancer Care helpline free on 0808 800 6000 (textphone 0808 800 6001) or visit www.breastcancercare.org.uk for more information or to find out other ways you can support the charity.